Avoiding Esther

JENIFER CARLL-TONG

WOULD YOU LIKE A FREE BOOK?

~

Have you read Book 1 in the Love in Lansing series? Would you like to stay up to date with all the latest news and upcoming releases? Sign up for Jenifer's newsletter and receive *Searching for Anna* as a free ebook download! Visit https://goo.gl/Qur2sU today!

DEDICATION

In memory of my grandmother, Dorothy Virginia King, who instilled in me a love for historical Christian romance, and my grandfather, Reverend Donald Keith King, whose life inspired so many people, and inspired the creation of a very important character in this series. Together, they shared with me the love of Jesus Christ. There is no way I could fit into one simple paragraph all that I owe to them. I miss them both every day but look forward to seeing them again in the presence of our Father.

"But as for you, continue in what you have learned and have become convinced of, because you know those from whom you learned it." ~ 2 Timothy 3:14

1

WOUNDED

Chateau-Thierry June 1918
     "That was easy."

Everything moved in slow motion as John's bayonet sliced through the chest of the German soldier. He had expected there to be more resistance, what with the thick wool service coat the soldier wore, not to mention the layers of skin, muscle and bone found underneath. But the weapon met with little more resistance than the grain-filled burlap sacks used for training back in the States. The thought was sobering; John's own uniform would not offer any more protection.

Thoughts often outrun actions. The body hadn't even hit the ground before John had finished his musings. *"Another corpse for rotting, along with all the rest."*

He heard the grunt first, then felt the blow. Something – no, someone – hit him in the calves and sent him face down into the dirt. He felt no pain. John scrambled back to his feet just in time to see Will bring his bayonet down into the chest of another German. *"Good,"* John thought. *"Will's still alive."*

This strange internal conversation continued, void of all

emotion, while John's external being continued the onslaught. How many men had he taken down? He had no idea. He just focused on one at a time, not stopping to think about the one before or the one coming after. Not until an enemy's blade sliced through his left bicep did John snap out of it. Fear at how close the weapon had come to its intended target quickly turned to anger. With a growl, John swung his rifle around. The German had raised his again, but John was quicker. He thrust his bayonet upward into the enemy soldier's middle. It stuck, but John did not give up. He doubled his efforts, creating so much force that he lifted the man off the ground as the blade finally sliced through his chest.

It was the first his bayonet had met with resistance. And it was the first time he had looked at the face of his enemy.

"My God! He's just a child," John thought. He had to have been younger than Will.

The German, eyes wide, stared in disbelief at John. Both faces, only inches apart, grew pale – one from losing his life, the other from taking it.

John grabbed the front of the falling boy's uniform and gently lowered him to the ground. He stood mesmerized, no longer emotionally disengaged from the act of killing.

He didn't hear the German behind him, nor did he feel the pain at first. He only felt the pressure as the bayonet slipped easily through the fabric of his doughboy uniform, piercing his skin and pushing deep into his body. John fell forward and landed face to face with the young German boy whose life he'd taken. Fitting, he thought, that this would be his dying view.

Something moved. John rolled to see a German soldier standing over him, his rifle aimed at John's head. Powerless to defend himself, John closed his eyes and waited. They were surrounded by gunfire. He doubted he would hear the shot, but surely, he would feel it, unless death was merciful and came quickly. He waited, but no pain came, just a loud grunt and the weight of another man falling on him. Before he could wrap his mind around what was happening, Will was there, lifting the body off of John.

"Can you walk?"

Could he? He wasn't sure. Walk where?

"Stay with me, Johnny!"

Johnny. That's what his mother used to call him. Before she left.

He was drifting, to where, he wasn't sure, but the noise of rifles and grenades began to fade somewhere off in the distance. He felt nothing...

But then, it returned – pain. A searing pain like he had never experienced before shot through John's lower back as Will hoisted him onto his shoulders. John was completely back to reality now.

"Leave me, Will," he pleaded. "You'll get yourself killed."

Will ran, hunkered down, with John on his back. The jostling caused so much pain that John began to beg.

"Please, Will. Just let me die."

Will tripped and stumbled, landing on his knees between two rotting corpses.

"Save yourself. Leave me."

"No. I won't leave you," Will said. "We live together, or we die together. But I won't leave you behind."

Will got up and kept going. John opened his eyes and could see the bunker just feet ahead. Safety was within reach. But a noise – like a large, metallic mosquito – buzzed past him. Will made a strange sound, then stumbled, and he and John fell, head over heels, down the inside wall of the trench. The last thing John saw was Will, face down in the sludge of the trench, blood pouring from his head.

"We die together," John said, then his world went black.

LANSING, Michigan June 1918

Her father would kill her if he ever found out, but she had to see for herself. The knife-like pressure in her chest was too much to bear. If she were to be cut, then she would be the one to thrust the blade.

Her hand trembled as she knocked – one, two, pause – three. A rustling on the other side of the door and then it creaked open. A large man with a little mustache appeared in the frame.

"Lil' missy, I believe you have the wrong door."

"Dub sent me."

The man's thick eyebrows shot up. "Dub? You don't look like no girl Dub would know."

She was a terrible liar and her confidence began to waiver under the man's scrutiny.

"Well, are you going to let me in?" she asked, trying to maintain her composure.

He eyed her one last time then shrugged his shoulders.

"What do I care who sent ya, as long as ya got money to spend. C'mon in, missy."

She stepped through the door and found herself in a small, windowless room containing only a table and a couple of chairs. Fear seized her for a moment as the man shut the door behind her, leaving the two of them alone in the dimly lit room. Within a moment, however, a door to the back opened and she was ushered into a much larger room full of people.

She quickly looked around. She hadn't expected there to be this many people gathered in an illegal drinking establishment in the middle of the day, but she was having a hard time finding the man she sought amongst the crowd of people gathered here. The thick fog of cigarette smoke wasn't helping the situation.

"Speakeasy?" she muttered under her breath. "There's nothing easy about this."

Worse than having to scan the dark room for the familiar face was having to suffer through the looks she was receiving from the patrons of the seedy establishment. Everyone eyed her suspiciously – everyone, that is, that wasn't face down on the table drunk or absorbed in a game of cards.

"You lookin' for someone?"

She breathed in sharply as she spun toward the voice. She hadn't realized the doorman had followed her into the bar.

"Uh, no, I mean – yes, but I don't see..."

But then she did see. Sitting in a front corner booth, with his hand half-way up the skirt of another woman, sat her fiancé.

Anger replaced trepidation as she pushed the burly door keeper out of her way. She marched to the table but stopped short. Her fists clenched, her body trembled, but she said nothing. A hundred words swirled her tongue, but her lips could voice none of them.

The woman noticed her first. Surprisingly, she actually appeared embarrassed. *'Do prostitutes experience such emotions?'* she thought.

The woman pulled away from Richard and pushed her skirt down.

"What's a matter, baby?"

The answer came in the form of an engagement ring hitting his head.

"Esther!" he cried, toppling the prostitute to the floor in his haste to leave the table. "It's not what you think!"

But Esther was already halfway to the door, determined to distance herself from the scene of dishonor. She rushed through the two doors and into the waiting car before Richard could reach her. She heard him calling her name as the cab pulled away, but she never looked back.

She clutched her heaving chest, certain that she would find an actual dagger there, slicing her heart in half. But there was no real blade, and no blood gushing from the spot. There was only the painful striking of her heart against her ribs. She looked up toward the heavens.

"Why does this keep happening to me?"

2

STILL ALIVE, BARELY

$\mathcal{H}$e wasn't dead. The searing pain radiating throughout his lower extremities told him that. But he didn't quite feel alive, either.

How many days had he been here? Two? Three? A week, maybe? John didn't know. He didn't even know where he was. He spent most of the day slipping in and out of a fog of consciousness, but he had noticed windows at one of his more lucid moments. Light streamed through them, making the thunder in his head beat even more painfully, but the colorful display the light produced didn't make sense to him. A constant rainbow? More likely a hallucination.

Doctors had come and gone several times. John had heard much of the same words over and over – tendon damage, severed muscles, spinal something, lucky. Something about barely missing his spine. A few inches to the right, the injury would have left him paralyzed. As it was, though, he would walk again. He heard talk of therapy and of hard work, but he distinctly heard someone say he would walk.

"Ward. Johnathon Ward? Can you hear me?"

John stirred in his bed and tried to focus on the man speaking to him.

"I'm Lieutenant Doherty," said a man in a white coat hovering over John's bed. "You gave us quite a scare at first, but you are going to be all right. You've been under heavy sedation, so your body could heal better, but we're going to start to reduce your pain medication now. Need to get you sitting up and moving a little. Do you understand what I'm saying?"

John blinked, but only the man's mustache and receding hairline were discernible to him. John nodded his head.

"Good. I'll be back in a few hours to check on you and see how much mobility you have."

The doctor patted his shoulder then turned to leave. He stopped at the foot of the bed to speak with someone sitting there. John concentrated on the figure despite the drug induced fog still affecting his vision. He could tell that it was another injured soldier, apparent by the bandage wrapped around his head, but he was too far away to make out anything else. The doctor walked away, and John watched as the man pulled something out of his pocket and rolled it around in his hand.

"Will," he breathed, dropping his head back on the pillow. Relief flooded his veins. Will Caffey was alive.

At the sound of John's voice, Will jumped and pulled his chair to the head of the bed.

"Glad to see you awake, John. I was beginning to worry."

"You were worried?" John groaned. "What about me? Last time I saw you, you were face down with a hole in your head."

Will smirked and touched his bandage. "Just a flesh wound. They say they'll have me back in the trenches in a couple of weeks."

"Hmmph, I wonder how long before they're sending me back?"

Will half chuckled dand shook his head. He looked at his hand and started rolling a marble around his palm.

John tried to sit up. Fire emanated from his back and shot down his right leg. He swore under his breath.

Will laughed.

"You think this is funny?" John winced, swearing again.

"Your medication is wearing off. They've kept you pretty drugged up until now."

John let out a long sigh as he straightened himself back onto the bed. "It didn't hurt this bad when it first happened."

"You were still in shock, I imagine."

He nodded his head. He probably had been in shock. They probably all had been in shock since they first stepped onto French ground. He turned his head toward his friend.

"What's the deal with the marble? You always have it with you?"

"It's an aggie," he answered, shrugging his shoulders. "And it belonged to her."

"Ah, I see," John smirked. "Your girl back home that isn't actually yours."

"Her name is Phoebe," Will chuckled. "Phoebe Albright. And she'll be mine someday – if I ever make it home."

"She must be pretty special," John said, with a hint of cynicism.

"She is."

"And beautiful?"

"The most."

"Aren't they all," John chuckled.

"Why do you hate women so much?" Will asked, aggie paused mid-roll.

"I don't hate women. They fulfill a very important role in society. They fill certain – needs," John said with a wink.

Will's jaw clenched, and he returned to the business of rolling the aggie between his fingers. John had gone too far, and he knew it. He squeezed his eyes shut and took a deep breath. He liked the kid, really, he did. He even kind of respected the dedication he had for his religion. They were so different, these two men. But somehow, they had hit it off from the first days of training at Camp Funston. John had taken a liking to the young soldier, seven years his junior. Will Caffey was a fascinating mixture of childlike innocence – an innocence he seemed to carry into every situation, including battle – and a maturity far beyond his years that was present at the same time. With Will, the glass was always half full, and his easygoing smile and good-natured humor almost made John feel as if his glass should be half full as well.

In the early days, John had worried about Will. He worried that the toils of war would wear away at the pureness of the young man. Life might have made John distrustful and cynical, but something in him wanted to keep Will from becoming like him. However, rather than ruining him, the battlefield seemed to have cultivated Will into a greater man. He had proven his marksmanship during their training days in Kansas, but on the field, it became apparent that the boy had exceptional talent with a rifle. And despite the fact that John was five inches taller, Will was broader through the shoulders and every bit as strong. But Will's physical strength paled in comparison to his inner strength. How many times had John witnessed Will comfort a frightened comrade or pray with a dying soldier during his last moments? Too many to count. Will had witnessed things that would make much older men weep, but, much like John, he seemed stronger because of it.

John opened his eyes and turned his head back toward his friend. Will continued to roll the aggie, but now his eyes were closed.

"You praying again?"

"Me?" Will chuckled. "Always."

"What do you have to pray about now? Life in the trenches, I understand, but here...hey, where are we anyway?"

A slow smile spread across the clean-shaven face of the younger soldier.

"A church. You did say *'over your dead body,'* and you were almost right."

John looked all around the makeshift hospital now, at the rows of cots filled with injured soldiers, the nurses and doctors tending them, and the windows behind them all – the colorful sunshine hallucinations were stained glass. How had he missed it before? A church, of all places. God must have a sense of humor after all.

"I was praying for you."

John looked at Will in shock.

"Didn't you hear the doctor? I'm going to be alright."

"I wasn't praying for your health. Well, not your physical health, anyway."

"Hmmph," John groaned. "Don't waste your time on my spirit, kid. I'm a hopeless cause."

"Psalm 62 says that hope comes from God, if you'll just let your soul find rest in him."

"And then will I profess unto them, I never knew you, depart from me, ye evildoer."

"Now, see, that gives me hope. You know the Bible. It's hidden in your heart, just waiting for you to allow it freedom in your life."

"Hidden in my heart? More like beaten into my flesh," John scowled.

Will's smile faded. "Your father isn't God, John."

"Tell him that," John laughed.

"You're judging your heavenly Father by your earthly father's actions."

"Actions motivated by scripture."

"Scripture distorted by a sinful man."

John didn't respond. Will was wrong, but he didn't want to

be the one to educate him about the truths of the world. Another part of that innocence he felt obligated to protect in his young friend. Besides, Will's deluded faith was obviously helping him survive this disgusting war. Let him keep his fantasies. What did it matter to John?

3

UNEXPECTED VISITOR

"Really, mother. I don't want to discuss it any more. I'm not forgiving him. It is over between Richard and me."

"I know, dear, but I'm still confused about the whole ordeal. I know what you've told me, about him being unfaithful and all, but how are you so certain that it's true?"

Esther blushed. It had been nearly two days since her parents had returned home and she had informed them that the engagement was off. To her surprise, they had asked very few questions, other than to inquire into her well-being. She was relieved that she had not needed to go into much detail, only that Richard was seeing another woman and that Esther had ended the relationship. She made no mention of the speakeasy, or of the type of woman Richard was 'seeing,' and her parents seemed uninterested in the actual details. Until now.

"I – I confronted Richard, and – he couldn't deny it," she said, keeping her eyes diverted. She prayed that would be enough to satisfy her mother's curiosity.

"Well, I say it's for the best. He wasn't right for you. And it wasn't like you really loved him, anyway."

"How can you say that?" Esther cried in frustration. "Of course, I loved him!"

"No, dear, you didn't," her mother said calmly, flipping the pie crust on the floured table.

"I was engaged to him!"

"I can't argue that fact," Mrs. Albright said, laying the rolling pin down. She wiped her hands on her apron and sighed.

"Trust me, Esther, it would hurt so much more if the love were genuine."

"I am hurt!" Esther said, raising her voice. She had never disrespected her mother, but she was being impossible.

"You are hurt, but not broken-hearted. Angry? Yes. Betrayed? Certainly. But that doesn't mean you loved the boy."

Mrs. Albright sat down next to her daughter and reached for her hand.

"Esther, how many times have you cried since you discovered the truth?"

"That's not fair. You know I'm not as emotional as other girls my age."

"How many times?"

Esther lowered her head. She had not shed a single tear in the past two days since the discovery of betrayal.

"Even emotionally strong women cry over the loss of love, Esther."

Esther sat pondering her mother's words. She wanted her to be wrong, but she knew she wasn't. Somewhere, deep inside, Esther had known all along. She wasn't in love with Richard. She never was. Just like she had never been in love with Leonard.

"It still hurts," Esther said, locking eyes with her mother.

"Of course, it does," her mother smiled gently. "I was never arguing that. I just want you to see that you will be alright. The sting of what he has done to you will fade and you'll move on. And then, someday, when you find the right man –"

"Oh, no!" Esther interrupted. "That's it for me. Two failed attempts is my limit."

She spoke with a confidence she did not feel, for even though she had recently told God she was willing to submit her whole life to His will, even if that meant a life of loneliness, it still stung to hear the words come out of her mouth.

"Oh, you don't mean that."

"Yes, I do. I'll run away to become a nun before I fall for another man!"

Mrs. Albright rolled her eyes. "One problem with that plan. You aren't Catholic."

"Now Momma, when have I ever let some little detail like that keep me from getting what I want?"

"God help the Pope if you're serious!" her mother said, throwing her hand in the air. Both women laughed.

"That sure is a sweet sound to hear in this house! Been far too little laughter over the past couple of days," Reverend Albright said, his large frame filling the kitchen doorway.

"It will return soon enough," her mother said, rising and returning to her pie crust. "Especially when your oldest shows up to dinner in a nun's habit!"

The reverend's eyebrows shot up.

"I'd like to hear that story, but it will have to wait. Esther has a visitor."

"If it's Richard again, please tell him to leave. I don't want to see him. Ever."

"It's not Richard," her father said, taking a seat at the table and snatching a piece of pie crust. "It's a young woman."

ESTHER'S CURIOSITY turned to anger when she stepped through

the door of the parlor. Of all the women in Lansing, she never expected her visitor to be Richard's harlot.

"You have some nerve! What in the world are you doing here?" she said, shutting the door to the parlor behind her. She had a few choice words for this woman that she did not need her parents hearing.

The woman's nervousness was apparent by her shallow breathing and twisting hands. She looked different somehow, and it was several moments before Esther realized what had changed. Makeup. Gone were the henna outlined eyes and red, powder-dusted cheeks, leaving wide, green eyes and freckled skin. She looked much younger, much more innocent than the woman Esther had first encountered at the bar.

"I came to speak with you, and to apologize," the young woman said, averting her eyes.

"That's rich!" Esther said, crossing her arms. "Are all prostitutes in the habit of apologizing to the women they've wronged?"

The young woman breathed in sharply. Tears welled in her eyes as she tugged on the handkerchief in her hands.

"I know I wronged you, Miss Albright, and I know you are hurt, but you've got no right to call me a prostitute."

"Well, what would you call yourself?"

"Stupid. Naïve. Loose, even," she said, tears falling freely down her cheeks. "But to insinuate that I did that – with other men – and for money..."

The sobbing woman broke something in Esther's heart, and it angered her. She was the one who had been hurt. Why should she feel pity for the woman who'd ruined her life?

"I didn't know about you," she said, finally looking up at Esther. "I swear, I thought I was the only one. He – he told me he loved me."

That last was almost a whisper, but Esther heard it clearly. She had no cause to believe her, but for some reason – she did.

"I – I thought..." Esther stuttered. "When I saw you at the speakeasy, and what you were doing...I'm sorry. I just assumed..."

"I asked him to stop, you know, in public, but he always got mad and threatened to leave me. I was just so afraid of losing him. I loved him."

Guilt flooded Esther's soul as she recalled the horrible things she had thought – and said – about the girl.

"I know now what a fool I've been," the woman said. "He never loved me."

"Did he tell you that?" Esther began, compassion growing by the minute. "I mean, now that I'm out of the picture, are you sure that Richard doesn't foresee a future with you?"

She nodded. "He laughed at me and told me he wanted nothing to do with me. He called me names much worse than you just did."

He's the devil, Esther thought. "Well, you're better off without him," she said.

At that, the girl began sobbing again. Esther moved to her side and guided her to the settee. She patted her on the back.

"There, there. I know it hurts now, but someday you will be over it. You'll forget why you ever had feelings for the man."

"You may be right," she said, her doe-like eyes glistening. "But what about the child I carry?"

4
____

GOING "HOME"

"They're sending you back already?" John asked, shifting his weight in the chair.

Will laughed. "Well, I'm not wearing this doughboy uniform for the fashion of it."

John had assumed that he and Will would return to the front together. It had only been a couple of weeks. Surely Will needed more time to heal before they sent him back to the slaughter fields. John hadn't considered the idea that Will would have to return to the fight without him. And even though it had been Will who had saved his life, John felt responsible for the kid and his safety.

But that isn't what the doctor had in mind, as John learned later that same afternoon. John wasn't returning to the front. He was returning to the States.

"Your injuries, though much improved, are more serious than we can handle from here. Stateside, you'll get the care you need. With therapy – and time – I am confident you will be able to walk pain free, maybe even without a cane, eventually."

John sat pondering the doctor's words long after he had

walked away. Eventually. Maybe. John hadn't taken the time to think about his injury long term. He had assumed they would patch him up and send him back in. But he was so broken, they couldn't fix him. And they were sending him home in hopes that someone else could. But what if therapy didn't work? What if he remained broken? Was he destined to be half a man, limping from one place to another, the rest of his life?

He was so deep in thought that he hadn't noticed Will return. He stood, staring off at something no one else could see, hands shoved deep into his pockets. John had never seen Will look so serious.

"You worried about returning to the front?" John asked.

"Me? No. Actually, I'm anxious to get back. I'm afraid that the other boys haven't had anyone to lean on while I've been gone."

"Then, why the long face?"

Will smiled weakly. "You're going home."

John's heart sank. Poor kid. "And you wish you were going home as well?"

"Well, of course I want to go home, but not until everyone else gets to go as well."

"So, you're sad about missing me? I'm touched," John said, poorly attempting to joke with the young man.

"And why would I miss your ugly mug?"

John smiled a half smile. "I told you your God is all screwed up. This is exactly the opposite of how it was supposed to happen. I thought I was looking out for you, and you ended up saving my life. And I should be the one returning to the front instead of you. You actually have something – someone to go home to."

Will absentmindedly pulled the aggie from his pocket.

"You gotta make me a promise," Will said.

"Promise? I'm not much for promises," John laughed.

"I'm serious, Johnny. You said you owe me, right?"

Now John became serious, too. "You know I would do anything for you, Will. Just ask and it will be done."

Will pulled a chair close and rested his forearms on his knees. When he looked up, tears brimmed in his blue eyes.

"If something happens – if I don't make it back..."

"Don't be ridiculous, Will."

"I'm serious. If I don't make it back, you gotta promise me – you'll find Phoebe."

"Alright," John said, perplexed.

"And you have to tell her – everything."

"Everything? I don't understand."

"Everything I've ever told you – about how I feel about her, about my plans. All those days we've spent in the trenches – you shared your past, I shared mine. I told you all about my dreams, my plans for a future with her. All that stuff – I've never told anyone any of that. Only you."

"Do you mean to tell me you've spent your entire life carrying a torch for this girl, and you never once told her how you feel?"

"Nope," Will chuckled.

"She must have some idea, though."

"I would think that she does, but I don't honestly know. When we were kids, I pestered her like crazy, chasing her on the playground, pulling her pigtails. I used to tell her all the time that I was going to marry her someday."

"What would she say?"

"She'd tell me to shut up or she was going to make me shut up."

John laughed. "Sounds like she had spunk."

"Still does. That's part of what I love so much about her. She's a little on the shy side, but she doesn't put up with any nonsense from anyone."

"Except from you?"

"Oh, no, she doesn't even take it from me," he laughed, his eyes drifting off to somewhere far from France. "When we were in high school, my favorite thing to do was to get her to laugh in the middle of class. She'd try so hard to ignore me, but I knew just how to get at her. Then, when she couldn't take it anymore, she would laugh out loud. Of course, everyone would turn and look at her. Then the blushing came – partly from embarrassment, partly from anger. Man, she'd get so mad at me. But I couldn't help myself. When she blushes, it's like a fire has ignited in her cheeks. She becomes even more beautiful – if that's possible."

John smiled. Even a cynic like himself couldn't help but be endeared to the boy. John's heart warmed listening to him talk of home.

"Shy and spunky – that's quite the combination."

"Yeah. She gets the spunkiness from her dad."

"The preacher?"

"Yeah. You'd really like him, John. He's been like a second dad to me since my own dad died. They were good friends."

John had a hard time imagining a man as generous and as kind as Will described. When he spoke of Phoebe's father, something inside of him yearned to meet the man, but he wasn't certain if it was because he wanted to prove to himself that a dad like that could exist or to prove to Will that he couldn't.

"So, do you promise?"

"How will I find this girl?"

"That's easy. She lives in the parsonage next door to Lansing First Church. And you're going to write my mother when you get stateside, right? So she can contact you if anything happens to me? Then, you'll have to travel to Lansing from wherever you are. Are you going home?"

"I don't have a home."

"I meant New York. Are they holding your job at the Times?"

"I didn't ask them to. I don't know. I could go back there, I'm sure, but I could also use a change as well."

"You know, the State Journal in Lansing could use a good journalist like you."

"I don't think I'll have difficulty finding a job. I'm sure newspapers will clamor for some reporting from the front lines."

"Yeah, but if you are in Lansing, you'll already be nearby if – you know."

John reached out and clasped Will's shoulder.

"No matter where I land, if the time comes, I'll make sure and get to Lansing to fulfill your request. You have my word."

"Thank you, John. I still think Lansing would be good for you. The Albrights would accept you as their own, as would my mother. You'd have family."

"I'm the only family I need, kid. Keeps me from getting disappointed. It also keeps me from disappointing others."

Will looked down and picked up his helmet from the floor. He frowned as he rolled it through his hands. John felt bad. Why did it mean so much to the kid that John not be alone?

"Listen, I promise I'll write to your mother. I've got to give her my information, right? But, I hope to God she never has to use it."

"Hey," Will chuckled. "Was that a prayer?"

"Hmmph! More like a curse. You do the praying. I'll do the cursing."

Will just shook his head as he scribbled something onto a scrap of paper. "My mother's address," he said, handing it to John.

The two shook hands, half smiling, neither saying a word. Then, without warning, Will leaned over and wrapped his arms around John. John couldn't remember the last time he had been hugged, but after the initial shock, he found himself returning the embrace. As quickly as it had begun, it ended and Will left. The pain in his back was nothing compared to the pain John felt as he watched Will walk away. It should be him going back to war, not that innocent kid. If Will's God was real, he must not have his head stuck on straight, because he got this all wrong.

"Well, soldier, I hear you're leaving me."

John smiled at the pretty nurse as she slid around the foot of his bed. Although he knew she flirted with all the injured soldiers, her sweet smile and flattery had been a nice distraction from the constant pain in his back.

"I'm afraid that is true, my dear. How will you ever survive without me?"

"I'll do my best, but my days won't be as bright. It's not often men as handsome as you and that friend of yours come through here. And now you're both leaving me."

"Actually, Will's already gone."

"That's too bad," she pouted playfully. "Without a goodbye kiss?"

"Not from that one – unless your name is Phoebe, he won't be interested."

"And what about you? Are you interested?"

John smiled at the buxom brunette. How he wished he weren't injured so he could show her just how interested he was. But he wasn't sure he'd ever again be in a position to offer a woman anything more than a smile.

"Maybe in a different place and time, sweetheart."

"And where would that place be? Where do you call home, soldier?"

"I'm what you might call an orphan of sorts. I don't like to stay put in any one place for too long."

"Well, you gotta have some place to call home."

"No, I don't."

"What am I supposed to do with this paperwork?" she asked, waving a clipboard in the air. "We gotta send you somewhere. So tell me, handsome, where are we shipping you?"

John thought for a moment, then sighed.

"I suppose Lansing, Michigan is as good a place as any."

5

SPINSTER SCHOOL

*E*sther entered the house and ripped off her hat in one fluid motion. She threw it on the table that sat nestled against the stairs in the entry of the small parsonage that the Albright family called home. Her scalp stung a little and the pompadour she had worked so diligently on earlier that day stuck out from where the hat pins had been ripped, but she couldn't care less at the moment. All she cared about was that classes were over for the day and she was finally home. One more day completed and one more day closer to receiving her certificate. Not that she was excited about a future as a secretary. She was simply looking forward to never again having to step foot in Yvonne Rock School for Secretaries, or, as she was prone to call it, Spinster school.

As she walked past the dining room, she caught a glimpse of her reflection in the mirror hanging over the buffet. She couldn't help but laugh at the ridiculous picture she presented, wads of hair pulled free of her coif and sticking out in all directions.

"Well, at least my dress looks presentable," she said.

"I would say your dress is far more than presentable," came

a voice from behind her. "But as the designer of said piece of clothing, maybe I'm just a little biased."

Esther whipped around and nearly knocked over her mother's vase of roses sitting on the side table.

"Anna!" she squealed, rushing to her friend and gathering her into an embrace. "What a pleasant surprise on such a dreary day!"

"Dreary day?" Anna Mallory laughed. "Are you well? The sun is shining. There isn't a cloud in the sky."

"I wouldn't know," Esther said, pulling back from her friend. "I've been trapped indoors. I suppose it is my time in spinster school, rather than the weather, that has clouded my happiness."

"Spinster school?" Anna searched her friend's face. "Now I am certain you are unwell."

"Secretary school. Spinster school. They are one and the same."

"I hardly believe that at twenty-two you can be labeled a spinster."

"My age doesn't matter. My enrollment in this silly school has sentenced me to spinsterhood."

Anna rolled her eyes. "You hate it that much?"

"It really is a drudgery. I am counting down the days until it is all over, but then, what do I have to look forward to besides a lifetime of the same?"

"Oh, stop being so melancholy. You just need some handsome man to sweep you off your feet and you'll forget all about this nonsense."

"The way Warren swept you off yours? You are married, yet you continue to work."

"That's different. I'm following my dream, not a paycheck. Warren doesn't care if I work or if I tend his home, as long as I'm happy."

"Marriage and happiness don't always coincide."

"It will for you, someday. You just have to find the right person."

"Easy for you to say. There hasn't been a day since you met him that you haven't been in love with your husband. How is Warren, by the way?"

"Busy. After our honeymoon on Mackinac Island and the trip to New York, he came back to such a backlog of work at the paper that I have seen very little of him since we returned."

"That's terrible, Anna. Surely his employees can do something to ease his load in light of his new marriage."

"I'm sure they would if they could, but three more employees were drafted while we were gone. There simply aren't enough hands to accomplish the work. But Warren assures me that it will get better. In fact, he has hired a new man, a soldier returned from the front with journalism experience. He says he is working out really well and thinks this gentleman will do a great deal in lifting the strain placed on him."

Esther was glad to hear that things were going so splendidly for her friend and her husband. There was a time when Anna's heart had been just as broken as Esther's, maybe worse, when mistaken identity and misunderstandings threatened to keep her from the man of her dreams. But God had cleared up the confusion and mended their relationship, and Esther had a difficult time remembering that Anna's life hadn't always been so bright.

"So, tell me, how was your trip to New York? Was it everything you had hoped?"

"Goodness me, I nearly forgot!" Anna laughed. "I came here with the express purpose of showing you something I brought back for you." Anna picked up a parcel wrapped in thick brown paper and handed it to Esther. "I brought something home for Phoebe as well, but I'm saving it until she comes for a visit. Will she be home for Thanksgiving?"

"I'm not certain. Last year she stayed at school to help a local church distribute food to needy families. I'm planning on writing to her this week, so I will ask. Maybe if I hint that you have a surprise for her, it will entice her to come home."

"I hope she does. I'm dying to tell her about the female evangelist we heard speak while we were in New York. She was so inspiring, and all I could think of was how exciting it will be to hear Phoebe share the gospel."

Phoebe, unlike Esther, had never set her sights on marriage. From a young age, Phoebe had known she wanted to minister to the lost and had wasted little time in enrolling in Bible College after graduating high school. Esther was proud of her sister and all she had accomplished, but she missed her more than she had ever expressed. She missed the camaraderie the two of them shared and yearned for someone to pour her heart out to, especially now that her life had changed in a way she had not expected. Esther's other sister, Sarah, was far too young to understand, and her mother, although a good listener and a loving parent, was still, well, her mother, and it simply wasn't the same as having your sister to cry out to. The summer had been a dismal season, with Phoebe off helping with revivals and Anna honeymooning with her new husband. And that dreariness was only made worse by the stuffy dark rooms and incessantly clattering typewriters at spinster school.

"I'm so glad you're home," Esther said, sighing. In the absence of her sister, her best friend was exactly what she needed.

"So am I." Anna smiled at Esther and placed her hands on her shoulders. "Now, open that package. I'm nearly bursting with anticipation!"

Esther laughed as she untied the string. As the wrapping fell away, it exposed the most delicate lavender silk Esther had ever set her eyes on.

"You wouldn't believe the stores in New York City. They put

our Arbaugh's and Knapp's to shame." Anna unfolded the fabric onto the table. "I found this in a high-end store on Fifth Avenue and thought of you immediately. It will be beautiful with your coloring. I was thinking an afternoon dress, but it's delicate enough that I could make you an evening gown if you prefer."

"I seldom am in need of an evening gown," Esther said as her finger lightly traced the silk. "I would so love a new afternoon dress, but when would you have time?"

"For you, I will make the time. Besides, fittings will be a great excuse for us to catch up. I felt just awful leaving you this summer, after how horribly Richard treated you."

"You have nothing to feel awful about. Besides, if you hadn't gone, would I have this lovely fabric?"

"I'm so glad you like it, but just so you know...I did not pick out this silk for a dreary, old spinster. I picked it out for my beautiful, full-of-life friend, so unless that friend decides to show up and kick this sad excuse for Esther out of your body, then this dress may never get created."

Esther laughed. "Just the thought of a new dress is enough to shake me out of my gloom. Come on and help me pin my hat back into place. I could use a cherry phosphate and a long talk. Let's head to the drug store."

In truth, Esther's spirits were lifted with the return of her friend. Maybe she wasn't happy with the way her life was turning out, but she was certainly happy with those she got to live her life with. And a cherry phosphate wouldn't hurt, either.

6

———

NIGHTMARES

"*S*top!" John yelled, bolting upright. Sweat poured down his face as his eyes searched the darkness. It took him a moment to realize where he was, but soon the sparse furniture of the small apartment he rented in North Lansing came into focus and his breathing slowed to a more normal pace. He was in Michigan, not France.

He tossed off the covers and threw his long legs over the side of the bed. He leaned forward, rested his elbows on his knees and rubbed his face. He was haunted, not by real ghosts, but by the ghostly image of Will running from him, straight into enemy lines. *It was only a dream,* John tried to reason, but the image of his best friend's body jerking unnaturally from the force of ammunition connecting with human flesh would not leave his mind. It wasn't the first dream he'd had of his friend, nor was it the most graphic, but something about this dream made John feel more unsettled than the rest.

John was slowly coming back to full consciousness, as the fog that is the dream world dissipated, but John struggled to remain in the dream, trying to capture the memory of what was different about this one. So much was the same: the fear, the despair, the inability to reach Will in time. John had almost grown accustomed to the sleepless, nightmare-filled nights that now outnumbered the dreamless ones. So why did this dream disturb him so? He was about to stand up, give up his futile attempt at grasping for fog, when it came back to him. Words. Will's words. John's dreams were always filled with sound - the thack-slurp, thack-slurp of heavy boots through muddy trenches, the pop-pop-pop sound of gunfire echoing across the open fields, the grunt-thud of soldiers' limp bodies hitting the ground — but never words.

Will lay, arm outstretched toward John like in all John's dreams, and, this time, he spoke.

"You left me. You weren't here to save me." A small river of blood trickled out of the corner of his mouth. "How could you forget me?"

John crossed the room and poured himself a glass of water, wishing it were something much stronger, and once again cursed his stupidity for moving to the dry region of Ingham County. Not that alcohol would make a difference. If it could, last night's visit to the speakeasy would have solved all his problems. Instead, he was left a pair of new ones — cotton-mouth and a headache. No, John realized, alcohol solved nothing. It couldn't even make John forget. Not even for a moment.

John pulled the curtain back and looked at the street below. By the amount of activity on the streets of his neighborhood, he judged it to be about midday. His pocket watch on his bedside table could confirm or deny John's suspicion, but he saw no need for that. It was Saturday and he had not a single plan for the day.

Out of practice rather than purpose, John dressed for the day. Maybe he would take a walk down by the Grand River. The therapy the Army doctors had prescribed was going well, and the more he moved, the better his mobility seemed to be. He couldn't wait until he could throw the blasted cane in the river, and he knew he would never get to that point if he didn't put in the effort. With a renewed sense of purpose, John donned his overcoat and reached for his cane.

As he reached for it, it slipped out of reach and clattered to the floor. He swore. While walking was getting much easier, bending was still a difficult endeavor. He placed his hand on the wall to steady himself and slowly bent over to retrieve the cane. With every inch he came closer to it, the dull ache in his lower back that he had almost grown accustomed to intensified. His outstretched fingers had nearly reached their intended target when his balance, hindered by the leftover alcohol in his system, faltered. His hand on the wall slipped and John found himself on the floor, excruciating pain shooting down his legs.

John remained on the floor for several minutes, cursing loudly and slamming his fist against the wooden floor slats. Slowly, the pain began to subside, but, knowing the effort it would take to rise would cause just as much pain as he had experienced getting into this position, John had little motivation to move. Maybe he would just spend the day here, lying on the hard floor, staring at the cracks in his ceiling. It was more of a plan than he had when he had first risen for the day. He could always go for a walk tomorrow, or next weekend, or next month.

John's head dropped to the side and his eyes settled on the offensive walking stick that had gotten him into this mess. He was determined not to live the rest of his life chained to the cane. It had been more than twenty years since he'd had to rely on anything, or anyone, else. He wasn't about to allow an inanimate object to control him any more than he had allowed his father to. He gritted his teeth and rolled onto his side. As he reached for his cane and steadied it on the ground for leverage, he noticed a piece of paper sticking out from under the furniture. He wondered how many other items had fallen under the dresser, but when he swiped his cane beneath it, the action only brought out the one piece of paper.

John put the cane aside and opened the folded scrap. Inside, an address was scribbled. He didn't recognize the address, but he did recognize the handwriting. It was Will's handwriting.

He squeezed his eyes shut as he clutched the paper in his fist. He had avoided the visit long enough.

With a new mission on his mind, John rolled over and, with the help of his cane and a nearby chair, pulled himself to standing. He was amazed at how little pain it caused. In fact, he felt no residual pain from the fall, only the dull ache he had grown accustomed to. He thought it was strange but dismissed the tiny miracle as nothing more than a result of the hard work he was putting in during therapy. He looked once more at the note in his hand.

"I haven't forgotten you, Will," he said, grabbing his fedora and heading out the door.

7

MRS. CAFFEY

"**W**ell, Esther, this is a surprise!"

"I'm sorry, Mrs. Caffey. I know it's been ages," Esther said, following the older woman into the parlor. She led her to a yellow loveseat.

"Oh, I know you're busy, what with your studies and all."

Esther squirmed in her seat a little in an attempt to loosen the stiff muscles in her lower back. Another souvenir from 'spinster school.'

"Yes, well, I'm nearly finished with my schooling, so hopefully I will have a little more free time to visit."

"That is, until you find employment as a secretary."

"Yes," Esther sighed. "I do have that to look forward to."

"You aren't happy with your career choice, are you dear?"

"Choice? What choice do I have?"

"You have all the choices in the world, as far as the Lord will allow, that is."

"Well, it seems as if the Lord is allowing me to be nothing more than an old-maid receptionist."

"Oh, Esther!" Mrs. Caffey laughed. "You are one for dramatics. I'm sure it won't be half as bad as you believe it will.

Besides, it's not as if you have to spend the next fifty years behind a typewriter."

"Only until I die."

"Or marry," Mrs. Caffey said, eyeing Esther knowingly. They'd had many talks on the subject of marriage since Esther's last breakup.

"You know I am cursed when it comes to men."

"One bad breakup is not a curse."

"But I've had *two* failed engagements."

"Oh, you cannot compare your breakup with Richard with what happened with Leonard."

There were undeniable similarities between the two breakups, but Mrs. Caffey was correct. Esther could not put Richard in the same category as Leonard. Yes, she had discovered Leonard in an embrace with another woman, but as he'd later explained, the encounter was intended to be a farewell to that woman, even though his heart truly belonged to her and not to Esther. Being a good and kind man, Leonard had fully intended to keep his promise of marriage to Esther, but God knew what was best for the both of them. Esther could never have been truly happy with him, and Mabel was clearly God's plan for Leonard all along. They are so well suited for one another, and so in love. Esther was actually grateful that God had caused her to stumble upon the two.

But Richard was different. Richard was dallying with another woman in a seedy establishment, not innocently saying goodbye to the woman he loved in a church classroom. But the one similarity that Esther could not push from her mind was that the two men, although completely different in personality and intent, had both rejected her for another.

"I don't think I will ever find love, a man who will choose me above all others."

"Just because you've had a bit of a bad time with love doesn't mean you won't find it someday. But you must put God first, in everything. Something tells me that in the area of love, you haven't been doing that."

Esther lowered her eyes, knowing Mrs. Caffey had discovered a truth she found difficult to admit.

"Do you remember when that woman evangelist visited our church several years ago?" Esther said.

"The one from Boston?"

"Yes, that's the one. I was so fascinated by everything she said. I had never seen a woman preach before, and it was as if I were looking at a grown-up version of myself. I don't feel called to be an evangelist, mind you, but her sense of humor, her boldness, even the way she prayed – it was like I had finally found someone like myself."

"Yes, I can see that," Mrs. Caffey chuckled.

"But then she started sharing how God had told her that she was going to be single her entire life, and I think something inside of me started to panic. What if that was God's plan for me? What if he didn't have a husband for me? What if I was supposed to live my life alone? The thought was terrible to a young teenager – it's still terrible to me. I think that's when I put up a wall between God and my love life. I knew I had free will in this life, and I guess I decided then and there that I would exercise that free will and find my own husband."

Mrs. Caffey listened quietly but said nothing.

"You must think I'm silly to worry about whether or not God wants me to live my life alone."

She still said nothing.

"You are being unusually quiet," Esther said nervously.

Mrs. Caffey inhaled deeply and released the breath slowly.

"I'm sorry, Esther. I was just praying. I want to make certain that I answer you with God's words, not my own. Do you want to know what scripture God gave me this morning in my Bible study?"

"Of course."

"It was Philippians 4:19. 'But my God will supply all of your needs according to his riches in glory by Christ Jesus."

It was Esther's turn to be quiet. She turned the scripture over and over in her mind, trying to decipher God's meaning for her. When she finally spoke, it was a mere whisper.

"So, you think God is saying that it won't be a man who fulfills my needs, but that He will?"

"Maybe. I don't know for certain. What I do know is that you need to trust him to fill your need for love, and that when he does, it will be according to His will, His riches, not your own."

"But – it could also mean that I'm to live my life as a spinster."

"Yes, dear, it could."

Esther took a deep breath. "Well, I suppose there's one good thing about being a spinster."

"What's that, dear?"

"No more broken engagements. You can't be left at the altar if you're never asked to go there in the first place."

JOHN STOOD on the corner and looked at the street sign, then he looked at Will's note. Cherry Street. This was the place. He crossed the street and headed in the direction of the descending house numbers. Walking seemed easier this afternoon and he found he had to rely on his cane very little. Maybe that fall had done something to improve his condition.

He passed each home, taking note of the house numbers. He looked ahead and counted the houses before him. If his calculations were correct, Will's mother's home was the last one on the block. It was still several houses away, but even from this distance, the small bungalow was exactly what John had expected it to look like. Pristine, white pickets adorned the fence, bordered by fall mums of various colors. White trim gleamed against the wood siding, painted an especially happy color of yellow. A picture-perfect house. Yes, that is exactly what John expected from the home that produced Will Caffey.

He was still several houses away when the door opened and two women emerged. The shorter one wore an apron and no coat - Mrs. Caffey, John assumed. The other woman wore a stylish overcoat and feathered hat, making John assume her to be much younger. The angle gave John a slight glimpse of her mouth, which was spread in a wide smile. If the rest of her face matched that smile, John judged the woman to be a beauty.

She walked down the little sidewalk and out the picket gate, but, to John's disappointment, turned the other way. He really wasn't interested in meeting the lady, but thought he'd have enjoyed the view that passing by her would've afforded. However, watching her slender form as it walked away wasn't a bad option either, he decided. *If this is what this side of town had to offer,* he thought, *I might find myself visiting Will's mother on a regular basis.*

When John finally took his eyes off the departing figure, he looked back at the house and saw the other woman still outside. It was then that he realized that she was looking at him. Being closer now, he could see she was smiling. Her hair, pulled tightly in a low knot at the back of her head, was mostly gray, but the dark brown strands that streaked throughout the chignon hinted at the hair color of her youth. He entered through the picket gate and as he drew near, he could see that her eyes, a bright blue, were unmistakably familiar to John. There was no doubt about it. This was the mother of Will Caffey.

John removed his hat and was about to introduce himself when the woman, smile still in place, rushed off her porch and threw her arms around him.

"John Ward! What took you so long?"

He used his cane to steady himself and keep from tipping over, although he wasn't certain what was more surprising, the fact that she knew who he was or the act of physical affection.

"How - how do you know who I am?" he asked.

Mrs. Caffey pulled back and clasped her hands. "Will's letters. I would have recognized you anywhere."

"I suppose," John said, tapping his cane on the ground, "this makes me rather recognizable."

Mrs. Caffey scowled and looked at the cane as if she had just now noticed it. "Oh, that. No, dear, I was talking about your height. Will said you were taller than most men in your platoon. He also said you spent most of the time scowling. So, when I saw you, I just put two and two together."

"Scowl?" John asked, but even as he did, he knew she was right. Leave it to Caffey to write to his mother about facial expressions. John chuckled and shook his head.

Mrs. Caffey laughed and clapped her hands in front of her chest. "Will also said that when you do smile, your whole face lights up and it's hard to believe you ever frowned a day in your life. Yes, indeed. You are without a doubt John Ward."

The woman was so open with whatever thoughts flooded her mind, a character trait John had seen very little of in his lifetime. In his experience, people attempted to do and say what they thought would make them look good. This woman, however, found joy in expressing exactly what she thought.

"Come, come. Let's not stand out here to catch a cold. We have so much getting-to-know-you to do. Are you hungry, dear? I have leftover roast. I could make you a sandwich."

"You don't have to trouble yourself," John said. He was in fact very hungry, the effects of last night's drinking making eating impossible up until this moment, but he didn't intend to spend very much time with the woman. Stop by, introduce himself, then make some sort of excuse for a quick exit. He felt an obligation to visit her, for Will's sake, but he didn't want to get too friendly.

"It's no trouble at all. And I have a chicken for dinner this evening. Don't tell me you can't stay. I won't take no for an answer." Mrs. Caffey turned and walked into the house, holding the door for John to follow her. He sighed. His quick visit was apparently turning into an all-day event.

The inside of the Caffey home was just as bright and cheery as the exterior. Flowery, wallpapered walls made the perfect backdrop for the decidedly feminine furniture and tables covered with crocheted doilies. It was so different from the masculine, wood-paneled walls and leather seating of his childhood homes. There were no expensive pieces of art or tapestry on the walls, but there was a fairly extensive display of photographs chronicling Will's childhood, which John found strange for a family of such modest means. John came from a wealthy family and he wasn't certain there was a single picture of his youth.

After a sandwich made from possibly the best roast beef John had ever tasted, Mrs. Caffey led them to a small parlor off the front hallway. She motioned for John to sit in a large, wing-back chair made of a rough, brown fabric, the only piece of furniture with any masculine appeal.

"My late husband's chair," she said as she seated herself in a smaller, gold rocker. "For months after his death, I would wake in the morning and find William curled up on that seat, fast asleep. I know that he cried himself to sleep many nights, but he was so brave and tried to hide it from me. He was so young, poor Will, when his father passed. I think the chair brought him comfort. You know what I mean?"

John didn't. He didn't have that kind of relationship with his own father. In fact, John was certain he wouldn't shed a single tear when news of his own father's death eventually came.

John cleared his throat. "Have you heard from Will?" he

said, hoping to change the subject. He was angry that he had allowed his thoughts to travel to his past.

Mrs. Caffey reached for a box on the floor next to her chair and placed it in her lap. When she opened it, he could see it was full of letters. From Will, he supposed. There were many nights, holed up in a bunker, that he had watched as Will had penned a note to someone back home. That box contained a large portion of those letters.

"Let me see...ah yes, here is the most recent. Shall I read it?"

"If it wouldn't be an inconvenience."

Mrs. Caffey laughed. "Inconvenience? I read them over and over when I'm alone. It will be nice to have someone to share them with!"

Mrs. Caffey opened the envelope and unfolded the paper. It looked very worn, evidence that she had spoken the truth about rereading the letters.

"Dear Ma," she read. "He always calls me Ma. Never mother or momma. Always Ma. 'Dear Ma, Well, my French vacation continued along the Marne river. We're fighting alongside the Poilu - what we call the French soldiers. It means 'hairy', not a particularly flattering term, but neither is Doughboy, the name they call our US boys. But we all get along alright. It was strange at first, since most of our boys don't speak French and most the Poilu don't speak English, but fighting Jerries is a universal language, I suppose."

John had been following Will's division through news received from the front. Marne was six weeks ago.

"I've heard rumors that we're headed to a place called St. Mihiel. It's a two day walk, but I hear it's beautiful country, so at least I'll enjoy the scenery."

John sighed inwardly. He had hoped for some new information, especially some sort of hint as to Will's location. Although clearly written to cheer his mother, this letter didn't sound too different from the last correspondence John had received from him. Of course, John's letter from Will said nothing about vacations or scenic walks.

"Well, I should probably try to get a quick wink or two while it's quiet. Give my love to everyone back home. I miss you. Love, Will." Mrs. Caffey carefully re-folded the letter and placed it back in the worn envelope. "Well, that's the last I've heard from him."

"What date was that written?"

Mrs. Caffey turned the paper over and read. "The third of August."

The same date as John's letter. He had hoped she had received something more recent.

"You're worried," Mrs. Caffey said softly.

"No," John lied. "Of course not."

A kind smile broke across the older woman's face. "John, dear, don't trouble yourself. Will has a lot of prayers going up on his behalf. He'll come home safely to us."

It took every ounce of willpower that John possessed to not scoff at Mrs. Caffey's statement. Her blind faith was foolish, but that gave him no cause to disrespect the woman in her own home.

"Besides," she continued, "if there were bad news from the front, wouldn't the newspaper be one of the first to hear of it?"

"Of course, you're right," he said. At least he hoped she was right, but John knew firsthand that the US government wasn't always forthcoming in their reports on the Great War. He couldn't believe the misinformation, as well as lack of information, that he encountered when he returned stateside. It seemed the military preferred to paint a pretty picture for the folks back home, rather than give an honest portrayal of the horrors actually happening at the front.

"Let's pray together for him. It always makes me feel better."

"No, ma'am," John said, shaking his head. He may allow her to express her faith while in her own home without his criticism, but he'd be darned before he would be forced to join in her fantasy world. "I don't believe in that."

Without flinching, she smiled warmly and extended her delicate, wrinkled hands toward him. "That's fine, dear, but you won't object if I pray, will you?"

Staring into her kind, blue eyes, eyes so like her son's, John could find no words to object. Before he knew what he was doing, he found himself holding the old woman's hands and staring at her bowed head as she spoke words of petition for Will to God - a God that John had not spoken to for over twenty years.

As she prayed, the hair on John's arms stood on end. Did a cool breeze just kick up from the open window across the room? He wasn't certain, but he did know one thing. The soothing sound of Mrs. Caffey's words did have a calming effect on him, no matter what words she chose or who she chose to pray them to. He decided he liked the feeling. John also decided, despite his initial feelings on the matter, that he was going to make a habit of visiting Will's Ma.

8

CONFRONTATION

The next Saturday turned out to be an especially bright and sunny day, a rarity for Michigan in early October. Esther had been cooped up in the stuffy upstairs classroom of her secretarial school all week and she longed to take in the fresh air this unique day afforded. So, when her little sister Sarah begged her to take her to feed the ducks, Esther jumped at the chance to get out of the house.

When they arrived at the Grand River, they discovered that they were not the only Lansing residents eager to enjoy the beautiful weather. As Sarah skipped toward the waterfront, the bag of stale bread swinging from her hand, Esther's gaze searched the park for a vacant seat to rest on. Every bench was taken, but one bench, not far from Sarah's perch on the riverbank, had only one woman seated on it. Surely, she wouldn't mind sharing with Esther for a while.

As Esther neared the woman, she thought there was something familiar about her. Something about the wavy, red hair and long, slender neck that reminded Esther of someone she had met. As she came closer, the wind blew a loose strand of hair into the woman's face, and as she reached up to tuck the errant lock behind her ear, she turned her head enough for Esther to realize that she had in fact seen the woman... once in the speakeasy and once in Esther's own home.

For a split second, Esther stopped and considered retracing her steps, but the look on the woman's face as she stared at the ground in front of her, so solemn on such a bright and sunny day, compelled her to move forward. She walked steadily toward the bench and stood next to it.

"Hello," Esther said.

The young woman looked up and made no attempt to conceal her surprise as she recognized Esther. She quickly recovered and quietly replied. "Hello."

"May I?" Esther asked, motioning to the bench.

"Oh, yes. Yes, of course."

Esther sat down and scanned the crowd for sight of her sister. Sarah was near and had found another little girl with whom to share her duck feed. The two young girls stood giggling, tearing pieces of hard bread off the old loaf and tossing them toward the grateful flock of ducks. Esther turned back to the other woman who had been fidgeting with the strings of her purse since Esther's arrival.

"I never got your name," Esther said, breaking the silence.

"Oh, yes, I'm sorry. I'm Katherine. Katherine Feegle, but my friends call me Katie."

"So, does that mean I may call you Katie?" Esther asked with a smile.

Katie's face visibly relaxed.

"I would like that very much, Miss Albright," she grinned with a sigh.

"Well, if you are Katie to me, then I am most certainly Esther to you. No point in formalities at this point."

"Alright, Esther."

"Well, Katie, tell me, what are you doing here? Did you come to feed the ducks as well?"

"No," Katie laughed. "I'm just taking a break. I've been looking for work all day. There was an opening for housekeeper at the hotel across the street there that included a room. I was really hoping to get it, but they filled it before I got there."

"Housekeeping? Wouldn't that be strenuous work for someone – well, in your condition?"

"Miss – I mean, Esther, in my condition, I can't be choosy. I need a job and a place to live, and I need it now. My friend Rhonda said I could have a job at the speakeasy, but it doesn't come with a room. Well, not unless I'm willing to do more unsavory work."

"More unsavory than housekeeping?"

The redhead blushed nearly the color of her freckles. "Yes. The rooms they are offering are only for girls willing to entertain gentlemen, you know, in the way you assumed I already did."

"Oh," Esther said, eyes wide. "I'm sorry. I should have understood your meaning without you having to go into detail. I'm not familiar with that – well, lifestyle. I'm sorry if I embarrassed you."

"It's alright. You didn't know."

"How long do you have before your lease is up on your current residence?"

"I didn't have a lease. I was living with my parents."

"Was?"

"Yes. I'm not really showing much yet, but enough for my Mama to notice. My Daddy kicked me out last week."

"Onto the streets? You must be joking!"

"No, I'm not. But good riddance, I say. With me gone, he won't have anyone but her to beat on, so she sealed her own fate when she ratted me out to him."

Dear Lord, how much has this woman had to endure? Esther wondered.

"But a week ago? Where have you been living, Katie?"

"Oh, here and there, but mostly with Rhonda above the bar. But the owner made it very clear to her that I wasn't to spend another night unless I was willing to go to work for them. So, here I am."

"But – but what will you do if you don't find a place?"

Tears glistened on her pale lashes.

"I'm not sure. I'd rather sleep on the streets than sell my body, but who's to say that I won't be accosted on the streets? Maybe Rhonda is right. Maybe working upstairs is better than starving out here. I mean, Richard used me for my body. What difference would it make if anyone else did as well?"

Katie held her head high, but Esther could see the fear in her eyes. *Darn you, Richard,* Esther thought furiously. If only he were here right now.

"You're not sleeping on the streets, Katie, and you certainly aren't prostituting yourself."

"Trust me, it's the last thing I want to do, but I've put myself in this position. God's only punishing me for the bad choices I've made."

"God doesn't work that way." Esther thought for a moment. "Sarah, it's time to go," she called, rising from the bench. "Come with me," she said to Katie.

"Where are we going?"

"Just trust me. I've got a plan. "

"ESTHER, What a pleasant surprise! And Sarah! I'm so glad you came to visit." Mrs. Caffey hugged the youngest Albright sister to her chest and kissed the top of her head.

"Me too," Sarah said. "Do you have any cookies?"

"Sarah!" Esther chastised.

"Oh, you leave her be," Mrs. Caffey scoffed. "I just baked

some fresh to take to the hospital for the soldiers. They are cooling on the stove. You go help yourself to some."

The older woman smiled as Sarah skipped off in the direction of the kitchen, then turned her attention back to the two young women.

"Hello dear, I'm Mrs. Caffey," she said to Katie.

"I'm sorry," Esther apologized, embarrassed that she'd overlooked introductions. "This is my friend, Katie."

"It's a pleasure to meet you," Katie said.

"You as well. Come, come. Let's have a seat. I've been standing at the oven for hours and could use a bit of a break."

She led them to the parlor just as Sarah came skipping in.

"You sure made a lot of cookies. Do you think the soldiers really need that many?"

"Well, there are a lot of soldiers, dear. Why? What else should I do with them?"

"Well, I could eat a bunch of them for you, you know, so you had less to carry all that way."

"Sarah, Momma would tan your hide if she heard you!"

"Awe, hush now Esther. Sarah knows she can speak as she pleases in my house. You and Phoebe always did. Why should things be any different for her?"

"You know, she only comes here to eat your cookies."

"I only bake cookies so she can come over and eat them. Go on, Sarah, but don't make yourself sick. I don't want your mother upset with me."

Esther remembered all too well the times she had returned home with a stomach ache after visiting the Caffeys. Mrs. Caffey baked the best cookies.

"So, what's on your mind Esther?"

"Am I that obvious?"

"To me, yes. But I've known you a long time."

Esther smiled at her and took a deep breath.

"I was hoping you would allow Katie to move in with you for a while."

Both women looked at her in shock. Esther continued undeterred.

"She's been put out by her parents and she needs a place to stay until she can get on her feet. And since Will is away fighting in the war, I thought you might appreciate the company. Katie is actively looking for work, so she won't be underfoot much. And, she can help you around the house, if need be."

"I see," Mrs. Caffey said, eyeing Katie. She fell silent for several moments and Esther feared that she had made a mistake asking the woman for such a big favor.

"So, Katie, who's the boy?" Mrs. Caffey finally asked.

"Wha – what do you mean?"

"The one that got you pregnant?"

Esther and Katie gasped in unison.

"How did – how did you know?" Katie stammered.

Mrs. Caffey sighed and smiled sweetly. "You've been kicked out of your home, your cheeks are glowing and you keep placing your hand on your stomach. I'm no Sherlock Holmes, but I can decipher those clues."

Katie dropped her hand to her lap, twisting the fabric of her skirt between her palms. A tear fell silently onto the folds.

"Richard," she finally whispered.

It was Mrs. Caffey's turn to gasp. Esther felt herself sit up straighter and her chin lift a little as the woman turned in shock to her.

"Your Richard?" she asked Esther.

"I didn't know he was her Richard, I swear," Katie gushed before Esther could respond. She never looked up, just shook her head as the tears flowed freely.

Esther reached out to grab one of her trembling hands. "He

was never my Richard. He wasn't either of ours. He played us both for the fool."

Mrs. Caffey sat staring at the floor shaking her head. "What happened to that boy? He was always such a good and loving kid when he was little."

"He's evil," Esther muttered.

"We're all evil," Mrs. Caffey said, the gentleness returning to her face. "His sin is no different than your sin, Esther, or mine for that matter."

Esther would never disrespect Mrs. Caffey by arguing with her, but she could not agree with her right now. Of course, Richard was evil. Why else would a man willfully sin against God, then discard another human and leave her to deal with the consequences alone?

"Give me a moment," Mrs. Caffey said, rising and leaving the room.

Katie looked at Esther, eyebrows raised, but Esther had no answer for her. It was several minutes before the older woman returned with a tea tray. She sat it down, poured a cup and offered it to Katie.

"Oh," Katie said, "I'm sorry, but I don't think I could right now."

"It's peppermint tea, dear. It will settle your stomach."

Katie smiled and accepted the cup. "Is it that obvious?"

"You're greener than a cucumber. The peppermint will do wonders. Don't worry, the first trimester is always the worst – especially the mornings. But there are things you can do to help, like getting plenty of rest. Once you finish your tea, I'll show you to your room and I want you to lie down."

"I can stay?"

"Of course. Esther knew what she was doing bringing you here. Now, go on, finish your tea."

Sarah skipped in, a cookie in each hand, and plopped down on the floor at Mrs. Caffey's feet.

"Sarah!" Esther scolded. "Where are your manners? You are dropping crumbs everywhere."

"Oh, never you mind," Mrs. Caffey said. "Nothing that can't be cleaned up. Leave the child alone."

Esther watched as Mrs. Caffey winked at the little girl, grabbing a golden curl. She sat stroking Sarah's hair, just like she had always Esther's and Phoebe's. There was never any doubt when Mrs. Caffey loved you, and it was impossible not to love her in return.

Watching her sister blissfully munch cookies while having her hair stroked caused Esther to smile. Sarah was so like her – a miniature version of herself in fact, but still so innocent, still too young to understand the evils of this world and hurt that awaited her in life. She took a sip of her peppermint tea as the thought of someone hurting her little sister made the acids in her stomach roil. If anyone ever treated Sarah the way Richard had treated her – and Katie – she would find a way to make them pay.

Esther shakily sat her cup and saucer back on the tray. She clenched her fists, trying to keep the fury building inside of her under control.

"Mrs. Caffey, could I leave Sarah with you for a while? I have an errand I need to run."

JOHN'S CANE clicked along as he made his way down the sidewalk. He hated using the blasted thing, but therapy had been especially painful today, so there was no getting around it. Besides, where he was headed no one paid much heed to him, much less his cane.

He turned down a side street not much bigger than an alley. He knew the way well. His life had fallen into a simple pattern since moving to Lansing. Work, therapy, drink, sleep, repeat.

Had he known that Ingham County had passed prohibition laws years ago, he might have thought twice about accepting the job at the State Journal, but it wasn't so bad. It hadn't been difficult at all locating an underground establishment near his new home.

As he neared the entrance, a taxicab pulled up outside.

Strange, John thought. This bar wasn't the kind you would travel a great distance for. Its patrons were mostly locals. *Why would someone take a cab here?*

His curiosity increased when a slender leg, followed by another, slipped out of the backseat. John sighed with disappointment when the owner of those legs adjusted her dress and the hem fell just above her two-toned boots. Her rolled-brim hat blocked her face from his view, but he could tell by the way she was dressed – pretty, but conservative by the day's standards – that this was no speakeasy regular. *Maybe she was visiting someone in the neighborhood?*

But she was in fact here for the saloon. She walked straight to the door, gave the knock and passed through easily. Something in John's journalistic nature perked up. He picked up his pace, ignoring the increased pain in his back.

John walked through the door just in time. The woman stood facing the bar speaking to a man seated there. He couldn't hear her voice over the noisy crowd, but the man was facing John, and he could hear what he was saying.

"Baby, I told you. I'm sorry."

John chuckled from the doorway. So, the wife had caught him, but at what? Drinking at a bar? That was certainly enough to upset a woman of conservative values.

John watched as the woman's shoulder drew back.

"*Poor sucker*," John thought. "*He's about to get slapped, and he doesn't seem to –*"

But she didn't slap him. To John's astonishment, and the

man's, the young woman punched him very squarely in the nose.

The man went flying off the stool, whether by the force of the hit or from pure shock, John wasn't certain. He laid on the floor holding his nose and swearing at her.

"You broke it! You broke my nose, you, you –"

The woman didn't wait for the insult that was forthcoming. She stood over the poor sap, lifted the pretty leg that John was only moments earlier admiring, and brought the heel of her boot sharply down between the man's legs.

John winced, as did every other man in the bar, and the man cried out in agony from the assault. The entire establishment fell silent.

Having accomplished her mission, the woman spun on her heels and walked straight toward the door. It wasn't until she was mere inches from running straight into John that she finally looked up and came to a grinding halt.

It was the first John had seen of her face. Everything around them faded away as the sound of his heartbeat echoed in his ears. Never had he seen a woman more beautiful. Her hair was covered by her hat, but a stray curl had fallen across her forehead – blonde. It suited her skin, he thought. And even in the dimly lit room, there was no mistaking her eye color – bright green with specks of amber stared back at him from behind long, thick lashes. He followed her straight, strong nose down to a pair of full, pouty lips that were moving, saying something to him.

"You're in my way. Move," the beauty commanded.

John burst into laughter. She was feisty. He liked that. He stepped out of her way, bowing ceremoniously, despite the pain it caused him.

"Of course, Milady. Anything you say." He looked up at her and grinned. "I wouldn't want to end up like your gentleman friend."

"He's no friend of mine," the fiery blonde grumbled as she swept past him and out the door.

John stood for several moments staring at the door, wanting badly to follow her and find out more about this woman that made his heart race. He moved toward the door, but felt the all too familiar fire in his lower back and changed his mind. What would a woman like her want with an invalid like him?

The man on the floor was just beginning to pull himself back to his stool when John sat down and ordered a drink.

"I'll take another one, too, Jimmy," said the younger man.

"Yeah, you need it." Jimmy laughed. "This one's on me."

John sipped his drink, trying hard to not laugh at the boy. He sat clutching a rag with ice between his legs, a sour scowl on his face. John knew he was better off staying out of the man's business, but the journalist in him couldn't resist getting to the bottom of the story.

"Wife not happy with you?"

"Not my wife, my fiancé. Or, ex-fiancé I guess."

John was happy to hear that the beautiful blonde was not married to the pretty boy sitting next to him. He turned and looked at the door again but realized that her taxicab was likely far from the speakeasy by now.

"What did you do to screw that up?"

"Another girl."

"Another girl?" John asked in disbelief. "She must be a real looker to choose her over that one."

"Nope. Not even close. But that one expected me to wait until the wedding night." He thrust a thumb in the direction of the door. "The other one didn't. So, it really didn't matter what she looked like, if you know what I mean."

John wrapped his fingers tightly around the handle of his mug. His jaw flexed as he eyed the arrogant jerk. It wasn't that long ago that he'd made an equally disrespectful remark to Will, but for some reason this man's comment set John's temper afire. He took a deep breath and focused on the foam of his amber colored drink.

"I didn't expect her to show up like that," the pretty boy continued. "I expected some sort of beating, or worse, but not from her. I kind of figured I'd be staring down the barrel of her father's shotgun. The Reverend is pretty protective of her, and he's got a temper."

"A gun-toting pastor?" John chuckled. Was this kid spinning stories for his sake?

"Yeah, well Reverend Albright isn't like most preachers."

John nearly dropped his beer. "What did you say?"

"I said, her dad isn't like most preachers."

"No, who did you say her father was?"

"Reverend Albright."

John dropped his head into his hand. So, that was Phoebe Albright.

Of course, John thought. *The first woman to ever truly turn my head turns out to be Will Caffey's girl.* He ran his fingers through his sand-colored hair and motioned to the bartender.

"I'll take another," John said, then, deciding he needed something stronger, "and a double shot of whiskey."

9

———

LANSING FIRST CHURCH

*J*ohn had no idea what he was thinking. It had only been a few short months since he had scoffed at being drug into a church as an unconscious wounded soldier, yet here he was walking toward the doors of a church on his own accord. He had fought the idea all week, telling himself that the last place he needed to be was sitting in a pew listening to some religious zealot babble on about sin and condemnation. But he hadn't been able to shake the image of the beautiful pastor's daughter, cheeks flushed and eyes blazing, and he couldn't resist the temptation to drink in a little bit more of the heaven that was Phoebe Albright.

So, here he was, awake early on a Sunday morning and walking down the sidewalk toward the Lansing First Church, the last place he wanted to be but the one place he knew he'd find her. The medium sized brick building loomed before him, strange and unassuming, so unlike the massive, stone clad churches of his youth. But just the sight of the building began to bring back memories he didn't want to face and John nearly turned around and headed to a less holy, but more enticing, establishment.

Just as he was about to go, he saw her. Dozens of people milled around the entrance, each taking their turn to enter, but somehow, amid the crowd, he saw *her*. The day was overcast, quite different from the sunny fall days they had been experiencing lately, but at the moment he noticed her, a crevice broke in the clouds, allowing a ray of sun to penetrate the gray and illuminate her golden hair, unadorned with any covering today. John laughed. This couldn't be happening, could it? It was like a terrible scene from a poorly written novel. But it was happening, and John found himself once again mesmerized by the beauty of this pastor's daughter. Everything in him warned him to leave. This was dangerous business, and he knew it. This was Will's girl, at least in Will's mind. John shouldn't be admiring her this way.

Will's girl. Yes, that's how Will saw her. Poor, miserable kid. Fighting at hell's front door for his country, the memory of his love helping him through the bleak devastation that only war can create. Meanwhile, the woman is back home agreeing to marry any man that asks her. This made John angry. He'd love to tell her just what he thought of her careless handling of a love as pure as Caffey's, but how could he without betraying Will, who'd never even told the girl how he felt?

John had finally made up his mind that he was on a fool-hardy mission and stopped. He was about to turn around when she spotted him. Their eyes met and for a moment, John stood transfixed. She looked surprised, or fearful? Before he knew what was happening, he found himself climbing the stairs of the church and standing face to face with Phoebe Albright.

"You!" she whispered. "What on earth are you doing here?"

"Here? Well, this is a church not a private club, am I correct?"

"But – you were at that place. Why would someone like you go to church?"

"Hospitals aren't for the healthy, are they sweetheart? And do I need to remind you that *you* were also at that place?"

He was hoping to unsettle her, embarrass her even, but rather than elicit a blush from the fair-haired beauty, his comment only seemed to anger her.

"I wasn't there for the same reason you were," she quietly spat back at him, the amber specks in her green eyes flaming.

"Oh? And what reason were you there?"

"That's none of your business," she hissed.

"Then you shouldn't have aired your drama in front of a bar full of onlookers."

"You have no..."

"John! I'm so happy to see you!"

They both turned to see Mrs. Caffey approaching.

"Ma'am," John greeted her with a nod.

"My dear," the woman turned her attention to Phoebe. "Are you alright? You are positively flushed. You aren't feeling ill, are you?"

"No, I'm fine," she said, smiling at Will's mother.

"Well, we can't spend all morning chatting out here. Come you two. It's time to go in."

Within moments, John found himself shuffled through the double doors and into the sanctuary. The sound of a pipe organ wafted through the air. Mrs. Caffey led them to a pew about halfway down the aisle. *Well, at least she doesn't sit in the front row*, he thought. To John's relief, Phoebe continued down the aisle. But his relief was short lived as Will's mother grabbed her hand.

"Sit next to me, dear. I have something I need to discuss with you."

John watched as Mrs. Caffey pulled Phoebe into the pew behind her, leaving John no other choice but to sit next to the blonde.

The moments passed slowly. *How long before this thing starts, anyway?* People kept flooding in, chatting as they did so, crowding into each of the pews. Others wormed their way into the one occupied by Phoebe and John, forcing him to slide closer to her. She was still whispering with Mrs. Caffey, but John could tell by the way her body tensed that she was very much aware of his presence. He certainly was aware of hers. Sitting this closely, shoulder to shoulder, he could feel her upper body move ever so slightly with each breath she took, stirring a longing in him he hadn't known could be there. The scent of lavender and citrus drifted from her in the subtlest of ways. He looked straight ahead, trying with all his might to not be affected by the feminine presence at his side, but even the sight of her hands laying delicately in her lap made him miserable with desire. It took everything he had to not reach out and touch them.

But, this is Will's girl, he reminded himself. How could he sit here fantasizing about touching his best friend's girl? Still, it was only looking. He would never act on these feelings, no matter how undeniable the draw to this woman was.

Finally, the service began, and John chuckled to himself. No matter the year or the town, nothing ever changed in church. He didn't expect anything ever would. All the same songs, same uncomfortable benches, same judgmental stares – it was as if he had been transported back twenty years. He half expected to turn to his right and find his father scowling at him.

If it hadn't been for the latecomers who had crowded into their pew, John very well may have walked out of the service. Why had he expected anything to be any different here, just because he was in a different town? Religion, and all its trappings, was never going to change. But in his position, there was no way he would be able to gracefully exit. Maybe if he had never been injured in the war he might be able to slide past the others, murmuring some sort of apology, but his cumbersome gait kept him anchored in his seat. He was stuck, and the thought of suffering through the service frozen twenty years in the past, sitting next to the most enticing piece of forbidden fruit ever placed before man began to wear on his nerves.

Just when he thought he could take no more, something unusual did happen. A large, barrel-chested man dressed in a dark blue serge suit walked from the back of the church, grabbed a guitar from behind the organ and began playing and singing in the background behind the music director. No one, except for John, seemed surprised by this. The music leader never missed a beat, no one in the choir seemed unnerved. It was as if they all expected this gentleman to join them at any random point during the music. John casually looked around for a disapproving glance but found none. Just smiling faces, as if the members of this congregation welcomed the unusual man and his unorthodox behavior. John had to admit, the robust gentleman and his smiling rendition of the otherwise dry hymn was rather entertaining. He wasn't being disrespect-ful, just much more lighthearted than John was accustomed to witnessing in church.

The music ended eventually, and John searched the plat-form for anyone resembling a pastor. There was no one dressed in robes and no one seated on the high-backed 'throne' John always remembered the ministers of his youth using — just the guitar gentleman replacing his instrument in the stand. When that same man stepped toward the pulpit and placed his hands on either side of the podium, realization finally dawned on John. The unconventional music man was none other than the Reverend Albright.

Once the shock began to fade, John found himself surveying the preacher. It was obvious that Phoebe must favor her mother, because she looked nothing like her father. The reverend's hair, although thinning somewhat, was still dark as night, and his eyes, though John couldn't be certain from this distance, seemed just as black. John couldn't imagine a more unlikely man to have fathered the fair Phoebe.

John had spent most of his life ignoring the 'Bible Thumping' tirades of preachers, but try as he might, he could not tune out the words of the charismatic pastor. His casual style of preaching was so engaging, so unlike the stiff, rehearsed preaching John had been raised on. In fact, John wasn't so certain that this preacher was even using notes. It wasn't until he was bringing the sermon to a close that John realized that speaking off the cuff was just the man's comfortable style of preaching, not a lack of organization, and that this casual approach had been what created the air of relaxation. As the preacher reiterated his three main points, he called for the congregation to rise and for those wishing to pray to come forward.

John's heart beat so violently against his chest he worried that Phoebe would hear it. *What am I doing here?* he asked himself. He had gone where he had sworn he would never go again, and for what? A few minutes in the presence of a woman? John had no use for women, especially one that belonged to someone else.

He looked down and found Phoebe peering at him cautiously through thick eyelashes, the way his mother used to look at him at the end of each service. He could almost feel his father's grip on the back of his neck, almost hear the scraping of his own shoes along the tiled aisle as his father dragged him toward the front of the church. The room closed in around John and he found it hard to breathe.

The congregation rose for the final hymn and John wasted no time in taking the opportunity to exit. He needed some fresh air, maybe even something stronger from Jimmy's, but whatever he needed, he knew it wouldn't be found within the walls of this church, and it certainly wouldn't be found in the presence of the beautiful, but disconcerting Phoebe Albright.

ESTHER FELT like she was suffocating. She was so distracted by the man sitting to her right that she barely heard a thing Mrs. Caffey was saying before service began. Who was he? And why was he here?

"I've tried asking around for a position for Katie, but nobody is hiring. I don't care, mind you, whether she has employment or not, but I believe that sitting around idle with no one but me for company is beginning to wear on the poor girl's nerves. Esther, do you hear me?"

"Hmmm," Esther's attention snapped back to Mrs. Caffey. "Oh yes, I'm sorry. I know. I spoke with Katie, and she is getting frustrated. But I don't know what I can do."

"Well, all we can do is pray, and that is enough, isn't that right?"

Esther smiled her agreement. "I've been praying every day for her."

"So, how did you come to meet John?" Mrs. Caffey asked, nodding toward the man sitting next to Esther.

Esther held her breath for a moment, choosing her words carefully. "I haven't really met him. He just started speaking to me on the sidewalk." It wasn't a complete lie. It wasn't the entire truth, either, and it made Esther feel horrible.

"Oh, I'm sorry. I should have introduced you. I guess I just assumed that Will had written your family about him as well."

"Will?"

"Yes, dear. John Ward served alongside Will in France. They became very close."

Esther tried to not act surprised, but she couldn't have been more shocked. This man not only knew Will, but they were friends? It didn't make sense. Will would never be caught dead in a place like a speakeasy. How in the world could these two men be close?

Esther felt the man named John press in closer to her as the pew filled and she breathed in deeply the scent of musk and soap. He sat with his arms crossed and she wondered what he had to be so angry about.

She wasn't certain if the service was actually longer than usual or if the visitor made it feel that way, but relief flooded her when, as the last song began, the man scooted himself out of the row. She turned and watched him exit out the back door. But her relief didn't last long. When she turned back around, she found her father walking briskly down the aisle behind him.

Her heart quickened. Did the man know who she was? He hadn't seem shocked that she knew Mrs. Caffey. Her stomach churned as another thought occurred to her — if this John Ward spoke with her father, would he tell him about her visit to the speakeasy?

Without another thought, Esther excused herself and followed the two men out of the building.

10

INTRODUCTIONS

"John? Wait," Reverend Albright called out as he bound down the stairs.

John stopped at the bottom of the stairs and eyed the robust man suspiciously. His heart still beat erratically within his chest and he longed to put as much distance between himself and this preacher, but the fact that he knew his name kept him rooted in his spot.

"You are John Ward, aren't you?"

"Yes, sir, I am. But how do you know that?"

"You fit the description in Will's letter, and you were sitting with his mother."

"Will's letter?" He wondered how many people Will had written to about him.

"Yes, he wrote me to tell me you were moving to Lansing and to keep an eye out for you."

"Hmmph," John grunted. "And he said to expect to see me in church?"

"No, not exactly. But I have been expecting you."

"And Will's letter gave you that expectation?" John asked incredulously.

"Guess I just felt it in my heart. Will had lots of great things to say about you. I'm glad to finally meet ya."

"Will has told me much about you as well, sir."

"He's a special lad."

"That he is."

"Where are you off to in such a hurry? My wife and I would love to have you to our home for lunch today."

As John searched for the right words to excuse himself from the invitation, he saw Phoebe quietly step out of the sanctuary. Her green eyes were wide as she watched John speaking with her father. Why was she so fearful? In an instant, he wanted nothing more than to spend the afternoon with her, to talk with her, to learn more about her.

Get yourself together man! This is no innocent pastor's daughter. This is a conniving vixen intent on trifling with the heart of any man that comes her way. And even if she wasn't, Will thinks she is an angel, and he is in love with her. How could you betray him?

"I'm sorry," John began, never taking his eyes off Phoebe, "but I have other plans."

"Well, then how about next Sunday?"

"Well, sir, I'm not certain I'll be back to church."

"Really?" Reverend Albright said, lifting an eyebrow. He and John watched one another, but he didn't say another word. The conversation hung silent for a few seconds. Finally, John sighed.

"I'm not a God-fearing man, Reverend."

"Then why did you come here today?"

John's eyes once again lighted on Phoebe. "I'm not really certain, sir."

"Well," Reverend Albright said, extending his hand toward John, "the offer for lunch stands. We'd be happy to have you whenever you're ready to accept it."

John didn't answer, just shook Reverend Albright's hand and turned away.

THE CONGREGATION POURED out of the building as Esther watched John Ward walk away from her father. John had looked at her with such gravity that she still could hardly breathe. She worried her fears were coming true — that he'd told her father about where she had gone and what she had done. But when her father turned toward her and smiled, she knew he'd learned nothing. Had he been informed that Esther had visited a speakeasy, there would have been no containing his anger, congregation milling around or not.

Esther, satisfied that her father was too consumed with shaking the hands of his parishioners to notice her absence, slipped down the side stairs and hurried after John. He was a tall man, and she worried that his long legs would have taken him too far down the sidewalk for her to catch up, but to her surprise he was only about a block and a half away. It was then that she saw why. She hadn't noticed the cane earlier, nor the stiff gait which necessitated it, but walking behind him as she was now, she could see that he had a rather severe limp. Other boys she knew had tried to enlist but had been turned away because of physical ailments. This limp was not something he had been born with. John Ward had been injured in the war.

"Mr. Ward," Esther called out after him. He kept walking. She tried again.

"Mr. Ward!" she yelled louder.

She was within a few feet of him by this time. Surely, he could hear her. Why was he ignoring her?

"MR. WARD!" she yelled finally, grabbing his arm when she reached him. "Surely, you are able to hear me."

John Ward stopped. His eyes, the color of a stormy sky, glared intensely down at her.

"Yes, Miss Albright. What can I do for you?" he asked, appearing more than a little annoyed.

His irritation caught Esther off guard. Apparently, it wasn't only his eyes that held a storm at bay.

"I'm sorry to bother you, but I just wanted to thank you."

"Thank me? For what?"

"For not telling my father. You know, about the speakeasy."

John tapped his cane against his shoe and smirked. "What makes you think I won't tell him?"

"Well, I – I suppose out of respect for our mutual friendship with Will."

His face darkened, and the storm swirled behind his eyes.

"Since when do you have respect for Will?"

His question confused her, but he didn't give her time to answer.

"Tell me, Miss Albright, did you respect Will enough to inform him of your engagement?"

"Well, no, I guess I didn't tell him, but he's been away at war..."

"And you couldn't take a minute to write him a letter? Don't tell me about respect for friendship."

John turned to walk away, but Esther wasn't finished.

"Excuse me, sir, but I don't understand where all of this animosity is coming from."

"Of course, you don't. I suppose that you expect your beauty to captivate me the way it does every other man you come across."

"What are you talking about? Wait, did you just call me beautiful?"

John laughed outright at this.

"I suppose you have a certain appeal, to lesser men. Might that be why you frequent establishments such as Jimmy's – to find men with less discriminating taste?"

Esther gasped. "How dare you? How on earth is someone like you friends with Will?"

"No accounting for taste, I suppose."

With that, John Ward tipped his hat, turned and left Esther alone and mouth agape.

11

LUNCH DATE

"**S**omeone's here to see you, Mr. Ward."

"Thank you, Miss Hagerman," John sighed, pushing away from his desk. He had been struggling unsuccessfully to write a small piece about the coal being released from Illinois to cover the shortage in Michigan, but he couldn't get the words on paper. He had been distracted ever since the news came in that 159 sick and wounded had returned to the U.S. Neither he nor Mrs. Caffey had received a letter from Will in weeks. Maybe, if Will were among the 159, he would be coming home soon.

But truth be known, it wasn't just Will on his mind. He couldn't stop thinking about Phoebe, and it was driving him insane. One minute he's thinking about Will and worrying about his safety, the next he is imagining touching the slender hand laying in the lap next to his, breathing in the soft fragrance of her perfume, getting lost in her eyes. Will's girl's eyes. What kind of friend was he?

This self-inflicted torture had continued all morning, and John should have welcomed the distraction of a visitor, but he didn't. He had no friends in Lansing, and no business he could think of that would require a visit to his office. Darn it anyway. He really needed to get this piece written. It was slated for the front page of the afternoon edition, and a visit from a salesperson or the like wasn't going to help to that end.

But to his surprise, it wasn't a solicitor, but Reverend Albright. John rose from his desk and extended his hand.

"Reverend. What can I do for you, sir?"

"Well, seein' as I was just in the neighborhood, thought I'd take you to lunch."

John stuck his hands in his pockets and leaned against the desk.

"I'm sorry, sir, but I am very busy right now."

"Awe, not that busy. C'mon. A man's gotta eat."

"Not before I finish this article."

"Can't it be finished after lunch?"

"No. It's due for this afternoon's edition. I'm sorry."

"Well, if you really can't..."

"I really can't," John said, placing his hand on the older man's shoulder and ushering him out his office door.

"Another time, then?" the Reverend offered.

"Oh – yes, yes. Of course, some other time," John answered.

John wasn't certain why he was so quick to dismiss the pastor's offer. Yes, he had a deadline to meet, but when push came to shove, he could have the article written in less than thirty minutes. It wasn't that he disliked the man. He barely knew him, and from what he could tell, he was a very likable person. Will held him in the highest regard, and that went a long way in John's eyes. There was something more to it, something intangible that made John uneasy around the clergyman. So, at least for now, he thought it best to avoid him.

But avoidance clearly wasn't on Reverend Albright's agenda, because the very next day, the office receptionist was back in John's office announcing a visitor.

"Is it the same man as yesterday?"

"Yes sir."

"Just get rid of him, would you please, Miss Hagerman?"

"Get rid of him?" she asked, eyes darting back and forth between John and the door.

"Yes. Just tell him I'm in a meeting."

"You – you want me to lie? To a preacher?" she asked, her hand flying to her throat. Her cheeks lost all color.

John sat back in his chair and crossed his arms. He needed to speak with his boss about finding him his own secretary. One with lower morals.

"How do you know he is a preacher?"

"Everyone knows Reverend Albright, Mr. Ward. And he would know I was lying. Preachers can sense that kind of thing."

"Not if you're good at it," he answered, rubbing his forehead.

"Oh, please, don't make me – "

John held up his hand. "I'm not going to make you lie. Tell him I'll be out in a few minutes."

John realized it was futile to keep putting the man off. He wasn't busy anyway. Might as well take advantage of the beautiful fall day and get out of his office. If what he had heard about Michigan winters was true, he needed to absorb as much good weather as possible before it was gone.

"John, my boy!" Reverend Albright greeted him. "I was afraid you'd be too busy again today."

"And I was afraid that if I didn't go to lunch with you, you'd keep showing up until I did."

"That was my plan," he said, smiling.

John laughed out loud, in spite of himself. Honesty. John liked that. No point in dancing around the truth when the truth is so easy to come by.

Reverend Albright led them to a restaurant around the corner from the Journal called Maudie's Diner. John had been here a couple of times. It was small, but the food was tasty enough and the service was quick. Good. This lunch wouldn't drag on forever.

Entering the little diner with the Reverend was an entirely different experience for John. Everyone present lit up at the sight of his companion and smiled or waved a greeting. And in turn, Reverend Albright greeted each personally, shaking hands, asking about their welfare, laughing at their answers.

He's a salesperson, John thought with a laugh. *He's selling God, and they're all buying it.*

But by the time they had settled into their own table, John's opinion had changed slightly. The Reverend was no cold, calculating salesman. He'd greeted each person by name, after all, asked them specific questions about their lives – questions that only someone who knows you personally would ask.

"How's your ankle, Bea? Is it healin' up good? Oh, that's good news. Listen, you let me or Ruth know if ya need anything, ya hear?"

"Any news from Charlie? Is he still in training, or has he been called up yet?"

Reverend Albright spoke to each person as though to a dear friend, which they all seemed to be. But he didn't save this kind treatment for only his friends. A young couple who had only recently moved to Lansing from up north also got a good five minutes of questions and conversation from the old pastor, followed by directions to the church – not for Sunday service attendance, but for assistance in finding work.

"I know a few people in this little town," John overheard the reverend say to them. "I'm sure we can find someone who knows someone who knows someone who is looking for a talented man such as yourself. Come see me later today or tomorrow."

John drummed his fingers on the table as he watched the older man order his lunch.

"I'll have the day's special. Oh, and coffee – black. And a little sugar, if you don't mind, Miss Maudie."

"Sugar? The last time you were in here with the missus..." the waitress said, eyebrows raised. Reverend Albright laughed heartily.

"Oh, don't you worry about Ruth. Leave her to me. Besides, without sugar in my coffee, I'm not nearly as sweet the rest of the day."

John ordered his lunch and gave the pastor a smile. *"Here we go,"* he thought. *"I wonder how he'll try to convert me? Hell and brimstone, most likely."*

"So, Will tells me you're not much of a huntin' man."

Caught off guard, John stammered, "Uh, no sir. My dad never had time for such things."

"Well, I always said a man who hasn't shot dinner for his family hasn't lived. What about fishin'?"

"No, well, not with my father. Will and I caught some fish in France, but that was more to keep from starving than for sport."

Reverend Albright laced his fingers across his broad torso and leaned back.

"I'm glad you had each other. I must say, I'm a bit surprised the two of you became such good friends."

"Never thought good boy Will would cavort with a heathen the likes of me?" John asked, taking a drink of the coffee just placed before him.

"I was referring to your age difference," the pastor responded unwaveringly.

"Sorry," John offered. "Thought you disapproved of me by your comment."

"Should I?"

"Probably," came John's simple and honest answer.

"Oh, I'm sure you're not as bad as you think. But, I suppose only time will tell," he laughed. "But it seems I'm not the only one curious about you."

"Sir?"

"I see you've met my daughter."

"Oh, yes. Yes sir." John wiped his hands on his pant legs, desperately, but unsuccessfully, searching his mind for a topic toward which to steer the conversation.

"I saw you sitting next to her in church, and I saw her chase you down after service. What did she say to you?"

"Oh, it was nothing sir. If I recall correctly, she was merely inviting me back for next Sunday's service."

The pastor's eyes held steadily on John. *Good grief,* he thought. *Could Miss Hagerman be right? Can this preacher sense I am lying?*

"Not surprised," the Reverend finally said. "She isn't one to shy away from newcomers. Not one to shy away from much of anything at all. Pretty outspoken, that one. But if you've had a conversation with her, you've probably already discovered that."

"She doesn't appear to be much of a wallflower."

Reverend Albright threw his head back as he laughed.

"True, true. Now back to fishin'. There's this great creek not too far out of town. It trickles off the Grand River, and for some reason, the fish seem to congregate there..."

John was relieved when the conversation turned away from Phoebe Albright. They spent the remainder of their lunch pleasantly discussing fishing, hunting, people in the community, and a hundred other topics. Once, when talk led to John's family, John diverted the conversation and the preacher didn't push him further. He just went back to sharing stories. John actually found himself disappointed when lunch came to an end and he had to return to the Journal.

"Well, son, I'm glad you had time to go to lunch today."

"Me too," John answered honestly. "Sorry about yesterday. Mondays are always hectic. Tuesdays are always much less so."

"Duly noted," the reverend said, nodding. "Nice talkin' with ya, John. You have a nice day."

And that was that. No "see you Sunday" or "I'll be looking for you in church." There had been no salvation talk, no fearful words or threats of damnation, no condemnation. Just lunch and talk. Lots and lots of talk.

John shook his head as he entered his office, not quite sure what to make of the unconventional pastor.

12

CHANGE IN PLANS

Reverend Albright apparently did take note of John's lightened Tuesday load, because he returned the next Tuesday, and the next, and the next. Each week the agenda was the same – lunch and conversation at Maudie's. Before long, John found himself looking forward to his lunch appointment with the pastor, even scheduling meetings and interviews around his weekly visit. It had become routine, one that John fell into comfortably.

So, John was understandably confused when on one of these routine visits, as the pair left the newspaper offices, Reverend Albright turned and headed right instead of left toward Maudie's. John stopped for a moment and stared at him, but when the pastor continued walking away from Maudie's, John hurried to catch up.

"No lunch at the diner today?" John asked.

"Not today. If it's alright with you, thought I'd take you somewhere else."

John shrugged. Lunch was lunch, as far as he was concerned. And, since his pain was so minimal today that he merely carried his cane, he thought he might actually enjoy the extended walk.

John's nonchalance was put to the test when the stark white steeple of the church came into view.

"We're eating at the church?" John questioned, eyebrows raised.

Reverend Albright laughed. "No, son. I just need to stop off and grab something."

John shoved his hands in his pockets and rocked back and forth on his heels as he watched the pastor climb the steps of the brick-clad building. Reverend Albright reached the door and called over his shoulder at John.

"Come on. You can help me," he said before disappearing into the church, not allowing John any time to protest.

John stood for a few moments, annoyed that the pastor would just assume that he would follow. He hadn't gotten very personal with the clergyman, but he thought he had made it clear enough that he didn't plan on stepping foot into any church ever again. Surely this was some sort of ruse to get John to break his pledge. Well, John wasn't about to fall for it.

But what if this wasn't an attempt to trap John? What if Reverend Albright wasn't trying to manipulate the situation or John's stance against the church? He hadn't attempted to push his religion on John before. Why would he start now? What if the truth were as simple as the Reverend presented it – he simply needed John's assistance?

John wrestled with these thoughts for only a few moments. Reverend Albright had been nothing but honest with him, had been good enough to buy him lunch once a week, and had never pressured him into falling for his religious schemes. The least John could do was help him with whatever errand he was about. He headed up the church steps, pleased that the climb only caused him minor pain.

When John entered the dimly lit sanctuary, he saw the

Reverend on the platform on his hands and knees, apparently struggling to rise.

"Are you all right?" He clutched his cane, and forgetting his own injury, rushed to Reverend Albright's aid.

"Me? Sure I am. Just trying to reach this sheet music I dropped on Sunday. It's slid under the piano."

Relieved that it hadn't been something more serious that had dropped the man to his knees, John crouched down to see if he could help.

"Looks to me like it's clear to the back. Might be easier if we roll the piano out away from the wall."

"I think you're right," the preacher agreed, rising to his feet. "Help me move this thing. It's a mite heavier than it looks, even with wheels on it."

The two men maneuvered the piano out until there was room for John to reach behind it and grab the two pieces of paper. He glanced at the music quickly as he handed it to the Reverend.

"Did you write this?" he asked, spying the handwritten notes.

"Yep, a long time ago, back in my saloon playing days."

John laughed at this, then realized the pastor wasn't laughing.

"Wait, you're serious? You used to play in saloons?"

"Yep. Saloons, dance halls, anywhere that paid. Thought I was going to be the next Arthur Collins. Why do you find that so comical?"

"Well, I don't know. I guess it's hard for me to imagine a man of God playing tunes for a bunch of drunks."

"Well, I wasn't a man of God back then," he said with a shrug of his shoulders. "I was spending most of my time at the bar anyway. I decided I might as well earn some coin while I was there."

This caught John off guard. This man – the one the entire

city seemed to have such respect for – was at one point in his life a heathen.

"You seem disappointed, John."

"Not disappointed, just surprised."

"Surprised that we have more in common than you once thought?"

John locked eyes with the Reverend. Had Phoebe told him where they met? Was he expecting some sort of apology or admission of guilt? If so, he'd be sorely disappointed.

"I'm not proud of my past, John, but I'm not ashamed, either, because it's the past. God has shown me great mercy, and for that I am thankful. I've dedicated my life to sharing the Good News, not because I need to earn the Grace that God has given me, but because I am busting at the seams with so much joy, I can't contain it."

Reverend Albright grabbed some more papers off the piano and handed the stack to John.

"Here. You carry these for me, if ya will, while I grab my guitar." He took the guitar off the stand and placed it in a ragged case hiding behind the organ. "You play any instruments?"

"No sir. No hunting, no fishing, no music lessons. No talking, no hugging, no loving. I was more of an inconvenience than a son to my father."

Reverend Albright stopped and turned toward him. "I'm sorry John."

"For what?"

"That you were treated that way. No child should ever feel as if they are an inconvenience."

"It's not your problem to apologize for, sir."

Reverend Albright half leaned, half sat on the altar and rested his arm on the guitar case. John couldn't help but wonder at the unconventional attitude of the pastor. At the church where John was raised, the minister would have had

John's hide if he'd so much as touched the altar, and here this minister was sitting on it.

"What about now? I'm sure your father is proud of you and all you've accomplished."

"I wouldn't know. I left when I was fifteen and I haven't been back. I'm sure he assumes I'm dead, or at least he hopes I am."

"John, you don't really think – "

"Yes, sir, I do. My father spent the first fifteen years of my life telling me how worthless I was, how God was going to punish me for my sin and how I was going to spend eternity in Hell. I've spent the last fourteen years proving him wrong by living the life I wanted to live, and I don't give a da– " John stopped. "Excuse me, Reverend, I didn't mean any disrespect to you. All I meant was, I've lived what you and others like you call a 'sinful' life, and I'm no worse off for it."

"Aren't you?"

Before John could answer, a door to the side of the platform opened and an elderly woman entered carrying a mop and a bucket.

"I'm so sorry," she said when she spotted the two men talking. "I didn't know anyone was in here."

"Oh, don't mind us, Mrs. Kinney. We were just heading out."

The woman smiled at Reverend Albright, but the smile quickly faded when she saw John. Her eyes grew wide and she quickly turned away, but not before John caught sight of a large, mottled scar marring the left side of her face. The valleys of the scar were an unnatural red color, while the top, which resembled melted wax, was nearly white. The scar drooped so that the woman's eye appeared closed, causing John to wonder if the poor thing even had use of the eye. John realized the woman's shocked reaction was likely a response to meeting a stranger, and it seemed Reverend Albright thought the same, as he ushered John out of the church.

Once back on the sidewalk, the pastor turned right and led

John to a small, two story home next door to the church. They stepped through the front door, and the first thing John saw was the profile of a woman sitting across the entry in what appeared to be a small parlor. Sunlight poured in through the window behind her, giving her silhouette an ethereal appearance. John knew the form well. He recognized the straight, strong nose, full, pouty lips, and golden locks tied into a bun at the base of her neck.

Phoebe.

It wasn't until this moment that John fully realized the preacher's lunch plans for him. This was Reverend Albright's home, and they were to have lunch with Phoebe.

"We're here, darlin'. I hope you're ready for us, because I'm so hungry, I could eat the north end of a southbound bear."

Phoebe placed the book she was reading on a small table and rose to meet the men in the parlor.

"I have no idea what that means, but I assume it isn't good," laughed a voice that John didn't recognize.

As she drew nearer, the light from the windows no longer disguised her and John found himself face to face, not with Phoebe, but her older replica.

"Hello John, I'm so glad to finally meet you!" beamed Mrs. Albright, extending her hand. "I thought my husband was never going to bring you by to meet me!"

"Had I known he was keeping such a lovely wife a secret, I would have insisted he bring me sooner," John teased as he took Mrs. Albright's hand.

"Ah," she blushed slightly. "I see you share the same charm as our William."

"I'll take any comparison to Will Caffey as a compliment, ma'am."

"As well you should. Now, come on you two. Lunch is getting cold."

Mrs. Albright led the men to a room just off the entryway. It wasn't a large dining room, but the Albrights had somehow managed to fit a very large table with eight chairs, as well as two sideboards and a table, into it. It was a little cramped, but welcoming, and the smell coming from the tureen in the middle of the table was already making John's mouth water.

"It isn't much," Mrs. Albright said as she lifted the lid, "Just some stew made from leftovers, but I thought you men could use something a little heartier than sandwiches."

As they sat down for lunch, Reverend Albright bowed his head and offered his customary prayer, and John took the opportunity to observe Mrs. Albright. On closer inspection, he could see that she was much older than her daughter, the temples of her hair greying slightly, and the corners of her eyes wrinkled just enough to prove that she was a woman who enjoyed her life. She was a beautiful preview of what her daughter would most likely look like at the same age, and the thought made John smile.

The prayer ended, and Mrs. Albright began dishing up the delicious smelling stew. It didn't take John long to realize that Mrs. Albright, although a far cry from what John would call shy, was much more reserved than her husband. She blushed easily when teased by the Reverend, much the way Will had described Phoebe's reaction to his own antics, and she didn't appear to always appreciate her husband's bluntness with John. They were just finishing with lunch when the Reverend asked a question so direct, so personal, John thought Mrs. Albright would have an angina attack.

"So, tell me my boy, how'd ya earn that cane?"

"James!" Mrs. Albright shrieked, a horrified look clouding her beautiful features.

"What? I just asked a question. John knows he doesn't have to answer anything he doesn't want to."

"That doesn't make it proper for you to ask."

"Awe, now Ruth, you worry too much about what is and isn't proper."

"Someone around this house ought to! My word, between your mouth and those of your daughters, it's a wonder the people haven't run us out of town!"

Daughters? John thought. *There's more than one?*

"Hey, speaking of which, where are my girls?"

"Mrs. Caffey invited them for lunch."

"Lunch?" Reverend Albright said with a huff. "Sweets are more like it. That woman stuffs more pastries down those girls' throats than Pershing has soldiers."

"Probably, but a little sugar never harmed a child, as far as I can see." laughed Mrs. Albright. "But we're about to find out. Here they come up the front steps."

The stew in John's stomach lurched. He hadn't seen Phoebe Albright since he had insulted her on the sidewalk outside of the church all those weeks ago. He wasn't certain how she would react to seeing him sitting in her home.

The front door burst open and John heard the excited voice of a child.

"Momma! We're home! And we brought company!" said a young girl running into the dining room. "Daddy! You're home too!"

The sprite-like child, a miniature version of her mother and sister, ran to Reverend Albright and threw herself into his arms. The Reverend, smiling just as brightly as the little girl, settled her onto his lap. It was then that she noticed John.

"Who are you?" she asked, furrowing her eyebrows.

John's answer was interrupted by a woman's voice.

"John!" exclaimed Mrs. Caffey from the hallway. "What a pleasant surprise!"

John rose from his chair and was immediately wrapped in an embrace. Will's mother said something about wishing he would visit more, but John didn't exactly hear her. Every sense he possessed was focused on the vision of beauty standing in the dining room entry and staring at him, wide-eyed. She stood as though transfixed, an angel draped in lavender from head to toe, and John felt like the devil himself invading her heaven.

"Good grief, girl," Reverend Albright laughed. "You look like you've seen a ghost."

The angel broke eye contact with John and turned a stiff smile toward her parents. John watched as her formerly bulging, wide eyes began to blink rapidly under her parents' perusal.

"Of course not, Father. I just didn't realize you had company. Had we known, we wouldn't have intruded on your lunch."

"Nonsense. It's no intrusion. You all pull up a chair. John here was just about to tell us how he became injured in the war."

"Oh, we came at the most opportune time," chimed in Mrs. Caffey. "Come dear," she said, beckoning to Phoebe. "Sit down and hold my hand. I became very emotional the last time I heard John share the story."

John watched Phoebe move hesitantly to the table and take a seat next to Will's mother, which placed her directly across from him. She looked at everyone in the room, except for him, which he found comical, until he realized the reason for her discomfort was his constant staring. He cleared his throat and averted his eyes.

It was now John's turn to squirm uncomfortably as he realized that he was the target of everyone else's stares. Each person, with the exception of Phoebe, was waiting for him to share the battle story. It wasn't the first time he had been asked to retell the events of that fateful day. Will's mother had asked him on one of his first visits to her house to tell her all about how her son had saved John's life. He had done so gladly, appreciative of the admiration Mrs. Caffey showed for her only child. If anyone deserved admiration, it was Will. But John had been careful to censure the retelling. Mrs. Caffey put up a brave front, but John knew she was worried about her son. John, unaccustomed to seeing a woman care about anyone but herself, had found himself taking great pains to not share any more details than he had to, so as not to worry the woman more than necessary.

John took a deep breath. He only hoped he could remember exactly how he had told her the first time.

13

___

REMEMBERING

$\mathcal{E}$sther could not have been more shocked if Satan himself had been seated at her parents' dining room table. Since graduating from secretary school, she had spent a little time relaxing and doing the things she had done before her engagement ended. So, after a pleasant lunch with Mrs. Caffey and her little sister, Esther had expected to return home to a quiet afternoon of tea with her mother. Instead, her day was turned upside down by the appearance of the unsavory Mr. John Ward. It was bad enough that she hadn't had the sense to guard her expression of surprise and had received a chastisement from her father, but the man would not stop staring at her. What was the matter with him? If it was his intent to make her uncomfortable, he was succeeding splendidly.

"Go on, John," Mrs. Caffey encouraged, squeezing Esther's hand. "I'm settled."

Esther refused to look up, choosing instead to concentrate on the intricate design of her mother's floral tablecloth. She heard John clear his throat.

"Well, as I told Mrs. Caffey before, it happened along the Marne River on our way to rendezvous with the 3rd Division."

His voice wavered a bit, and Esther couldn't stop herself from stealing a glance at the man. He no longer stared at her. His eyes fixated on the tablecloth, glassed over and distant. His body may have been sitting in her dining room, but his thoughts, it seemed, were more than three thousand miles away. As his deep voice continued the story, Esther felt herself swept away to the battlefield.

"WE HAD SPENT days advancing without a single sign of the enemy," John continued. This statement wasn't entirely true, because there had been evidence of the enemy's existence everywhere. Evidence in the form of rotting corpses, both German and Allied. Even now, months later, John could still smell the scent of putrid decay that hung over the entire valley. But, telling the whole truth was more than folks back home could handle. It was more than John could handle, and he had lived through it.

"We had just passed an abandoned French trench, and it appeared we still had miles to go before we found the front. We were all exhausted, and most likely not as alert as we should have been. Then out of nowhere, gunfire started raining down on us. Night was just beginning to settle in and no one could tell where the fire was coming from. Everyone scrambled for cover, and in the chaos, our platoon got split.

"Will and I and several other doughboys ran south and found an outcropping of rock to duck behind, but the majority of our boys were either dead or scrambling behind trees or small knolls, pinned down with nowhere to go. From our stand-point, we couldn't see for certain where the gunfire was coming from, but we knew they were overlooking us from some point to the east. We figured the Germans didn't know our location, since no fire headed our way. It was dark, and the trapped men were still front and center of the Jerries. We figured we had an advantage – they thought our entire platoon was trapped. We didn't dare fire our guns and give away our position, especially when we weren't a hundred percent certain of their position either. The only choice we had was to head toward the hill, just a handful of us soldiers, armed with only our rifles, which were at this point useless, and a few grenades.

"We inched our way up the hill and discovered we were much closer than we originally thought. We circled the machine gun nest the best we could. We had lost our platoon leader, so every single one of us looked for Will. I guess when push comes to shove, the man you respect the most becomes the man you look to lead. I spotted him around the same time as the rest of the men. He was on the other side of the nest. That crazy kid was right up on them. We waited for him, then he gave us the signal. The first thing in was the grenades. They didn't know what hit them."

How much should he share? Should he tell them about the blood, the screaming, the numerous men he had killed, the German boy?

"We followed close behind and tried to get some shots in, but at that close of range, our fists and bayonets were our best defense. So, we suddenly found ourselves in the middle of hand to hand combat. I lost track of how many men I took down. And I also lost track of Will. It wasn't until a German soldier was about to take my life that I saw him again."

John could hear the artillery, smell the smoke, feel the pressure of the bayonet slicing into his back.

"What about Will?"

John snapped out of his dream and locked eyes with her. Was that genuine concern pooling in her green eyes?

"Out of nowhere, Will appeared over me, taking that Jerry out. If he hadn't shown up, I wouldn't be here to tell the story."

John's heart beat wildly in his chest. It was the excitement of retelling the story, he lied to himself, not the fact that Will's girl's haunting green eyes held him captive.

"But then, what happened next?" Mrs. Caffey asked, interrupting the spell. She leaned over to Phoebe and nearly squealed. "This next part is the best part of the whole story."

"We were still a long way from safety, and I begged Will to leave me and save himself, but that stubborn son of a ..." John caught himself, "gun wouldn't take no for an answer. He hoisted me onto his back and ran at least seventy yards to an abandoned bunker, all the while, machine gun fire and large shells falling all around us."

"And that was when Will was injured, right before reaching the bunker. Isn't that right, John?" Mrs. Caffey interrupted. John was about to answer her when Phoebe spoke.

"Will - he was injured?" she choked out. Tears were streaming down her face.

"Oh, don't cry, dear. It was merely a scratch, isn't that right, John? A scratch?"

Confused over Phoebe's reaction, John took a moment to answer. "Yes, ma'am. Just a flesh wound."

"God be praised," Mrs. Caffey beamed. "Mark my words, my boy is going to come home a hero. I know all our prayers will be answered, because..."

John wasn't listening to her anymore, so mesmerized by the beauty sitting across from him. As she pulled a handkerchief from her pocket and began to wipe her tears, John began to see that Will may in fact be correct — maybe he did have a future with this girl. She certainly appeared concerned for his welfare.

Maybe this Phoebe that he carries a torch for does in fact have feelings for him, if it's possible for any woman to care for someone other than herself. John still thought him a fool for caring about her. But, then, why did he have this undeniable desire to gather the girl in his own arms and comfort her right now?

"I really must be getting back to the office," John said suddenly. He pushed away from the table and stood.

"Oh, must you?" Mrs. Albright asked. "I have some cake if you'd like to stay."

"No, thank you," he said, watching the still emotional Phoebe. "I have a lot to finish before the afternoon edition. Thank you for your hospitality, Mrs. Albright."

"Any time, John. And we mean that. Our door is always open to you."

He had to stifle a laugh when, out of the corner of his eye, he saw Phoebe's head snap up at her mother's open invitation. He was certain not every Albright would welcome his presence on a regular basis.

"I'll keep that in mind," he said, picking up his fedora and cane and heading for the front door.

"How about this evening, son? Your boss and his wife are joining us for dinner," the reverend said.

Again, Phoebe's stiff posture almost caused John to laugh. Part of him longed to accept, if nothing more than to enjoy her discomfort at his presence. She slowly looked up at him, anxious green eyes capturing his as she did so. John could feel his heart thud against his rib cage.

"I'm sorry, but I already have plans," he lied. He nodded and stepped out of the door into the brisk, October afternoon. He concentrated on the familiar tap of his cane as he hurried back to work, determined more than ever that he needed to keep as much distance as possible between himself and Phoebe Albright.

14

BE CAREFUL WHAT YOU WISH FOR

*J*ohn was deep into writing an article on the effect of war on oil prices when a rap on his office door interrupted him. He looked up to find his boss, Warren Mallory, opening his door.

"Got a minute?" the jovial newsman asked.

"Of course," John said. "Do any of your employees answer no to that question?"

Warren rubbed his chin for a moment. "Not that I can recall. Hey, do you remember our conversation about you having your own secretary?"

John had nearly forgotten. He had broached the subject with his boss shortly after Rev. Albright's second visit, but he'd since then had given up on the idea. He typed all his own articles anyway, and Miss Hagerman, the newspaper's receptionist, was more than able to help John with any of his other needs around the office.

"I do remember, but - "

"Good, because I hired someone."

"You hired someone?"

"Yeah. Is that a problem?"

"No, of course not. I guess I just assumed I would get to choose the woman myself."

"Well, the opportunity arose, and I jumped at it. She's a recent graduate of Yvonne Rock Secretarial School, so she's been instructed in all the newest technologies and I'm sure she'll be eager to please, since this is her first position."

Great, John thought. *Just my luck to get someone wet behind the ears.*

"And I'd bet you'd be hard pressed to find another more appealing to look at, since that is why, I assume, you wanted to pick out your own secretary," Warren said with a wink.

So, not only would John be dealing with a novice, but a pretty one at that. The last thing he wanted was some looker complicating things at work. He'd had enough complications in his life ever since he'd met... Actually, maybe a pretty girl around the office would be a nice distraction. He could use another face to replace that flaxen-haired vixen that had so often invaded his thoughts as of late.

"She's in my office. I'll bring her over and introduce you," Warren said.

John rose and grabbed his suit coat off the back of his chair. He slid it on and was just buttoning it when his boss returned. Warren Mallory opened the office door wide and motioned for the young woman to enter. She smiled at Warren from beneath a wide-brimmed hat laden with flowers, then slowly lifted her head, revealing sharp green eyes that John had come to know very well.

"Mr. John Ward, meet your new secretary, Miss - "

"You?" the woman hissed between clenched teeth.

John did a much better job at concealing his surprise. "Good morning, Miss Albright. It's a pleasure to see you again."

"You two know each other?"

John watched as Phoebe quickly recovered. She turned a radiant smile toward Warren Mallory.

"Mr. Ward is a friend of a friend."

"Ah, yes. Will Caffey. I forget how many people know and love that boy, my wife included. Can't wait to meet the fellow. Well," he said, nodding at John. "I'll leave you two. I am taking my beautiful wife to lunch. I'll check in when I return."

John watched as Phoebe Albright turned to watch Warren leave. She continued staring at the door and John wondered if she were contemplating following the man straight away. Working as John's secretary certainly couldn't have been at the top of her list of preferred jobs. She stood as still as a statue, though he doubted even Michelangelo could capture the beauty of her profile.

A knock on his door made them both jump.

"Yes?" John said. The door opened, revealing a massive, ruddy-faced man.

"I brought up a desk outta storage that Mr. Mallory requested. Where'd ye want it?"

John followed the man into the hall and looked at the old, dusty wood desk placed just outside his office door.

"That's fine right there," John said.

"Ok, Mr. Ward. Got some cleaner an' rags I'll bring back in a jiffy an' clean er up for ya."

"The rags and cleaner will be helpful, but my new secretary will be more than happy to clean her own desk."

The Irishman looked wide-eyed at John. "Oh, no sir. Ain't no trouble 'tall. Wouldn't want the lass gettin' her wee hands dirty."

"This wee lass would be more than happy to clean the desk," Phoebe said, stepping forward and smiling sweetly at the man. "Besides, I'm sure you have better things to attend to, Mister ...?"

"O'Brien, miss. Patrick O'Brien, but everyone calls me Paddy."

She reached out and shook his hand.

"It's a pleasure to meet you, Mr. O'Brien. I am Miss Albright. I look forward to working with you."

"Oh, you willna see much of me. I spend most of my time in the loading bay. Heavy liftin' is what I do best."

"Excellent. Now I know where to find you if I need anything heavy moved."

A huge grin spread across Paddy's face. "That's right, lass. Ya need anythin, anythin 'tall, you just head to the back a the building and ask for ol' Paddy."

"Well, Paddy, there is one thing I need," she smiled sweetly.

"Anythin', lass."

"Some cleaner?"

Paddy threw his head back and laughed. "I almost forgot! I told ya. Heavy liftin' is what I do best, not rememberin'. I'll be back in a jiffy."

John rolled his eyes. He had meant to anger the pretty blonde with the menial task. Instead, she had used the moment to endear the old goat to her. *What a conniver!*

Looking quite proud of herself, Phoebe walked over to the coat tree and hung her wool overcoat next to his. As she unpinned her hat, John took notice of her dress. The pale green fabric, a shade or two lighter than the green of her eyes, clung nicely to her figure without hinting too much at what lay beneath. The hem of the dress fell just above her ankle, concealed by her button-up boots, and John wondered if he would get another glimpse of her slender calf, as he had outside the speakeasy all those weeks ago, when she seated herself behind her desk.

John shook his head to get a handle on himself. He would have to be especially steadfast in keeping his thoughts above board now that he would be working so closely with Will's girl. Of all the secretaries graduating from all the schools in all the state, why did Mallory have to hire this one? He went back inside his office and returned to writing the article he had been working on before Warren Mallory had turned his world upside down.

Nearly an hour passed before Phoebe was standing in front of his desk again. He looked up at her, annoyed at the interruption.

"Yes?" he said curtly.

"The desk is cleaned. What would you like me to do next?"

He turned back to his typewriter. "You'll need a typewriter - "

"Already taken care of."

He looked at her again, eyebrows raised.

She shrugged her shoulders. "I asked Paddy where I might find one, and he brought one to me post haste."

"Of course, he did," John said, turning once again to his work. He typed for a few more minutes, then realized she still stood on the other side of his desk.

"Yes?" he said, turning back toward her and folding his hands on his desk.

She sighed. "The desk is clean. I have a typewriter. What would you like me to do next?"

John looked at her face, set in hard lines as she waited for him to respond. Her cheeks were a heightened pink, most likely from the exertion it must have taken to clean years of grime off the old desk. A brown smudge adorned her cheek, evidence that the job had not been easy.

John rose from his desk and handed her his handkerchief. She looked at him quizzically and he just pointed at her face without saying a word.

"Thank you," she said, taking the offered handkerchief.

As she wiped her face clean, he noticed that her dress had met with the same fate as her face. Brown smudges dotted the front of her once spotless outfit. John felt a twinge of regret but dismissed it as quickly as it had appeared.

"Apparently, your school did not instruct you on how to dress for your position."

"What do you find so offensive about the way I am dressed?" Phoebe looked down at her outfit, brushing some of the dirt away. "My instructors said that we should strive to always look beautiful, but not provocative. Do I not look beautiful or is it that you find my dress too provocative?" she said, placing her hands on her hips. She looked him square in the eye.

John found himself in a rare state of speechlessness. She was actually daring him to either call her beautiful or to call her provocative. His mouth hung slightly agape as he searched for an answer that would not incriminate him, but no words came. As he struggled, he watched one perfectly arched golden brow slowly rise in defiance.

"Your dress is passable, I suppose, for an afternoon tea," he finally said. He crossed his arms and lifted an eyebrow in response to hers. "But not for a day at the newspaper. I suggest tomorrow you wear something more appropriate, like a dark skirt and plain blouse, unless you want to ruin your wardrobe with ink smears."

She folded her hands in front of her and smiled. "Certainly, Mr. Ward. Is there anything else you wanted before I take my lunch?"

"That is all for now," John said. Although she had conceded to his wishes, he felt somehow as if he had not won this battle. The bottom of her skirt swished as she walked toward the door, and swished some more as she reached back to shut it behind her.

"Oh," she said, smiling icily. "I will make certain to let Mrs. Mallory know that you found the dress she designed for me to be 'passable.'" She slammed the door.

John leaned on his desk and squeezed his eyes shut. Working with his new secretary was not going to be easy.

15

THE LETTER

"*P*assable! Can you believe that, Anna? He called my dress 'passable.' Not only is he a reviler and a misogynist, he clearly is void of any fashion sense."

It had been a week since she began working at the State Journal, and today was the first chance she had had to spend any time with her best friend. It was also the first she had spoken with anyone about her horrible new boss.

"Most men are, Esther," Anna Mallory said with a shrug. "Why, before he met me, Warren had all of his clothing picked out by his tailor. Luckily, his tailor has good taste, but it wouldn't have mattered. If the man had told him to wear knickers to the opera, he would have. He has absolutely no sense when it comes to fashion."

"Even so, Warren would never call anything you, or any other woman, wore 'passable.' And did you know that my father has been meeting that man once a week for lunch? You could have knocked me over with a feather when he showed up at the office and greeted John Ward like they were old friends! I only put up with the man because I'm paid to. Why would anyone do it for free?"

"You forget that I've met him, on more than one occasion. I find the gentleman to be quite pleasant."

"Pleasant? It's a ruse. I'm telling you, Anna, I don't know how I'm going to survive working for that man. He's rude and obnoxious and... and..."

"Extremely handsome?" Anna interrupted with a smirk.

"I hadn't noticed," Esther said, stuffing a bite of sandwich into her mouth.

Anna threw her head back and laughed. "Of course, you haven't. Man, how I wish Phoebe were here to see this."

Esther swallowed. "See what?"

"This. You." Anna motioned at Esther. "I've never seen you like this."

"Like what? Angry? You've seen me angry plenty of times."

"No, silly. Flustered. This John Ward has really gotten under your skin. I think, maybe, you've finally met your match."

"My match? You aren't making any sense. He has the personality of a badger, and the intelligence to match. He is so horrible, he makes me wish I were back in secretary school."

Anna took a sip of her Vernor's, unsuccessfully masking a smile.

Esther crossed her arms. "I mean it. I can't stand him."

"Really? Then why have you spent our entire lunch talking about him?"

Esther swallowed hard. She didn't have a response to that.

Anna laughed. "You're falling for him. You mark my words."

With Anna's words still ringing in her ears, Esther returned to the office. She approached her desk and braced herself for whatever snide remarks her new boss would hurl at her next, but to her surprise, he was nowhere to be found. In the week she had worked for him, John hadn't taken a lunch longer than thirty minutes, except for Tuesday when he had lunched with her father.

She busied herself with the few tasks she had left over from before lunch, but when an hour passed and still no John, she found herself with nothing to do. Rather than sit and twiddle her thumbs, Esther decided to ask Warren's secretary if there was anything with which she needed assistance.

"Good afternoon, Miss Hagerman. Mr. Ward isn't in, so I was wondering..." but Esther stopped short when the woman looked at her, worry etched across her face. "Miss Hagerman, is something wrong?"

"I'm not sure. I mean, I think so, but I really don't know." The woman's forehead wrinkled even further and she squeezed her hands together until her knuckles were pure white.

"Well, something has happened that has upset you. Why don't you tell me, and I'll see if I can help?"

"Oh, dear. I'm not certain I should say anything."

"I think you should tell someone, and I seem to be the only one around. Come, now. What has happened?"

Miss Hagerman's eyes darted around the empty reception area, then finally settled once again on Esther. "It's Mr. Ward," she said.

She had Esther's complete attention now. "What about Mr. Ward?"

"He received a letter a couple of hours ago. He was in a pleasant mood when I handed it to him, but the minute he looked at the return address, his features changed. It was like a dark cloud descended over him. He looked fit to be tied before he even opened the envelope. Then he read the letter, crumpled it up, and threw it in the trash basket. He stormed out of here and he hasn't been back since."

What could that letter have said that could have caused such a reaction? Esther wondered.

"I'm really worried about him, Miss Albright. I've never seen him like this."

Esther thought a moment. "You said he threw the letter away? Which trash can?"

Miss Hagerman pointed to a small, metal basket on the other side of her desk. Esther looked in, and right on top, just as Miss Hagerman had said, was a crumpled piece of paper. Esther reached in and retrieved it.

"Oh, Miss Albright! I don't think we ought to be reading Mr. Ward's mail!"

"How else are we going to solve this mystery? Isn't this what Sherlock Holmes would do?" she asked. Esther had seen Miss Hagerman slyly reading the Conan Doyle books behind her desk on more than one occasion.

"Yes!" she replied enthusiastically. "That is exactly what he would do!"

Esther smiled and unwrapped the paper. A small part of her felt like she was intruding into John Ward's personal affairs, but considering the way the other secretary was acting, she felt she should do something. She smoothed out the wrinkles and read the typed note.

Esther gasped. "Mr. Ward's father has passed away."

"Oh, mercy! Poor Mr. Ward. No wonder he was so upset. Do you think he rushed off home for the funeral?"

"I don't think so. It appears he's already been buried."

"Maybe to comfort his Ma?"

Esther scanned the letter again. "It doesn't look like she's alive. This letter says that Mr. Ward is the sole survivor."

"Well, then where in the world do you think he's stormed off to?"

Esther refolded the letter and stuck it in her pocket. "I'm not certain, but I may have an idea."

She returned to her desk to grab her coat, hat and handbag. She spoke to Miss Hagerman on her way out the door.

"If anyone asks, tell them I went on an errand for Mr. Ward."

~

"Sorry, missy, but I can't let you in."

Esther wasn't expecting this. She had easily gained access to the speakeasy in her two previous visits.

"I don't understand. You've let me in before."

"We don't want no trouble in here, and you caused quite the ruckus the last time."

"Let me get this straight," she said as innocently as possible. "You aren't going to let me, a frail female, inside because you are worried for the safety of your patrons?"

The big man smiled. "Missy, after seein' you in action the last time you was here, I'm more afraid for my own safety than anyone else's."

"What's your name, sir?"

"Name's Charlie. Charlie Ross, ma'am."

"Well, it's a pleasure to officially meet you, Charlie Charlie Ross. I'm Esther. Esther Albright. Now that we are friends, Charlie, I give you my word as your friend, that I will cause no harm to any of your patrons. In fact, I'm here out of concern for the welfare of someone I believe to be inside."

"Albright? As in the preacher Albright?"

Why does everyone in this town know my father? Esther sighed. "Do I have to answer that question?"

Charlie rubbed his forehead. "Why do I get the feeling you're gonna cause me more problems than I need if I keep lettin' you in here?"

"Please," Esther asked sweetly.

"C'mon. I'll help you find whoever you're looking for."

"Oh, you don't need to bother yourself..."

"What are friends for," he said with a smirk, shaking his head. "After you," he sighed.

He opened the door and ushered her through the small, dimly lit ante room and into the bar. It took a few moments for her eyes to adjust to the darkness, as well as the fog of smoke that hung over the room.

"All right, what's this fella look like?"

"How do you know it's a gentleman?"

"I've been doin' this job a long time. Let's just say it's intuition."

Esther's eyes were just beginning to focus but it didn't take long for her to locate John. He sat at the bar, his back facing the door, but she recognized not only the cut of his suit, but his cane leaning against the bar next to him. "There he is."

"That one?" He laughed. "You won't be the first woman today to try an' pull him away from his drink."

Something inside Esther bristled at those words. "Other women?"

"Yessum. Turned them all away, and they was professionals, if ya get my meanin', ma'am."

"Yes, Charlie," she said, blushing. "I understand. Is – Is this gentleman in the habit of keeping company with 'professionals'?"

Charlie looked down on her and his eyebrows knitted together as he considered her question. "Now, missy, I wouldn't be keepin' my job for long if I talked about the customers and their habits, would I?"

Esther swallowed hard. Charlie's avoidance of her question could only mean one thing.

"But," he continued, "just between us friends – ," he said, winking again, "I don't ever recall that particular fella payin' attention to them ladies. When he first started comin' around, they tried, but he never seemed interested. Only seemed interested in the liquor, but lately, not even that. Haven't seen him around here for some time, well, until today, that is."

"Thank you for your help Charlie."

"I'll be right over here if ya need me."

"Oh, I don't think that will be necessary."

"Right over here," he repeated, pointing at a stool next to the door. "He's got quite a few under his belt."

Esther slid onto the stool next to John just as the bartender passed him another beer.

"That seat's taken," John grumbled without looking up.

"Obviously," she said. "I can see you are socializing with all your friends," Esther laughed, gesturing at the empty seats surrounding John.

John's head shot up. He swore under his breath. "What are you doing here?" He turned back to his beer and took a hearty swig.

"I came to retrieve you."

"Hmmph. I'm not going anywhere."

"Well, then I guess I'm staying right here as well. Excuse me, sir," she said, motioning for the bartender. "Do you have cherry phosphate?"

"You kiddin' lady?" the man snorted.

"Well, what do you have that isn't alcohol?"

"How 'bout a Vernor's ginger ale?"

"That will do nicely, thank you."

She turned to find John staring at her, mouth agape.

"You come to a speakeasy and order a ginger ale? You're a piece of work."

"I'm not here to drink."

"Then why are you here?"

"I told you. I'm here - "

"Oh, that's right. You're here to save me from myself." John turned on his stool and leaned closer to her. "What if I told you that I don't want to be saved."

His words were slurred, and she could smell the alcohol on his breath, but she resisted the urge to pull away. He was trying to intimidate her, and she wasn't about to let him win. She leaned in even closer.

"I'd say that you are lying," she said quietly. "I'd say that you don't know what you want, and that's why you came here, to try to forget your problems because you don't have a solution for them."

A slow smile spread across his mouth. "I see daddy isn't the only Albright with wise words."

"Come on, Mr. Ward. I have a cab waiting outside. If we - "

"I said I'm not going anywhere. Listen, you might think that just because you're beautiful, you can bat your pretty eyelashes and hypnotize me with those gorgeous green eyes of yours and I'll do anything you ask, but I'm not a fool like other men. I know what kind of woman you are." He pulled away and took another swig of beer.

"You think I'm beautiful?" she asked incredulously.

John's head swung back around, and his eyebrows shot up. He brought his face close to hers again.

"I think you are the most beautiful creature I have ever laid eyes on. Even when I'm not looking at you," he began, reaching out and caressing a loose curl between his fingers, "my dreams are haunted by your golden hair, your emerald eyes, your perfect lips."

Esther's heart beat rapidly as John spoke huskily, only a few inches from her. She would only need to lean in slightly and...

"Everything okay here, missy?" Charlie's voice boomed behind them.

John shook his head several times and squinted at the large man towering over them.

"Yes, Charlie. Everything is just fine," Esther said.

"Yes, Charlie," John said, slapping him on the meaty arm. "Don't mind us. The lady here is just trying to save me from inevitable destruction."

Charlie scowled at John. "You just keep your hands to yourself, you understand?" he said, then returned to his post at the door.

John looked back at Esther. "I see you have yet another

admirer. Tell me, Miss Albright, how many men are you stringing along right now?"

"We really should be going, Mr. Ward. Come on, let me help you out."

"What about Will?"

Esther stopped. "Will? Will Caffey? What about him?"

"Is he just another of your conquests or is he someone special."

John wasn't making any sense and Esther was losing patience. She stood up. "It's time to go. You've had too much to drink and you aren't thinking straight." Esther reached down and grabbed his cane.

John stood also, but instead of his cane, he grabbed Esther's arm instead.

"I've never thought straighter in all my life. Will Caffey is the best man I know, and you treat him like a piece of-"

John never finished his sentence. Before either of them knew what was happening, Charlie descended on him.

"I warned you." The surly doorman grabbed John by the collar, drug him through the two sets of doors and threw him into the road. Esther followed quickly behind. She could tell by the look on John's face that Charlie's rough treatment had caused him great pain.

"Charlie, I appreciate your gallant protection, but he has a war injury."

"Sorry, missy, but I gave him ample warning. Besides, the pain will likely sober the fool up."

Esther crouched near where John lay on the ground. "Come on, Mr. Ward. Let's get you into the cab."

"You'd better do as Miss Albright asks, or I'll be the one helpin' you home, if you get my drift," Charlie threatened.

"I get your drift," John grunted, rising slowly and limping to the cab. Charlie held the cab door for Esther and helped her into the cab.

He moved to close the door, then hesitated. "I don't like this one bit. Are you sure you know what you're doing?" he asked.

"I'll be just fine," she assured him. "I think you are correct; your little moment of assistance seems to have sobered him quite a bit."

Esther and John traveled for several minutes in silence. Esther wasn't entirely certain that her companion was still awake. She was just about to poke him when he spoke.

"How'd you know I'd be at Jimmy's?"

Esther reached inside her handbag, pulled out the letter and handed it to him. His face was a mask of confusion as he took the letter, but it seemed to take only a moment for the truth to register. His head snapped in her direction.

"You're going through my personal belongings now?"

"Only if you consider the garbage can one of your personal belongings."

John swore but said nothing more about it. He stuffed the letter into his pocket, leaned his head against the door and closed his eyes.

"I'm sorry about your father," Esther said softly.

John grunted. "I'm not."

"You don't mean that."

John continued to stare out the window. "I do mean it. I can't tell you how many times I have wished the old man dead. That wish finally came true." He lifted his head and looked at her in such a penetrating way that she shuddered. "Does that make you think less of me, Miss Albright?"

Esther swallowed hard but refused to break eye contact. "Then, why all the drinking? Why try to drink away your sorrows, if you have none?"

John blinked a few times and shook his head. "I don't know," he said, looking away again and resting his head once more on the door. "I really don't know."

They rode in silence for the remainder of the trip. When

the car finally came to a stop, John lifted his head and swore once more, but this time he apologized.

"Sorry. Force of habit. But why in the world did you bring me here? I just want to go home and sleep it off. I only live a couple of blocks from Jimmy's."

"Well, I couldn't very well leave you by yourself. I don't trust you to not head back into that bar."

"But here?"

Esther opened the door and motioned for him to follow her.

"Come on. I can't carry you. You'll have to make your way on your own."

Grumbling under his breath, John snatched his cane from Esther's hand and stumbled out of the cab. He made it about twenty paces before he came to rest on the front stairs of Lansing First Church.

Esther paid the cab driver and turned back to John who was slumped over on the stairs.

"Wait right here," she said.

"Where else have I got to go?" he slurred and slumped even further.

Esther lifted her skirt and ran next door. She hadn't thought through her plan very thoroughly. All she'd known was her father would know what to do. The problem she was now discovering was how in the world would she explain the situation to him.

She rushed through the front door and found her father sitting in the parlor reading the afternoon edition of the Lansing State Journal.

"Good grief, girl. What has you in such a tizzy?"

"It's John Ward," she said, taking deep breaths in an attempt to slow her breathing.

"John? What about John?" her father asked, laying the paper aside.

"He's sitting on the front stairs of the church, and he's drunk."

"Drunk? How do you know that?"

Esther put her hands on her hips and tilted her head. "I may not be a very worldly woman, Daddy, but I know drunk from sober."

"Fair enough, girl. Fair enough." Reverend Albright rose from his chair and grabbed his hat and coat. "Get some coffee brewing and have your mother bring the pot over when it's finished."

"I can bring - "

"I said have your mother bring it," he said sternly.

"Yes, Daddy," Esther said. Her father didn't make demands very often, but when he did, his daughters knew better than defy them.

Esther watched out the front window as her father casually skipped down the stairs, as if a drunk man collapsed in front of his church every day. While she watched him, a dark dread began to build in the pit of her stomach. What if John told her father that she had entered the speakeasy to drag him out? After his drunken admission of being attracted to her, she doubted he would have the good sense to censure his story to protect her, not that she thought he would care to protect her reputation in the first place. John wasn't too fond of her when sober. As a drunk, he was bound to say anything.

Esther now realized that by saving John Ward, she had most likely just condemned herself.

16

WRETCHED

*J*ohn had just finished retching in the bushes beside the church stairs when a familiar voice spoke behind him.

"Well, I don't believe Mrs. Albright is going to take too kindly to that. She just transplanted those roses from her own garden."

John silently cursed Phoebe. What was she thinking getting her father involved?

"I just need to get home," he said, rising to his feet. He stumbled sideways a few steps and felt searing pain in his lower back. If he could already feel that after all the drinks he had downed this afternoon, then he was sure to pay for his run-in with Charlie tomorrow. "I just need my cane."

"See here," the reverend said when John faltered again. "You're not going anywhere until we get you sobered up. Where's your coat, boy?"

John looked dumbly down at his body. "I don't know. Back at the office, I guess."

"Come on." Reverend Albright grabbed John's arm and put

it over his shoulder while he wrapped his own arm around the younger man's waist. "It'll be warmer inside."

It was indeed warmer inside, and John wasn't completely certain that he was finished with the retching that the minister had interrupted. The heat of the sanctuary felt suffocating and he feared he would lose the rest of the alcohol right there in the middle of the aisle. Reverend Albright handed him a bucket.

"Just in case."

"Thanks," John muttered before heaving into the bucket.

John continued to vomit until his stomach had nothing left to give, then the dry heaving began. The bitter burn of bile coated his throat until the muscles of his stomach finally gave up their onslaught and John was left with a hard and hot throbbing inside his skull. He didn't look up when someone took the bucket from him.

"Thank you, Mrs. Kinney," he heard the reverend say.

The church custodian. "Thank you, Mrs. Kinney," John managed to choke out. His eyes opened a crack as he said this, and he saw the woman, her back to him, stop for a split second. He thought he saw her shoulders shaking before she ran from the room, her hand over her mouth. John cursed himself. That poor woman should not have had to deal with a pail full of his vomit.

"Here," said the pastor, placing a warm mug into John's hands. Coffee. Where had that come from?

"I don't think I can..."

"It'll help sober you. Come on, drink up."

John took a sip of the bitter drink. He had never been much of a fan of the stuff, but his empty stomach cried out for something to fill it.

"This your first time drinkin'?" Reverend Albright asked as he lowered his large frame onto the pew next to John.

"No, sir," John mumbled. He kept his head cradled in his hands in an attempt to keep himself upright in the pew.

"Didn't think so. Well, then shall I assume you had a hefty amount of alcohol this afternoon?"

"Yes, sir."

"Uh huh. I see. How much?"

"As much and as fast as they would serve it to me."

"Well, I don't need to tell you how foolhardy that was."

"No, sir," John said, rubbing his temples. "I've figured that out by now."

"Why?"

John slowly swiveled his head toward him. "Why what?"

"Why, all of a sudden, did you dive into the beer barrel and not come up for air?"

So, Phoebe hadn't told her father about the letter. What had she told him? Probably nothing, John reasoned. He didn't think the good pastor would be treating him so kindly if he had known how close John had just come to kissing his daughter.

Without a word, John reached in his pocket and pulled out the crumpled piece of paper. He handed it to Reverend Albright. The preacher read the letter and let out a long sigh.

"So, the man who treated you as an inconvenience has met his maker. Now I understand."

"No, I don't think you do, because I don't understand."

"Because you didn't love him."

"Exactly."

"But hating him doesn't feel so good either."

John was speechless. How had this man, whom John had known for such a short amount of time, pinpointed a problem that John had never figured out himself. Yes, he hated his father. But, hating him hurt more than any beating or bayonet had ever hurt him.

A wave of emotions that John had difficulty identifying — anger, fear, desperation — built inside of John until he could no longer contain it. A flood of tears burst from him and uncontrollable sobs shook his entire body. John hadn't cried since shortly after his mother left, and years of bottled up emotions came flooding out of him like a broken dam.

When the tears finally began to dry up, John realized the minister had wrapped an arm around his shoulders. He was talking quietly, but he wasn't speaking to John. He was praying.

"You're wasting your breath," John said, wiping his face with the back of his sleeve. "God gave up on me a long time ago."

"He's never left you, son. You just stopped looking for Him."

John shook his head back and forth but said nothing.

"John, all this pain you are experiencing, and the bitterness and emptiness, God wants to take it all from you."

"Well, then I wish he would just go ahead and do it!"

"Are you ready to let Him into your life so He can?"

John snorted. "I knew there was a catch. So, God wants to help me, but only if I'm willing to give up everything to him. Figures."

"It's the only way, son. The things of this world are only entrapments unless God is the center of our lives. Look at your father. He had everything a man could ever want, but he chose to 'play church' on Sundays rather than fully commit every aspect of his life to God. And where did that get him? He died alone, without his son or his wife by his side. What good did all the riches he'd amassed over the years do him at that moment? What good are they doing him now?"

"And you think I'm like him? I rejected his wealth and his way of life long ago, and that hasn't saved me from a life of misery. I'm nothing like him, and I'm still miserable."

"Aren't you, son? Your father clung to money and anger, yes, but you have your own vices. You cling to your bitterness and unforgiveness. You lament how miserable you are, but yet you wear it like a badge of honor. 'Don't mess with me. I'm John Ward. Leave me alone. I don't need anyone to care about me.'"

John's head only pounded louder as his heart began to beat

against his chest as well. He knew the pastor was right, but he wasn't sure he could change his life.

"That's just who I am," John reasoned out loud. "There's nothing I can do to change. After all these years, it's in my blood."

"You're right. You can't change it."

Confusion etched across his brow, John turned to eye the minister.

Reverend Albright continued. "You can't change it, but God can."

THE NEXT MORNING was especially bright and sunny, or at least it seemed so to John. He had to admit, however, that any brightness past pitch black was disagreeable to him and the splitting headache he was nursing. Never in his life had he felt so ill from drinking and he doubted he would be repeating the previous day's activity any time soon.

As he slowly opened the door to the State Journal, the familiar scent of ink and metal hit him like a slap across the face and a wave of nausea swept over him. He fought back against the urge to relieve his stomach of its contents, knowing that it would only result in the bitter burning of bile in the back of his throat and an increase in the intensity of the headache he was already suffering. He swallowed hard and trudged through the front reception area.

"Good morning, Mr. Ward," Miss Hagerman said cautiously.

John glared at her through hooded eyes. "Is it, Miss Hagerman? Is it a *good* morning? Because from where I stand, it is anything but."

"I - I was just trying to be friendly," she stammered.

"Why don't you try minding your own business," he snapped as he walked past her and stormed into his office.

John slammed the office door behind him, instantly regretting the action when a knife-like pain pierced his already throbbing head. He slowly slumped into his desk chair and cradled his head in his hands. This is how he remained until a cup of coffee appeared on his desk. He looked up and found Phoebe standing quietly, hands folded in front of her.

"Does everyone in your family think coffee cures everything?" he asked, dropping his head to his hands again.

"Miss Hagerman didn't deserve to be spoken to like that," she said softly.

"Didn't she?" he said sardonically. "Don't try to tell me that she isn't the one who led you to dig through the trash."

"I won't deny it. She was a nervous wreck yesterday, so worried about you that she couldn't hide her concern. Rather than your ire, she deserves your thanks."

"I'll thank her to keep out of my business."

She turned and walked toward the door. "If you don't need anything from me, I'll return to my desk."

"I still don't understand why you did it."

"Excuse me?" She turned and looked at him, her brow furrowed.

John stood and rounded his desk and sat on the front edge. He stretched out his long legs and crossed his arms across his chest. The position brought him almost eye level with her.

"Why did you do it? Why did you come after me?"

Phoebe's features softened as she held his gaze. He had expected pity or judgment or, at the very least, condemnation in her eyes, but all he saw was something he hadn't seen in a very long time...tenderness.

"We all need saving at some point in our lives," she said before closing the door behind her.

John stared at the closed door for several minutes. He knew that the saving Phoebe referred to was more of a physical nature than the spiritual salvation her father had spoken of last night, but it brought him back to the pastor's words none-theless.

John couldn't save himself. He hadn't realized he was trying to do just that until Reverend Albright had spoken those words, but it was true. He'd tried working hard, but that only made him successful, not happy. He'd tried redeeming himself by enlisting in the war, but that experience had only seemed to darken his outlook on life. Had he not met Will Caffey, he wasn't certain how lost he would have been coming out of that horrible war. Alcohol wasn't the answer, as evidenced by the splitting headache he was battling right now. No, John couldn't save himself. He was more miserable today than he had ever been.

John could almost buy into this salvation that the preacher was selling. He was tired. Perhaps there was something to this total surrender that both the pastor and Will had spoken of. It sounded nice to relax, and stop trying so hard. Neither Will nor Reverend Albright had much to speak of, in worldly terms, yet both of them had a peace about them that made John jealous.

One thing had kept John from giving in last night inside that church. Forgiveness. According to the Reverend, God wanted to forgive John of his sins, and God himself certainly knew how many sins John had. But when Reverend Albright had quoted Ephesians 4, John had known that this Jesus salvation wasn't for him. It was true, John had a multitude of sins, and he could almost believe that God wanted to forgive him, but his sins were nothing compared to his father's, and the idea that Jesus had not only died for John's transgressions, but for his father's as well was incomprehensible to John. And even more unbelievable was that God expected John to forgive his father as well.

"You'll never have true freedom, John," Reverend Albright had said. "Until you can forgive your father, you will always carry a weight that is too heavy to bear."

"How could God expect me to forgive that man, after all he did?"

"Jesus himself said that if you do not forgive others' sins, God will not forgive yours."

"Then I'm destined to remain a sinner."

"What punishment has carrying around that unforgiveness done to your father? Nothing, I tell you. The only person your unforgiveness has punished is you, son."

John had never considered his unforgiveness as a self-imposed punishment, but now it felt like such an encumbrance. Reverend Albright was right. John's father wasn't the least bit affected by John's hatred. Only John was. And he was continuing to allow that man's sins to affect him, even after his death.

John turned and looked at the untouched cup on his desk. Coffee. He didn't need the bitter brew any more than he needed a nosy pastor's daughter meddling in his life. He rose and took the cup to the window, fully intending to pour the contents out. But instead he found himself lifting the mug to his nose and taking in the woody aroma of the warm beverage. He sighed, trying not to think of the slender hands that had poured it, trying not to remember the desire to hold those hands as he sat next to her in her father's church, and most of all trying not to believe they'd likely folded together in prayer for him only a few short hours ago. As if drinking away the thoughts, he downed the entire contents of the cup.

John shook his head and opened his office door. Phoebe, Will's girl, he reminded himself, wasn't at her desk. It was just as well, John reasoned as he grabbed his coat off the hook and placed the empty cup on her desk. He didn't need her approval to leave the office. And he most certainly didn't need her knowing glances as he brought back both flowers and an apology for Miss Hagerman.

17

SAVING KATIE

*J*ohn typed furiously at his desk. Nearly everyone else had left, except the few workers in the loading bay finishing their shift, but John remained, trying to finish a piece about the latest outbreak of Spanish Influenza. He should have completed it hours ago, but no matter what he tried, he couldn't keep his mind focused when Phoebe was nearby. And since she was his secretary, she was nearby all day long. That is why for the past week, John had found himself alone at his desk for hours after the office had closed.

He had just finished typing the final sentence when he heard a rapping sound. He rose from his seat. He wasn't certain where the sound was coming from, but thought maybe the reception area.

Walking out of his office and down the hall toward the entrance, he heard the sound again. He looked at the front door and saw Mrs. Caffey rapping on the glass with her umbrella handle. He opened the door for her.

"This is a surprise, Mrs. Caffey."

"I've been knocking for quite some time. I was just about to give up."

"I was typing. The clicking of my typewriter must have drowned out the sound of your tapping. Miss Hagerman left hours ago, and I - Mrs. Caffey? Is something wrong?" John asked, noticing the woman's odd behavior. The usually placid older woman stood twisting the unused umbrella in her hands, as if she hoped to squeeze juice from it.

"Yes, I mean, I'm not certain. Oh, John, I didn't know where to go. I kept praying and asking God for wisdom, but I still didn't know what to do. All I kept thinking was, 'If Will were here, he'd know what to do,' but Will isn't here. That's when your face came to me. If I can't have Will's help in the matter, then surely you, his good friend, are the next best option."

"Alright, ma'am, slow down. Take a breath or two," John said, leading her to a set of chairs outside of Warren Mallory's office. "Why don't you try and tell me what this is all about."

"It's about Katie, the girl staying with me. Well, not exactly. I mean, yes, it's about Katie, but not just her. They both are gone, but I'm not certain where they've gone. So, can you see why I don't know what to do?"

John did not see. The older woman wasn't making any sense. He took a deep breath.

"They? Who are they?"

"Oh, dear, I'm just making things worse. Miss Feegle, the girl who lives with me, and Miss Albright. Do you remember her? Reverend Albright's daughter? You sat next to her that one time you visited church with me?"

"Yes, yes," John assured her.

"Oh, of course. I completely forgot that she works for you now. How fortuitous how that all worked out..."

"Mrs. Caffey, what about Miss Feegle and Miss Albright?"

"Oh, dear. Well, when Miss Feegle left my house today, she told me that she wouldn't be returning. She said that she had been unable to find work and that she was going to take a job that she deserved. I had no idea what that meant. So, when

Miss Albright stopped by this evening, I told her what Miss Feegle had said, and she turned white as a sheet, and said she knew exactly what Miss Feegle meant."

"And what did Miss Feegle mean?" John asked.

"I don't know. All she would tell me was that it was a place of ill-repute and that she was going after her."

"She said that?" John said, jumping to his feet. He wasn't certain, but he believed he knew exactly what place of ill-repute Phoebe had spoken of.

"John, dear, do you know where they've gone?"

"I might, Mrs. Caffey, and if I am correct, then it is a very good thing you came to me."

"Oh, dear, I knew this wasn't good. Oh, John, what are we going to do?"

"You are going to go home. I'm going to go retrieve the women."

Mrs. Caffey sighed and smiled. "Thank you, son. I knew that if anyone could help me, it would be you."

John grabbed his coat and hat. He paused as his eyes fell upon the cane leaning against his desk. What good could a partially crippled man do in an emergency? He hoped Mrs. Caffey had not made a mistake placing her trust in him. But what choice did either of them have? John was Phoebe's only hope, if she indeed was where he feared she was. If Will's God were in fact real, John thought, now would be a good time for him to show up.

John walked out of the office, leaving his cane behind.

Esther kept to the shadows of the hallway, inching her way closer to the door at the end. She wasn't certain what she had expected from this rescue, but when Charlie wasn't at his usual post, she'd almost lost her nerve. The man filling in for him was half Charlie's size and his appearance seemed much less fore-boding than the hefty friend she had made over the course of her three previous visits, but unlike Charlie, this man actually frightened Esther. He'd made no pretense about scrutinizing her body from head to toe, and the hungry way he'd taken in her figure had almost made her run from the speakeasy. But Esther was certain that Katie was inside, and she was not turning back until she had Katie by her side.

If her bravado had wavered at the front door, it nearly disappeared altogether as she crept along the dark hallway. There were so many doors, doors that led to rooms with people doing things Esther did not wish to imagine. How would she ever find Katie? She couldn't very well knock on every door asking for her. Could she?

"Dear God, please help me."

Esther could see no other way. If interrupting every - um, *patron* until she found the right room was the only way, then that is exactly what she would do. She only prayed that Katie were behind the first door.

She lifted her hand and was about to knock when she heard a scream. She couldn't be certain that it was Katie, but whoever it was, she needed help and she was in the room behind the next door.

In a rush, Esther ran to the door and threw it open. Katie was there, crouched in a corner crying. A man stood a few feet from her. He turned toward the now open door and pulled his pants up as he did. Esther wasn't certain who was more surprised, the half-dressed man or herself.

"Mr. Baxter?" she said incredulously. She stood, mouth agape, as the president of the church board grabbed the remainder of his clothing off the bed and pushed her aside as he ran out the door. Esther couldn't believe what she had just witnessed, but she took no time to think about it. She rushed to Katie, still crouched in the corner of the room.

"Oh, Katie, are you alright?"

Katie didn't answer. Her cries began to shake her entire body as Esther wrapped her arms around her. Esther felt completely helpless, a feeling she had very little experience in.

"Did - did he...did he hurt you?" she asked, her voice wavering slightly. She felt the other woman's head shake from side to side.

"Oh, Esther. What was I thinking? I thought this was my punishment, to live a life like this. I thought this was the only way. But when he came in here and started to undress, I knew I couldn't do it. I tried to tell him, but he just kept taking his clothes off and saying that he was going to get his money's worth. I didn't know what to do. I started praying, but when he dropped his pants, I just screamed."

Esther rubbed her back and kissed the top of her head. "Well, thank God that you did, because I don't know how I would have found you otherwise. Come, now. Let's not dawdle. We must hurry and get you out of here."

"She's not going anywhere," a voice said from behind them.

The women turned toward the door and found their exit blocked by two men. One, the bouncer with the hungry eyes, the other a man Esther had never seen before. He appeared out of place, with his expensive suit and impeccably shined shoes and Esther couldn't help but wonder why a man who dressed like Warren Mallory would be in an establishment as seedy as this one.

Esther swallowed back the fear rising in her throat and stood to face the men.

"She is going somewhere, and you aren't going to stop us. Step aside."

The man in the suit threw his head back and laughed, but Esther found no humor in his reaction.

"What do you find so funny?"

The man brought his eyes back to lock with Esther's. She

saw there a darkness that caused her heart to stop. "I find your arrogance hilarious. What makes you think we will do your bidding. No, little girl. I'm the boss around here. You'll do as I say, and I say she stays."

Esther placed her hands on her hips, hoping the action disguised the shaking that had taken them over. She spoke to Katie over her shoulder and told the girl to stand. It wouldn't do to have either one of them cowering in the presence of these brutes.

"Well, sir, if you are the boss, then you are exactly the person I need to speak with. Do you realize that one of your customers was about to rape this young woman?"

Again, the man laughed. Ice trickled down Esther's spine at the sound. "Rape? It isn't rape if it's been paid for."

"It's rape if she says 'no,' and I most certainly heard her scream the word. If I heard her on the other side of the door, the gentleman most certainly heard her as well."

The man in the suit stepped close to Esther and peered into her eyes. She could smell the putrid sweet of liquor from deep within his throat.

"I'm the only one who says 'no' around here, woman. If I say yes, then the answer is yes. And I say yes - yes she will take that customer, and the next and the next. I would have taken it easy on her, this being her first night. But I can see that she needs to learn a lesson. I think six customers should be enough to make her see her place."

Esther's blood ran cold. "Six men? You can't be serious."

The man turned to the bouncer. "Get this one out of here," he said, motioning toward Esther.

Esther looked desperately between Katie and the bouncer as he reached for Esther's arm. His strong fingers dug into the soft flesh of her upper arm as he yanked her toward the door.

"But - but, she's with child!"

With those words, both men stopped and looked at Esther,

then at Katie. The man in the suit stared at Katie's midsection in disbelief. When his eyes raised to hers, his face was red with anger.

"Is that true?" he yelled.

Katie didn't speak, just nodded numbly, her body still trembling. The man turned to the bouncer.

"Forget her, take this one. And don't let her back in."

Esther breathed a sigh of relief, but her relief was short lived. She watched the bouncer roughly drag Katie out the door. She started to follow, but her way was blocked by the man in the suit.

"I said she could go. Never said anything about you," he said, picking up Katie's suitcase.

Esther's heart beat rapidly. "Let me through."

"Now, why would I do that? Not a good business decision, if you ask me. See, I have customers expecting a new girl. I don't plan to refund their money, so I need a new girl. Not the redhead they were expecting, but I'm sure they won't be disappointed."

"You can't be serious," she said, but he wasn't listening. He turned and shut the door. Esther ran to it, but as she reached for the handle, she heard the sickening sound of a key setting the lock from the outside. She rattled the handle and turned it with all of her might, but it would not budge.

"You can't expect - I won't!" she yelled through the door. "You can't make me! I'll scream!"

Esther backed up from the door as panic rose within her. Katie had screamed at the top of her lungs, yet Esther was the only one who came to her rescue. Who would rescue Esther if she tried the same?

She began praying as she paced the floor. Surely there was a way to escape, she just needed to figure something out before the first 'customer' arrived. Customer. That was it — Mr. Baxter was most likely the first man waiting for the new girl. There is no way he would lay a hand on her. Maybe she could reason with him and he could help her escape.

While the plan was forming in her mind, she once again heard the scraping sound of key in lock. She turned toward the door, her plea for help on the tip of her tongue. But it wasn't Mr. Baxter who walked through the door. It was the hungry-eyed doorman.

"Boss said I deserve a bonus." He slammed the door behind him. "I tried convincing him ta let me take the other girl for a spin, ta make sure she was ready for customers, but he was hopin' it was her first time, so he charged extra for her first customer. If'n he'd listened ta me, we wouldn't have had any surprises. But, then again," he said, inching his way closer to Esther, "if I'd had her, then I wouldn't be here with you now, and if my guess is right, you is a cherry."

Esther slowly backed away from the man as he continued toward her. She desperately searched for a way out of the situation as he continued to taunt her.

"Yeah, I think you is a cherry, and a feistier one at that. I'm going to enjoy this."

He reached out to touch Esther's cheek and she swatted his hand away, but he only smiled and shook his head.

"Please," she pleaded. "Let me go. You know I'm not a working girl."

"C'mon, sweetheart, if ya give me half a chance, ya might enjoy it yourself."

He reached out and took her chin in his hand. He lifted her face to meet his mouth, but Esther turned her head and sunk her teeth into the flesh of his wrist. The man swore and released her. Esther took the split-second opportunity and bolted for the door, but his hands were on her before she could reach it. He twirled her to face him. Esther barely had time to straighten herself before he brought the back of his hand across her cheekbone. The force of the blow sent her flying backward and onto the bed. Shards of white light blurred her vision as the pain from the impact exploded in her head. She pushed herself onto her elbows and tried to focus on her assailant.

"Have it your way. I'll enjoy it more this way," he said as he unbuckled the belt of his pants.

18

SAVING ESTHER

ohn knocked and knocked on the door of the speakeasy, but nobody answered. He rattled the handle and threw his shoulder against the door, but nothing worked. He backed up and sized up the building. It was only two stories tall, but he could see no exterior staircase leading to the second floor. Maybe if he followed the building around to the back alley, he could find a second entrance.

"I don't even know if she's inside," John said out loud, removing his hat and running his fingers through his sandy brown hair.

"Don't know if who's inside?"

John turned to find the burly door keeper making his way down the street, eyeing John suspiciously. John hadn't been back to the speakeasy since his run-in with the man, and John could tell by the look on his face that the bouncer wasn't too happy to see him.

"The woman that came looking for me. I believe she is inside."

"Now, why in the world would Miss Albright come back here?"

"You're surprised? I assumed, since you know each other by name, that she was a regular here."

"Nope," the big man said as he crossed his arms. "Only been here a few times, far as I recollect. And only to give someone a piece of her mind. So, since you are out here, and that other fella is off to war, I don't suspect she's inside."

John let that information sink in. So, Phoebe wasn't a regular of the bar. But, if his gut instinct was correct, she was inside the building right now.

"Listen, I just want in to see for myself."

"I told ya last time not to come back." The large man's forehead wrinkled, and his eyes squinted at John. "You'd best be movin' along."

John sized up the man and knew there was no way he could take him, even if John weren't injured, but, if that was what he had to do to find Phoebe, then he would. Before it got to that point, John decided to try reasoning with the big man one last time.

"Charlie, isn't it? I'm not trying to cause any trouble, Charlie, but I have reason to believe that she is inside the building, but not in the bar. I believe she is upstairs."

The hefty man laughed, and his large belly shook with each breath. "That's a good'n, mister, but there's no way you're convincin' me that the lass would find herself up there."

"What if I told you she was foolhardy enough to think she could save one of the working girls?"

At that, Charlie raised an eyebrow. "Now, *that* I might believe. What makes ya think that?"

"Just a hunch, but we don't have any time to waste."

Charlie scratched his chin with one meaty paw. "If you're wrong, I could lose my job."

"But what if I'm right?"

Before Charlie could answer, they were interrupted by a woman screaming in the side alley. Both men frowned and ran around the corner. To John's relief, it wasn't Phoebe. But the woman did look familiar. John was about to turn away when the man pushed the woman to the ground and threw a suitcase on top of her.

"Hey!" John yelled and ran toward the woman.

"Mind your own business," the man growled when John reached them.

"Now, Mr. Sullivan, that ain't no way to treat a lady."

John was surprised to see that Charlie had followed close on his heels. For a large man, he was surprisingly sprightly.

"She is no lady, and I don't pay you to worry about what I do."

John looked at the girl and realized that he did in fact know her. She was the girl that had been boarding with Mrs. Caffey. He had met her once when he'd visited Will's mother. She recognized him as well, but rather than seeming relieved at his presence, she became even more frantic.

"Mr. Ward! She's upstairs! They won't let her go. You hafta hurry! He's going to - " but the girl was unable to finish before the man standing over her kicked her in the ribs.

"Shut your mouth, you slut."

Before the man knew what hit him, Charlie had him by the neck and lifted him off the ground. John knew the large man could kill the weasel in the suit easily with his bare hands, but he took little time to consider the man's fate. He bolted toward the open door and sprinted up the stairs to the second floor, ignoring the searing pain the movement made in his lower back. Without another thought, he started throwing doors open. The first few rooms were empty, the next few revealed very surprised couples staring back at him. The next door was locked.

John stopped. Each of the other doors had been unlocked, apparently a business policy. But not this one. He pounded his fists against the door.

"Help!"

Even at the heightened pitch, he would recognize Phoebe's voice anywhere. He threw his shoulder into the locked door with all his might. He heard the squeak of the wood as his weight heaved against it. He backed up and shouldered the door a second time, this time hearing the wood begin to splinter.

"Go away, or I'll make you regret opening that door," John heard a gruff voice bellow.

God, please help me, John prayed. He threw himself once more against the door. With a loud crack, it gave way and John's body flew into the room behind its splintered remains.

John straightened and saw a man standing between the bed and the doorway, belt unbuckled. Phoebe was on the bed, a bright purple mark under her left eye. He didn't know if he had arrived just in time or minutes too late.

"Who do you think y-"

The man never finished his sentence. In an instant, John plowed into him and both of their bodies flew into the wall. Not allowing him to catch his breath, John connected his fist with the man's midsection, doubling him over. Not pausing for a second, John grabbed the front of the man's shirt and threw him to the ground. He rolled over and John was on top of him, grabbing the collar of his shirt with his left hand and hitting him in the face with his right. Punch after punch, John pummeled the man with every bit of emotion he had coursing through his veins. He didn't stop, he couldn't stop. It was as if a force beyond his control had taken over his body. Somewhere in the distance he heard the popping of gunfire, smelled the decaying bodies, felt the pain of a bayonet in his back. He looked down and the face of the lifeless German boy stared back at him.

The sounds of war slowly dissipated and all that was left was the sound of John's own breathing echoing inside his head.

He squeezed his eyes shut, willing the images from his mind. Far away, he heard his name. A woman was calling him, beckoning him. He felt hands on his shoulders, felt the rocking of someone shaking him. He opened his eyes and the German boy was gone. He stared at the motionless man beneath him, bloody and unconscious, but still breathing. He heard the woman speaking, no longer in the distance, but just behind him, crying.

"Stop. You're going to kill him. You have to stop."

John turned to find Phoebe kneeling behind him, sobbing. He wiped his bloody knuckles on his suit coat and stood to pull her to her feet.

"Did he - " he began, unsure if he could finish the sentence, or if he even wanted to know.

"No," she cried, shaking her head. "But he would have, had you not - had you not..." Her words trailed off as her body began to shake.

Without another thought, John swept her into his arms and headed out the door. Her body, raked with sobs, melted against his chest as he carried her through the dark hallway. Her arms clung to his neck when his movement down the narrow stairway jostled her. He wanted to run, to get her away from this terrible place as quickly as possible, and he cursed his injury for keeping him from doing exactly that. For now, it would have to be enough that he held her in his arms.

"Don't worry," he whispered against her hair. "I have you. You're safe."

John kicked open the door and found Charlie still there, standing over the unconscious body of the man in the suit. John stopped momentarily and looked from Charlie to the man on the ground then back at Charlie. Charlie just shrugged his shoulders.

"He's just takin' a little nap, that's all."

John nodded. Charlie looked past him to the doorway behind John.

"What about your fella? Do I need to take care of matters?" Charlie lifted one eyebrow quizzically.

"He was still breathing when I left. Where's the other girl?"

"I put her in a cab. She's waitin' for ya."

"Thank you, Charlie," John said and turned toward the front of the building. Charlie put up a hand.

"Miss Albright, you alright? Did anybody hurt ya?"

She lifted her head from John's shoulder and shook it.

"No, Charlie. Mr. Ward arrived just in time."

Charlie's brow furrowed. "By the look of that shiner ya got, I'd say someone hurt ya a little."

She reached up and gingerly touched the bruise beneath her eye, wincing as she did.

"Who did that to ya, missy?" Charlie eyed her, the vein at his temple throbbing.

"I don't know his name, but he was at the door when I arrived."

Charlie's face turned red and the muscles in his jaw flexed. "I see. Well, ya best be gettin' home. Leave this mess ta me ta fix."

John didn't wait to find out what Charlie meant by *fix*. He carried Phoebe to the front of the bar where a cab waited for them, just as Charlie had said. He carefully placed Phoebe inside and crawled in beside her. The other woman sat pressed against the far side of the cab, shivering.

John gave directions to the driver then turned back to the women. He didn't know whether to hold them or shake them. How could Phoebe be so foolish? Did she really think she could save the world, one prostitute at a time? John couldn't bear the thought of what could have happened had he not arrived when he did. He was angry with her, and angry words bubbled up within him. He was about to speak when he saw Phoebe reach out and grab the other girl's hand.

"Everything is alright," she whispered to her. "You're safe now."

John sat in shock. Only moments earlier, Phoebe herself had been racked with sobs. But here she was, after all she had been through, transforming into the pillar of strength for someone else.

As John watched her transition from fearful to strong, Phoebe lifted her head and looked at him. Green pools of gentleness stared back at him, and any anger he may have harbored dissipated like fog on a windy day. His heart returned to a rapid beat, but this time it wasn't due to physical exertion.

Will's girl.

He turned back to the driver.

"I'll get out here."

The cab stopped, and John jumped out. He shut the door behind him.

"Where are you going?" Phoebe asked, leaning through the open window.

"Home," John said simply. He pulled a wad of money out of his wallet and handed it to the driver before turning back to her. "This will get you both home. Once there, do me a favor — stay there."

JOHN WASN'T certain how long he sat there, staring at his reflection in the mirror. All he knew was that he no longer recognized the man that stared back at him.

Before the war, John had been confident in who he was — a loner, a self-sufficient survivor who relied on no one but himself, unable to abide weakness, in himself or in others. And he had been no man of God. But in less than a year, he had become a near invalid, reliant on the help of medical professionals and others to teach him how to walk again. He had met Will Caffey and had learned to trust another human being, something that he hadn't done since he was a small child. And now, he feared, he was allowing his heart to do something he never thought possible. Love.

How could he allow this to happen? How could he fall for Phoebe Albright?

Will's girl.

A pastor's daughter, at that. Still, no matter how improbable it may have seemed a few months ago, he could no longer deny that he had feelings for her. Such strong feelings, in fact, that when he'd thought her life in danger, he cared enough to call out to a God he had long ago forsaken.

How had he gotten into this mess? How had he, like every other man in the vicinity of this woman, become so entangled in her trap? And, a trap it surely was, for John had never felt so ensnared in his entire life.

He rose from the chair and stepped closer to the mirror. A spattering of blood speckled the collar of his shirt and shirt collar. His coat was most likely stained as well, if he looked close enough, but the dark navy color disguised it well. John removed his coat and threw it over the chair he had just vacated. He removed his collar then his shirt and threw them on top of the jacket, intending to throw them all in the trash. One ruined suit seemed of little consequence after the events of the day.

John had just pulled on and buttoned a fresh shirt when someone knocked on his door. He looked at the calendar. Nobody knocked on his door except the landlord, and he only came on the first to collect the rent. After all that had just happened, John was a little concerned about opening his door, but when the light knocks repeated, he figured it must be the absent-minded proprietor.

When he opened the door, his elderly landlord was not on the other side. Phoebe Albright was.

He stood staring at her, confused, until she broke the silence.

"May I come in?"

She did not wait for an answer, and John stepped out of the way as she swept into the room. He knew it wasn't proper for her to be here alone, but the shock of seeing her standing in his doorway had been enough to make him forget all propriety. He closed the door behind her.

"What are you doing here, Miss Albright? I told you to go home. You need to stay away from this part of town."

Phoebe turned and looked at him. "I needed to come back."

"No, what you needed to do was listen to directions. Good grief, woman. Haven't you caused enough headache for one day?"

"Headache? Is that what coming to my rescue was to you? A headache?"

"It wasn't exactly a pleasant situation you got me mixed up in."

"I got you mixed up into nothing! I never asked you to rush to my aid!" Color flooded her cheeks, and John was reminded of something Will had said. *'It's like a fire has ignited in her cheeks. She becomes even more beautiful — if that's possible.'* John had to agree.

"Would you rather I hadn't shown up? Would you rather have been left to your own devices against that scoundrel?"

"I'd rather you not make me feel like such a burden, when my actions are no different than yours. I was only trying to save someone's virtue."

John swore. "It's not at all the same. You aren't a man. You shouldn't have gone there by yourself."

"Well, I'm glad to hear that you realize I'm not a man. By the coarse language you use in front of me, I was afraid you thought me a sailor home on leave!"

"If you don't like my language, then you know where the door is."

"I'm not leaving here until I say what I came to say."

John rolled his eyes. "This ought to be good. Pray tell, what in the world did you cross town, against my orders, to tell me?"

"I came to say thank you."

John felt as if the wind had been knocked out of him. Her beautiful face that only moments ago was wrinkled with defiance and fire, had settled into a soft innocence that John wasn't prepared for. He could handle her anger. He could handle her stubbornness. What he couldn't handle was her vulnerability. Every fiber in his being yearned to pull her into his arms and tell her everything was going to be alright, but the alarms sounding in his brain warned him of the foolishness of such an act.

"I'm sorry about my language. I'll try to control it in your presence." He walked around the chair, hoping futilely that the small piece of furniture would somehow serve as a barrier between the fair-haired woman and his churning emotions. He turned and faced her. "How on earth did you find me?"

"I watched you enter this building as the car pulled away. I asked the driver to bring me back after we dropped Katie off at Mrs. Caffey's. The rest was as simple as finding your name on the proper post box downstairs."

"You're quite the detective. First my letter out of the trash, now tracking me to my apartment. Are you certain your talents wouldn't be better suited for work with the police?"

She lowered her head and stared at her hands clasped in front of her. They twisted at her gloves. John smiled. She was nervous. He wasn't certain he had ever seen her in a state of nervousness. He cursed himself for finding it so endearing.

His eyes traveled up her arms to her face where the mark

below her eye had turned a decidedly ugly purple. Something in him twisted at the sight of her flawless face marred by such a painful reminder of what she had gone through. As if in a dream, John found himself rounding the chair and stepping closer to her. His hand reached up and his knuckles lightly brushed the stray strands of golden hair that had fallen across her face and over her bruised cheek. At his gentle touch, she looked up at him through glistening lashes.

"John," she exhaled.

It came out as effortlessly as her breath itself, and the sound of his name on her lips destroyed what little resolve he was clinging to. His arm snaked around her waist and his mouth descended on hers like a hungry animal in search of a long sought-after meal. The hair on the back of his neck stood on end when, rather than push him away, her own arms moved up to rest on his shoulders. She was kissing him back, and the realization had a heady effect on him. He lost all sense of where he was and what he was doing. All he knew was that she was in his arms and she was responding with just as much passion as he was releasing.

She gasped when John parted her lips and began to explore deeper. The kiss changed, and her actions became apprehensive, as if she had never been kissed like this before. Her apprehension was enough to bring John back to his senses. He pushed her away as quickly as he had drawn her near, and they both stood staring at each other, panting. She looked like such a little girl, staring doe-eyed at him, lips slightly parted, not the vixen he had always silently labeled her. John swore under his breath.

"You shouldn't have come here."

19

AFTERMATH

*E*sther's two days off did little to calm her nerves about returning to work. They did, however, afford the time needed for the bruise to heal sufficiently. Unless a person looked very closely, they would have no idea that she had experienced any kind of trauma to her face. She just hoped the rest of her mannerisms disguised the trauma she had experienced in her heart as sufficiently.

She arrived early, hoping to avoid Miss Hagerman and her attempt at her best Sherlock Holmes impersonation. She was not that fortunate.

The minute she spotted Esther, Warren's secretary jumped from her seat.

"Oh, Miss Albright! I'm so happy to see you've returned!"

Esther laughed, in spite of herself. "Did you fear I wouldn't?"

"Well, I wasn't sure, and I don't think Mr. Ward was either. Every day, he asked me if I had heard from you or if Mr. Mallory had any news. I asked him if he would like me to call on you, to see if you were well, but he insisted that I leave you alone. He said that if you wished to return to work, you would.

What did he mean by that, Miss Albright? Why wouldn't you wish to return to work?"

"I have no idea why he would say that," Esther answered honestly. "But, as you can see, I am all better and I have returned, so you need worry no further."

"I'm so glad. You didn't have the Spanish Flu, did you?"

"Goodness, no. Really, Miss Hagerman. If I had contracted the Spanish Flu, I wouldn't be returning to work so quickly."

"Of course. How silly of me." She returned to her seat behind her desk. "Well, I'm glad it was just some little bug. And I'm glad you're back. Mr. Ward just hasn't been the same without you."

Esther didn't stop to ask the woman what she'd meant by the remark but made her way quickly to her desk. She wanted to be settled into work before John arrived. She went to the coat tree to hang her coat and realized she hadn't arrived early enough. John's overcoat was already on its usual hook. She hung hers beside it and seated herself behind the desk. There was a pile of notes waiting for her to type, so she wasted no time getting to work.

She had barely finished typing the first sentence when John's office door flung open and he nearly fell out of the room, eyes wide. Was his expression one of shock or relief? Esther couldn't tell. He recovered quickly and straightened his jacket.

"Good morning, Miss Albright. I'm glad to see you're feeling better."

"Yes, sir. Much better."

He stood over her, staring, but said nothing. His expression wasn't quite blank, but she couldn't read any hint to what he was thinking. He finally broke the silence.

"I - I thought maybe you had reconsidered, you know, reconsidered being under my employ."

"Why would I do that?"

"Well," he said, moving closer and lowering his voice. "I thought that, after we, you know..."

Esther stood suddenly. "I think it best to continue this conversation in your office, Mr. Ward. Don't you agree?"

"Yes, of course," he said, sweeping his arm to allow her to pass in front of him.

Once the door was shut, she turned to face him.

"Was it your intent to embarrass me?"

"Embarrass? Of course not!"

"Then why mention the kiss out there, where others could hear?"

"Miss Albright, there wasn't anyone within hearing distance."

"You don't know that for certain, unless you are able to see through walls and around corners."

John nodded his head. "You're right. I'm sorry. I had no intention, nor will I ever have the intention, of embarrassing you."

They stood in silence for a few moments. John unbuttoned his suit coat and stuffed his hands in his pockets. He rocked back and forth and looked everywhere in the room except at Esther. She longed to be angry at him, but he looked so adorable, nervously standing there like a chastised schoolboy, that she couldn't muster a single angry thought.

"I'm sorry," she said.

He looked up and raised his eyebrows. "Well, it was pretty foolhardy of you to embark on such a mission all by yourself. Have you any idea what could have happened had I not found you when I did?"

"Oh, I'm certain I have a very good idea what would have happened," she said. Her hand touched her cheek absent-mindedly.

"I'm glad to see that it is healing nicely for you," John said. "How did you explain it to your parents?"

"I didn't have to," she said, smiling slightly. "My parents are out of town visiting friends. They don't return for a couple more days."

"That's fortunate."

"I suppose, though if my father had been home, I probably would have gone to him first. He would have had no problem barging into the brothel to find Katie."

John chuckled. "And how would you have explained how you knew where to find Katie?"

"That would have been far more difficult, I suppose. Speaking of which, how did you know to come to Jimmy's?"

"Mrs. Caffey found me. Said you were going to a place of ill repute. I made an assumption."

"The correct assumption, thank goodness. I really am very grateful. I know I tried thanking you before, but, well, we..." her voice trailed off. She could feel her cheeks growing warm, a sensation she seldom experienced.

"Yes, we..." John said. He ceased his rocking back and forth.

"That's what I am trying to apologize for. I mean, yes, of course I'm sorry I made the terrible decision to go after Katie by myself, and I am sorry that decision put you in peril. But when I said I was sorry a moment ago, I was apologizing for the kiss."

John withdrew his hands from his pockets and placed them on his waist. "The kiss? You are apologizing for the kiss?"

"Yes."

John shook his head and chuckled. "Miss Albright, I know that you experienced quite a shock that evening, so your mind may have been a little muddled, but you have nothing to apologize for. I kissed you. If an apology should be made, it is I who should be offering it."

Esther considered his words. Her mind had not been the least bit muddled. She remembered well him approaching her from across the room, the gentle way his knuckles slid across her tender cheekbone, and she most definitely remembered the desire that bubbled up within her when he took her in his arms and his lips captured hers. No, her mind had most definitely been very sharp.

"I'm not saying I started the kiss. I'm apologizing for whatever I did to offend you during it. I'm not certain what I did, since I am not very experienced in such matters, but whatever error I committed, I feel that I must apologize."

John ran his fingers through his hair and rested his hand on the back of his neck. He shook his head.

"You did nothing wrong. I pushed you away because it wasn't right, me kissing you. I shouldn't have done it."

"Shouldn't have kissed me?"

"Correct. I let my emotions get the best of me. You were in distress. I shouldn't have taken advantage of you, and you have my word that it will not happen again. I think it best if we both just forget it ever happened."

Esther stared at him for several moments, her mouth slightly agape. This man, the man she'd found so abhorrent when she'd first met him, and who seemed to find her just as distasteful, was now admitting that it was wrong to take advantage of her. She slowly moved closer to him and didn't stop until she was a mere foot from him.

"But, John, what if I told you that, in that moment, I wanted nothing more than for you to take advantage of me?"

She stood so close, she could smell the mixture of his soap with his cologne. She longed to reach out, touch the front of his jacket. Would he push her away again? Or would he pull her into another embrace?

A knock on the door interrupted their trance. John nearly knocked his desk over trying to get around to the other side of it. Esther stood still, trying desperately to calm her rapidly beating heart.

"Come in," John bellowed, straightening his jacket.

Warren Mallory stuck his head through the door and looked at Esther.

"Ah, Miss Hagerman was correct. You have returned! We were beginning to worry. Mrs. Mallory was ready to send out a search party if you didn't return soon."

Esther laughed. "You can assure your wife that I am well and back to normal. Now, unless you need anything else Mr. Ward, I will return to my desk. I have a pile of work to catch up on."

"I need nothing else," John said as he shuffled the papers on his desk.

Esther smiled. This man, whom only moments ago seemed about to kiss her again, was trying desperately hard to appear cold and aloof in front of his boss. And for some reason, Esther thought it was adorable.

20

MISERY

It had been several days since her adventure saving Katie and life seemed to return to normal, at least on the surface. Work returned to its usual pattern, her parents returned from their trip, none the wiser of her little escapade. But beneath the calm routine she presented, Esther was a jumble of nerves.

To anyone else in the office, John and Esther's interactions would appear normal. But she was well-aware of his change in attitude toward her.

John avoided Esther at all costs. Not to the point that anyone else would notice, mind you, but it was painfully obvious to her. He was never rude, always professional, but he was guarded, stiff almost. If he needed her to do something, he would write her a note and place it on her desk. If she came in to his office to speak to him, he was curt and to the point, and he never raised his eyes from whatever he was working on.

At first, Esther ignored it all. He was her boss, after all, and nothing more than a professional relationship should be expected. But as the days wore on, and John made more and more obvious efforts to distance himself from the one person he should be working the closest with, in Esther's opinion, the more annoyed Esther became. John had been the one who had kissed her, not the other way around. It wasn't fair that he aroused feelings in her that she never expected to have for him, then treated her like she had some sort of infectious disease.

Feelings. For John Ward. That was the most surprising outcome of her life-threatening adventure. Esther had thought that she was incapable of opening her heart to another man, let alone a man she found so repugnant. But she was beginning to have feelings for him. And there was no denying that, in spite of his efforts to rebuff her, John Ward was at least attracted to Esther. Still, he seemed to be growing farther and farther from her emotionally. Why was Esther always falling for men that were emotionally unavailable to her?

Deep in thought considering this very question, she didn't hear John come out of his office. She had no idea how long he had been standing there, leaning against the frame of the door, staring at her. But when she did discover him, her heart missed a couple of beats when she saw the almost gentle way he was regarding her.

"You always look so miserable," he said simply.

"You are talking nonsense," Esther scoffed. She wasn't certain what facial expression she had been wearing before she'd noticed him standing there, but she doubted it was anything other than confusion. She tried to regain some sort of composure and smirked at him. "I am seldom without a smile on my face."

"I mean when you think no one is looking. Those times, when you haven't put on a mask, you look sad."

"I'm not sad right now. Just a little frustrated."

"I wasn't talking about right now."

The realization that John Ward had been stealing glances at her when she was unaware made her heart race. His next words made it stop beating all together.

"Is it really that awful working for me?"

Esther looked up into his blue-gray eyes. The walls that he had always maintained so diligently behind them were gone, replaced by a raw vulnerability she had never seen before. No, that wasn't completely true. She had seen behind them one other time. When he was intoxicated and confessing his attraction to her. Esther forced herself to breathe.

"No, Mr. Ward," she said softly. "It isn't at all awful working for you."

She held his gaze, refusing to allow her growing heart rate to weaken her resolve to break through whatever barriers John had built between them, for whatever reason he had built them.

John took a breath and was about to say something when something beyond Esther caught his eye.

"Ah, I see you have survived your first day on the job," John said to someone. Esther turned to see to whom he was speaking and couldn't believe her eyes.

"Charlie!" Esther exclaimed. "What are you doing here?"

"Got me a job downstairs. Mr. Ward put in a good word for me."

"Oh," she said, turning a raised eyebrow toward John. "Did he now?"

John just shrugged his shoulders. "A man's gotta work."

Esther turned back to the hefty man. "I'm so sorry, Charlie. Did you lose your job over, well, over my interference upstairs of the speakeasy?"

"Missy, everyone lost their jobs. Seems someone with a guilty conscience alerted the authorities to the location of a certain illegal establishment," he said with a wink.

Esther gasped. "You? You called the police?"

"I couldn't let a place like that continue to operate. It's one thing to look the other way when everyone involved is doing so of their own free will, but to think that they were willin' to force some nice girl like yerself or that sweet Miss Feeney into that type of work, well, I couldn't stomach that no way."

"Aren't you concerned that someone will come after you?"

Charlie laughed, his large chest bouncing up and down. "Missy, who's brave enough to come after Big Charlie? Ain't no one from Jimmy's, that's for sure. Most of them is in jail now, and any that got away, well, they're all too afraid of me. There's only two people ever been willin' to stand up to me, and they both standin' right here, so I think I'm safe."

The only two people standing with Charlie were herself and John. She turned to John, wondering what had transpired between her boss and the former doorman. She was about to ask, but he quickly changed the subject.

"Well, Charlie, I'm glad you were able to gain employment here. It will be nice to have another set of eyes to keep track of Miss Albright. I'm afraid she's more excitement than one man can handle."

Charlie laughed again, and although she knew the men were laughing at her expense, Esther couldn't help but smile herself.

"Both of you gentleman can rest assured, I've spent my last moments in any bar. Probably more than the two of you can say," she said, crossing her arms.

"Not me," Charlie said, shaking his head. "I'm a teetot'ler m'self."

Esther laughed, but when she realized the man wasn't laughing along with her, she sobered quickly. "Are you teasing me?"

"No, ma'am. Never cared much for what drinkin' did to men. I just took the job to support my family. But, can't justify workin' for a place like that no longer."

Esther placed a hand on the man's meaty arm. "Well, now you won't have to. I'm certain you will much prefer working for Mr. Mallory."

"Already do, missy. Everyone is real nice, and the pay is much better. So, no, you won't see me darkenin' the doorsteps of any speakeasies ever again."

Their conversation was disrupted by Miss Hagerman. "I'm sorry to interrupt, but Mr. Mallory would like to see you in his office, Mr. Ward."

"Certainly," he said before following the woman to the reception area.

Esther watched him walk away.

"Penny for yer thoughts, missy."

She turned a sweet smile back to the man. "Oh, it's nothing. I was just realizing that he made no pledge against visiting speakeasies in the future."

"Aw, I wouldn't worry about that one. Don't think they are his cup of tea anymore, really. Other than that night he and I had our run-in, he really didn't spend much time there. Come to think of it, if it hadn't been for rescuin' you, I don't think he'd a ever stepped foot inside Jimmy's again."

Esther hoped the man was correct.

"You wanted to see me?" John said as he stuck his head into his boss's office.

"Yes, come in. And shut the door behind you."

John did as he was told, noting that the usually jovial man seemed much more serious than normal.

Warren motioned for the chair opposite his desk and John sat in it. It wasn't the first time he had been summoned to Warren Mallory's office, but for some reason, this time felt as if he were about to be chastised, or, worse yet, relieved of his job.

"John, I'm not a man who minces words. I am honest to a fault, and I expect the same kind of honesty from those around me, especially those in my employ."

"I understand," John said, though he really wasn't certain where this conversation was going. He had a lot of sins he could be held accountable for, but dishonesty wasn't one he considered a problem.

"Good. So, when I ask you a question, I expect an honest answer."

"Have I ever given you anything but honest answers?" John asked. He was becoming irritated. Was the man accusing him of something?

"I don't think so, but I wanted to make certain that we were on the same page before I began. I have a question for you and I want you to answer me honestly, no matter what you fear might be the consequence."

John swallowed hard. "You have my promise."

Warren leaned back in his chair and folded his arms across his chest. His eyebrows knit together as he eyed John. "What's going on between you and Miss Albright?"

John's heart stopped beating. "I - I don't know what you are talking about?"

"You promised honesty."

"I'm trying to be honest, but I don't understand what you are asking me. Are you insinuating that something inappropriate is happening between me and my secretary?"

Warren leaned forward and rested his forearms on his desk. "A little over a week ago, Miss Albright missed a couple days of work. Not an unusual occurrence during flu season. What I did consider unusual was your reaction. You acted like a chicken locked out of the hen house, like a lost boy whose breadcrumbs had been eaten by the birds. But when Miss Hagerman offered to call on Miss Albright, you panicked and called her off. Then, when your secretary did return, the tension between the two of you was thicker than molasses in the middle of January."

"Mr. Mallory, it is no secret that the relationship between

my secretary and myself is at best strained. Our personalities clash sometimes..."

"Did you clash to the point that you'd strike her?"

John breathed in sharply. "Excuse me?"

"When she came back to work, she returned with the remnants of a bruise beneath her left eye. What I am asking you is, did you hit her?"

"No!" John said, jumping to his feet. "I'm a lot of things, Mr. Mallory, but I am no woman beater."

Warren eyed his best reporter for several moments. "I want to believe you, John, but something is fishy about the events of the last couple of weeks. First the shiner, then the tension between the two of you. Now, I see both of you speaking with the new guy Charlie like you're old friends. It's one thing for one of my male employees to know a man of Charlie's, well, background, but quite another for someone of Miss Albright's rearing to know the man intimately. I'm having a difficult time wrapping my mind around all of it."

John didn't know how to answer Warren without betraying Phoebe. He decided to only answer the question that was asked of him.

"I did not, nor would I ever, lay a hand on Miss Albright."

"Do you know how she came to have such a bruise?"

John was silent for a moment. "Yes. I do know, but it's not my story to tell. But I can promise you that it did not come by my hand."

"Charlie?"

"No!" John said, shaking his head and laughing. "I think the only man more concerned with Miss Albright's wellbeing than me would be Charlie Ross."

Warren slowly lifted one eyebrow at John. "So, you are concerned with Miss Albright's wellbeing? Have a seat, John."

Cringing inwardly, John once again seated himself across from his boss.

"I think I know the answer to this question, but I'd like to hear you confirm or deny my suspicions. Tell me John, how do you feel about Miss Albright?"

John felt cornered. He had promised honesty, and he prided himself on being a man who kept his word. He took a deep breath. "My feelings for her go deeper than they should."

Warren scowled. "What is that supposed to mean?"

"I mean that, although I know it isn't right, I still can't help having feelings for the woman."

Warren chuckled and shook his head. "This is not where I thought this conversation was going to end up. I'm happier with this ending, mind you — just surprised. But tell me, what would be so wrong with you having feelings for her?"

"Well, sir, I believe there is another who cares for her, making it impossible for me to do the same."

"You aren't speaking of that popinjay, Richard? My wife has told me all about him. Trust me, there is nothing there that should hold you back from pursuing the girl."

"No, not Richard. I'm speaking of Will Caffey."

Warren's eyebrows shot up. "Caffey? What on earth makes you think that?"

"Caffey himself told me how he feels."

"Interesting," Warren said. "But have you considered Miss Albright's feelings? She is my wife's best friend. From my observation, she has nothing but sisterly affection for the boy."

John considered his boss's words and felt a familiar twang of sympathy for his good friend — this had been his observation as well.

"Listen, John. That secretary of yours is beautiful. She is also strong-willed and opinionated. If you have feelings for her, I suggest you act on them, whether or not some young man halfway around the world thinks he has some sort of claim on her. Because, trust me, she isn't the kind of woman to be told that she belongs to someone she doesn't have feelings for. And, if my hunch is correct, her affections are placed much closer to home."

What could Warren mean? Was he saying that Phoebe had feelings for John? Had she revealed these feelings to Warren's wife?

As John left Warren's office, the emotions that he had struggled to deny for the past few months bubbled to the surface. His boss was right. Even if Will did have feelings for Phoebe, it was obvious those feelings were not returned. And if Phoebe wasn't in love with Will, and John missed the opportunity to tell her how he truly felt, would he regret his choice for the rest of his life?

21

RED ROSES

Will would forgive him. Eventually. It might hurt at first, but he would forgive him. Wouldn't he? He had to forgive him. John knocked on the door before he had any more time to consider the ramifications of what he was about to do.

"John," Mrs. Albright said, eyebrows raised. "This is a surprise. Come in." She opened the door wide, motioning for John to enter. "My husband isn't home. He is visiting with one of the church's shut-ins – a Mr. Randall. He lives near your newspaper offices. Do you know him?"

"No, ma'am," John answered, removing his hat and twisting it in his hands. "But I'm not here to see Reverend Albright. Is your daughter home?"

Her eyebrows raised once more, but settled quickly back into place. "She is. Why don't you wait in the parlor while I get her?"

John stood in the middle of the small gathering room, shifting his weight back and forth on his feet and continued to twist his hat. He struggled with what he was about to do. It's one thing to steal your best friend's girl, but quite another thing to do it while that friend is off fighting Germans in France. But this was no ordinary woman. John had never felt like this about anyone. And, besides, she clearly did not feel for Will what he felt for her.

"Please forgive me, Will," he breathed, looking around the room for anything to occupy his mind until Mrs. Albright finally returned with Phoebe.

He saw them the minute he turned around. Roses. Red roses. They stood out amongst the pale neutrals of the faded furniture and leather-bound books the way stained glass windows stand out against the cold, stone walls of cathedrals. They stood out the way Phoebe did everywhere she went. A rose among the thorns of his life.

He crossed the room to get away from them, but the over-powering scent of the blooms followed him no matter where he stood. He fought the memories, but much like the unavoidable aroma that filled the room, he could not fight the images from long ago.

The older he grew, the weaker most memories became, especially where his mother was concerned. But some memo-ries, odd, ridiculous memories, glowed in his subconscious like a candle in a dark house. Such a light may not illuminate an entire room, but can give those items within its reach an unearthly glow. John didn't know why some memories slipped through his grasp like dissipating fog, while others stuck with him as if he were standing right in the middle of them. Memo-ries like the red roses.

She had loved roses so much, his mother. He couldn't remember a time that the drawing room was void of the red flower. Well, that is, until she left. The first morning, John had noticed the roses on the piano were wilting. His mother must still be abed. *Was she ill?* She always rose early and spent time in her garden, praying and singing before her morning tray was brought to her room. John knew to leave his mother alone until after her morning prayer time. The presence of fresh, red roses was a sign to him that she was finished in the garden and that he could call upon his mother's time.

That morning, however, the previous day's roses remained in the vase, and they stayed there long into the day. John had asked his father about his mother that morning, but all he would say was that she was ill. John wished to know more, but his father offered up no more information and he knew better than to question him further.

But when, by the next morning, his mother still had not replaced the roses, John began to worry. How sick was she? She had never gone this long without seeing John. Despite his fear of his father, John approached the door of his study quietly. He knocked so softly that he was certain there would be no response, but to his relief, and trepidation, a resounding "Come in," sounded from the other side.

John's little hands slowly turned the knob and he awkwardly shuffled into the room. How old had he been? He couldn't have been more than five, but he remembered how he felt standing there, halfway between his father's desk and the door, waiting for the elder to look up and acknowledge his presence. His little boy mind searched for the words his heart ached to ask, but fear of his father tightened his throat to nearly closed and he fought to keep breath in his lungs.

"She's gone," his father said gruffly, answering John's unasked question without looking up.

Fear seized John. Ice ran through his veins until he could no longer feel the tips of the fingers that clutched the buttons on the front of his shirt.

"M-Mother is dead?" The words tasted like salt as tears ran down his cheeks and into his mouth.

The senior Johnathon Ward looked up angrily and scowled at his only child.

"No, you idiot. She's not dead. She's gone. She left."

Left? It didn't make any sense. Where had she gone? When would she return?

"Leave me be," his father grumbled, returning to his ledger.

John stood transfixed, his childish mind trying to patch together the words his father had said with the fabric of reality around him. His mother was gone, but not dead. She had said nothing to John about leaving. Maybe she didn't think she would be gone long enough for him to notice. Surely, she would return soon, then she could explain everything to John the way she always did. Gently, kindly — so unlike his father.

John had been so caught up in his own mind that he hadn't noticed his father quietly rise nor had he seen him grab the heavy book off his desk.

"I said LEAVE," his father growled, grabbing John by his upper arm, digging his nails deeply into the flesh above the elbow. John squeezed his eyes tight against the impending blows.

When John was finally released from his father's study, and his grip, he limped, head held low, past the drawing room and toward his bedroom looking for solace. The red of the wilting roses gleamed out of the corner of his eye as he passed the room. He stopped for a moment, wanting with all his will to grab the horrible flowers from their vase and tear them into a million pieces, but he thought better of it when, as he watched, one wilted petal broke free from the spent bloom and fell to the shiny black surface of the piano. No, he would leave them. His mother would replace them when she returned. She loved her vibrant, red roses so much.

But fresh roses did not appear. One week, and three beatings later, the roses on the piano had turned the ugliest shade of black John had ever seen. Every day, as he watched them die, he alternated between the desire to shake the remaining life out of them until they were nothing more than green sticks with thorns, and the desire to replace them daily with new roses until his mother returned. He couldn't bring himself to do either. In the end, it wasn't John who destroyed his mother's blooms, but the maid his father had hired to pack up the drawing room, as well as the rest of the house, for their sudden move. John watched the young girl unceremoniously discard the dead flowers then wrap his mother's vase in paper, putting an end to his struggling emotions.

John hated red roses.

The scent of vanilla and citrus breaking through the aroma of roses pulled John back from his reverie. He didn't have to look to know who had entered the parlor. The faint smell of her perfume announced Phoebe's arrival before her voice did.

"Mother said you wished to see me?" she said quietly.

John turned slowly toward her voice. She stood in the hallway, appearing shocked by the sight of John standing alone in her parents' parlor. She was a vision in white and brown, colors that John would have otherwise thought dull and boring, but the plainness of her attire only accentuated her attractiveness. This is how she should always dress, John mused, in clothes that did not compete with her beauty.

She had apparently just returned from her mother's garden. She held in her hands more roses. More red roses. John shuddered. They were a beautiful, if stark, reminder to not fall victim to this conniving beauty. He could never love a woman that so callously disregarded the affections of a man as good as Will Caffey. And what kind of man was he to even consider falling victim to her trap? She was a woman, and like every other woman could not be trusted. A woman who, when given the opportunity, would leave John, if he chose to give her the chance. Which he did not.

"Excuse me, Miss Albright, but I've just remembered somewhere I need to be," was all he said as he brushed past her and walked straight out the front door.

JOHN DIDN'T WAIT for Phoebe's response to his quick departure but rushed down the stairs of her front porch and turned left on the sidewalk. Hailing a cab was not even a consideration. The long walk would do him good. His gimp leg may not appreciate the exertion, but his mind could use the time to clear itself.

He could feel a storm brewing inside of him that he wasn't certain he could manage. Getting as far away from Phoebe Albright was the only solution to that mounting storm. Why, then, did he all of a sudden find himself climbing the stairs of the whitewashed church and opening its doors?

Before he knew what he was doing, John rushed down the aisle of the sanctuary and dropped himself onto the kneeling bench of one of the altars. As a child, the wailing seat, as it used to be called, had always represented bondage to him, a place his father had drug John, in order to repent of whatever sin his father had decided to punish him for. A place that was a constant reminder of the rules of religion, rules John never seemed to be able to keep for any length of time. But Will had said that the altar was a place for freedom. John longed to be free, and he was hedging his bets that Will, not his father, knew the true purpose of the wooden kneeling bench at the foot of the podium.

John caught a glimpse of Mrs. Kinney out of the corner of his eye just before dropping his head onto his folded arms, but her presence was of little consequence to him now. The storm within him had burst through every barrier he had built up against it and his sobs shook his body so hard that he gripped the wooden rail to steady himself. Within moments, his arms and the altar beneath them were soaked with his tears, yet there seemed no end in sight to this burst of emotions. John was helpless, a state of being that he had very little experience in, with no idea how to pull himself out.

A strong hand gripped his shoulder. He felt the person lower themself to the bench next to him. He sensed who the person was, but the man's deep voice removed all doubt.

"It's alright, son. Let it all out," Reverend Albright said.

The pastor's presence seemed to bring more release and John's sobbing grew louder and more violent.

"I - I can't," he choked out between gasps of breath. "I can't. I can't do it anymore."

The minister didn't ask what John meant. He seemed to already know.

"You don't need to, John. It's time to let go."

John raised his head to look at Reverend Albright, whose right hand still gripped John's shoulder, like a lifeline feeding strength to John. He leaned on the altar with his left arm and looked at John with sincere, sympathetic eyes.

"I don't know how," John said warily.

"I can show you, if you'll allow me to. John, you've carried this weight around for so long, it's time to give it up to God. Give him the weight of your sins, the weight of your guilt, and, son, you need to give him the weight of your unforgiveness. It's all too heavy for one man to bear."

"You're right. I can't do it anymore. I don't want to do it anymore."

"I'm glad. May I pray with you?"

The large minister's voice echoed off the hammerbeam ceiling of the church, and John felt as if it reverberated inside his soul as well, as Reverend Albright led John in a simple sinner's prayer. There was no organ music, no choir singing, no crowded church witnessing the event, but something happened to John that was unmistakably real. It was as if a suffocating cloak that John never recognized was suddenly lifted from him and was replaced with a fullness the likes of which he had never before known. He laid all of his pain on the altar that day, and although he never dreamed it could really happen, he somehow knew that Jesus had taken it. And John realized that he never wanted it back.

22

ESTHER'S MISSION

*E*sther typed and retyped the same letter over and again, removing the paper and discreetly throwing it away before inserting a fresh sheet and beginning the charade all over again. She had nothing to do until her boss arrived at work but wanted to appear busy when he did. She had no idea why he had visited her house yesterday, nor did she understand why he had acted so strangely. If she were hard at work when he arrived, maybe she could avoid a confrontation with him in the office.

She knew of nothing she could have done to merit such treatment, and the more she thought about it, the angrier she got. It's one thing to treat her like an invisible inconvenience at their place of employ, quite another to seek her out in her own home to insult her like he did.

But when he arrived just a few minutes later, she was shocked to find that his mood was completely altered.

"May I have a moment of your time, please? In my office, if it's not too much trouble?" he asked politely.

Esther eyed him suspiciously. "Of course, it's no bother. My time is at your disposal. You are my boss, are you not?"

John laughed. "My dear Miss Albright, I think we both know that no man will ever truly be the boss of you."

Esther fought back a smile. She longed to hurl a much-deserved insult toward him but had been praying all morning that God would help her control her temper. She respected Warren, if not John, and did not wish to cause a scene for his sake.

She rose from her desk and entered the office. John followed her, shutting the door behind him. Esther raised an eyebrow. He never shut the door any more when they were alone.

"I'd like to offer an apology, if you'll allow me to."

"I will allow it," she said. "Although, I'd much prefer an explanation. I'm not at all certain why you were at my home in the first place, nor do I understand why you felt the need to rush out. If I have done something that offended you, I'd like to know what it was."

John laughed. "You'd like to know what you've done to offend me? Would you like the items listed alphabetically or chronologically?"

Esther crossed her arms. "I'd offer the same in return, but your offenses are too long to list. I'm afraid I'd run out of type-writer ribbon."

At that, John threw his head back and laughed. Esther was not amused. John must have sensed this, because he stopped laughing, cleared his throat and continued.

"You deserve an explanation, of both my intentions and my exit, but I'll begin with my exit, if that's alright."

Esther said nothing, only shrugged her shoulders.

John offered her a chair then drug his chair around the desk to sit facing her. He rested his elbow on his desk and stared at his fingers tapping on the desktop for a few moments before speaking.

"I assume your father said nothing to you about what happened after I left?" He still did not make eye contact.

"My father?"

John chuckled. "I didn't expect that he would. But I wish he had. It might make this conversation easier." He leaned forward in his seat and rested his arms on his knees. He stared at his folded hands for a few moments, then finally lifted his gaze to meet hers.

"I gave my life to Jesus yesterday."

Esther inhaled sharply. "Oh, John." Her heart beat wildly as his words sunk in. "I'm so happy for you. Truly, I am!" A quiet joy settled over her as she watched a smile spread across his usually solemn face. The crinkles around his silvery blue eyes gave his already handsome features an even more endearing appearance. She hadn't realized she carried a burden for the man, but the relief his words brought left her feeling lightened. It took every bit of willpower that she owned to not throw herself into his arms out of joy.

"I've never felt such liberation," he said, smiling fully now. "I had always rejected God and the salvation that Jesus offered because I thought that I would have to give up my life in exchange for the life he wanted me to live, and I guess that is true. But I finally realized that the life I was living wasn't life at all. It was a prison of my own creation. Once I was willing to give everything to God, even the things I had clung to for so long, I finally felt released. I've never been so happy, yet nothing in my life has really changed. I don't understand it, so I can't expect you to understand."

"Oh, but I do understand," she said enthusiastically. "Your circumstances haven't changed, but the way you view them has."

"Yes! That's exactly it. So, nothing has changed, yet everything has. But, I now realize that with this new-found freedom, there are certain responsibilities. Not obligations because of rules, but things I want to do out of gratitude for what Jesus has done for me. And one of those responsibilities has to do with you."

"With me?"

"I know it will come as no surprise that I haven't always been the kindest to you."

Esther realized her anger toward him had completely dissipated. "You have done more for me than any man I have ever known. You saved my virtue, maybe my life. I don't believe there could be any other act of kindness that could compare."

"I'm talking about my attitude. You must admit that I have often spoken curtly to you when you did not deserve it."

"Maybe, but I'm not exactly a defenseless victim. I'm certain I have met every curt remark you have made with an equally sour one."

"I wouldn't say that is true."

"That's because many of those remarks remained thoughts in my head."

John smiled. "I suppose I should be grateful for that."

"I'm the one that's grateful. Had I verbalized them, I surely would be looking for a new employer."

John chuckled again but sobered quickly.

"Is that your wish? To be under someone else's employ?"

"I was only teasing."

John looked at her for some moments before continuing. "Do you remember when I asked you why you always look so miserable?"

"Yes. And I told you then that it wasn't you."

"Then what is it? I have to know, before I finish telling you the rest of what I have to say."

Esther stared at her hands in her lap. He was being so open and honest with her, she felt obligated to do the same.

"It isn't you. It's - it's this job."

"Working for me?"

"No. Working for you makes it bearable," she said before she realized what she was saying. Esther wasn't one to blush but revealing this kind of information was still slightly embarrassing to her.

"So, you hate working for the newspaper?"

Esther sighed and lifted her eyes to meet his. "I hate being a secretary. I hate everything about it."

John's eyebrows knit together. "How long have you hated it?"

"Since the first minute of school."

"Then why continue?"

"What choice do I have? There are few career choices for a spinster like me."

The corners of his mouth twitched. "Spinster? I hardly think..."

"Do not laugh at me, John Ward."

"I'm sorry. I didn't mean to," he said. "It's just ridiculous that you see yourself that way.

"Well, maybe not a spinster yet, but I'm well on my way."

He looked at her with such intensity that she stopped breathing. He opened his mouth to say something, but, looking as if the thought bothered him, closed his mouth and looked away. After several moments, he turned back to her and spoke.

"I think that if you are unhappy, you should find something to make you happy. Take it from me, someone who has spent their life miserable because they felt it was just their lot in life. If you are unhappy, then you, and only you, are the one person who can change it."

"What other option do I have?"

"There are always options. Some options just take more bravery, I suppose."

As she pondered his words, someone knocked at the office door.

"One moment," John said, rising.

Esther stood as well and headed toward the door, but John

grabbed her hand. Shivers ran up her arm as she turned to look him in the eye.

"I've lived my life in misery for too many years. I don't want to do that anymore. Do you think it would be possible for us to start again?"

~

ESTHER RETURNED to her desk and had little time to process what had just occurred in John Ward's office when Miss Hagerman approached her.

"You have a visitor," she said.

"A visitor?"

"Yes. A young lady. She says you don't know her. Says she's a friend of someone named Katie?"

A friend of Katie's? Esther rose from her desk. "Thank you, Miss Hagerman."

Esther followed the receptionist to the front lobby. Standing near the door, nervously rocking back and forth on her heels, was a woman Esther had never met. By the amount of rouge she wore, Esther could guess from where Katie knew her. She approached the stranger with a smile and held out her hand.

"Good morning. I'm Miss Albright. Miss Hagerman tells me you are a friend of Miss Feeney?"

"Yes, ma'am," the girl answered without looking up. "My name's Rhonda. Don't know if Katie, er, I mean, Miss Feeney ever mentioned me."

"Yes, of course," Esther said warmly. Katie had mentioned Rhonda on more than one occasion. She could sense the woman's uneasiness. She turned to Miss Hagerman.

"I'm going for a cup of coffee. Please inform Mr. Ward that I will return momentarily."

Esther led the woman down the street to Steuben's cafe.

She opened the door, but Rhonda seemed hesitant. "It's alright," Esther said. "Frank and Bea are old family friends."

The two took a seat by the window. Esther ordered a cup of coffee, but Rhonda declined. Esther would have let it pass, assuming the woman wasn't in the mood for coffee, but something about the look on her face gave her pause. She reached out and touched the waitress's sleeve.

"Bring my friend some bacon and eggs...and some toast," she said, then turned back to Rhonda. "Would you like coffee, or would you prefer juice or milk?"

Rhonda leaned toward Esther and spoke in a low voice. "Miss Albright, I haven't any money."

Esther smiled. "I invited you, remember? It is my treat."

Rhonda visibly relaxed. "Coffee, please," she said.

Esther smiled and nodded to the waitress, then turned back to Rhonda, who sat staring at the tablecloth. Esther waited until the two cups of steaming coffee were placed in front of them to speak again.

"So, Rhonda. To what do I owe the pleasure of your visit?"

The woman looked at her cup and rubbed her thumb up and down the handle. She kept her eyes downcast as she spoke. "I'm sorry. I know that you don't even know me, but I've got nowhere to turn, now that, well..."

"That your place of employ has been shut down?"

Rhonda nodded her head. "I mean, there are other places that, well, you know..."

"Would hire a woman of your background?"

She looked up at Esther wide-eyed. Esther reached across the table and clasped her hand.

"I didn't mean that as an insult. I'm just trying to help you communicate. Let us not dance around the subject. I know what line of work you were in, and I am certain there are plenty other establishments willing to employ you. The fact that you are here tells me that you do not wish to continue in that line of work. Am I correct?"

"Yes, ma'am. But as far as I can see, I don't have any other choice. There aren't many options for a girl like me."

"There are always options," Esther said, remembering John's words. "Some options just take more bravery than others."

Rhonda smiled as the plate of food was placed in front of her, but the smile quickly faded, and a blush rose in her cheeks. She dropped her eyes, but not before Esther saw a look of humiliation cross them. Something had upset her. Esther turned to see what had caused Rhonda such distress. She turned just in time to see a man quickly leaving the cafe. Even though he was in a mad rush, Esther would have recognized Mr. Elmer Baxter anywhere.

It took very little persuading to convince Warren Mallory to hire Rhonda. She didn't have the secretarial training that Esther had, but Esther assured Warren that there was plenty of help that her new friend could offer, and Esther could teach her to type after work. Warren agreed heartily, citing the need for assistance in the typesetting room, now that another of his employees had been drafted.

"I must inform you, however, that this friend of mine does have a past."

"A past? Now you sound like John when he brought Charlie in."

Esther smiled. "Well, let's just say she and Charlie are acquainted."

Warren held up his hand. "Stop right there. I don't care about her past, only her future work here. I think it's best if I know as little as possible about your association with Charlie and this new friend of yours."

Esther suppressed a giggle. "That's probably a wise decision. It's much better to be able to say, 'I don't know' rather than 'I can't say.'"

"Agreed. It may not be very journalistic of me, but I'll remain happily ignorant in this situation, thank you very much." He laughed. "Have you any other friends looking for work? I could actually use a couple of extra hands in typesetting."

Esther couldn't believe she hadn't thought of it before. "I do have one friend, but she would be a temporary hire."

"Why is that?"

Esther folded her hands in front of her and squared her shoulders. "There's no reason to skirt the truth that will be obvious eventually. She is temporary because she is with child. She is unmarried, and the father of the baby has abandoned her."

Esther waited for a shocked reaction, or, at the very least, a stammering of excuses as to why he should not hire the girl, but Warren just nodded his head.

"Well, then, seems this woman is definitely in need of employment. If she is your friend, then that's good enough for me."

With sheer joy and Warren's permission, she hurried off to Mrs. Caffey's house and returned with a very eager-to-please Katie.

It was shortly before noon when John found Esther in the typesetting room with the two new hires.

"I've been looking for you everywhere," he said, stuffing his hands in his pockets. "Thought maybe you had changed your mind about finding a new boss."

Esther chuckled. "No. I was just introducing Mr. Nichols to his two new assistants," she said, motioning to Katie and Rhonda. "I believe you know Miss Feeney but let me introduce you to Miss Milford."

When John and Rhonda saw each other, Esther knew immediately that this was not the first time they had met. Rhonda dropped her gaze immediately and backed up a few steps. John, equally as nervous, said a quick 'nice to meet you' before making a lame excuse and quickly exiting the room.

Esther stood dumbfounded for several seconds. Katie and Mr. Nichols were deep in conversation about the mechanical workings of the typesetter. Rhonda looked up at Esther once, but dropped her gaze quickly, refusing to look her in the eye. No, this was not John and Rhonda's first encounter, and that realization nauseated her.

As she slowly made her way back to her desk, she tried convincing herself that it was none of her business. John's private life was his own. Besides, now that he had committed his life to Jesus, his sins were washed clean, weren't they? If God no longer judged him by his past deeds, then certainly Esther had no right to judge him. She just needed to return to her desk and focus on her job instead of obsessing over the past transgressions of John Ward.

But no matter how hard she tried to convince herself to forget what she had just witnessed, she couldn't erase the look of shame on John's face when he saw Rhonda standing in front of him. The longer she thought about it, the harder she punched the keys of her typewriter. It was that look that spurred her to storm into John's office and slam the door behind her.

"How could you?" she screeched. "How could you patronize such an establishment?"

John moved from behind his desk, confusion knitting his eyebrows. "What are you talking about?"

"Don't try to play innocent with me, Mr. Ward! I saw the way you looked at Rhonda, and I saw the way she looked at you! It is obvious that the two of you are not strangers!"

John ran his fingers through his sandy colored hair. "Let me explain..."

"Explain? You mean make an excuse!" Hot tears burned in her eyes. "You disgust me! There is nothing you could say that could excuse going to a place like that," she said before turning and yanking the door open.

Before she could storm through it, John was there, slamming the door shut. She whirled around and found his face inches from hers.

"Nothing could excuse my actions? How about the excuse that I was there to save you?"

"What? You came to save me and decided to spend some time enjoying the services of a prostitute first?"

"What I am trying to tell you is that, although I do not know the woman personally, we have, well, seen one another. When I was searching for you, I started throwing doors open. She was behind one of those doors."

Esther blinked rapidly, both in an attempt to stop the moisture from gathering in her eyes and to give her mind some time to digest what John had just said.

"You entered other rooms..."

"Looking for you."

"So, if you and she haven't...I mean, if you were never..."

"One of her customers?"

"Yes. If the two of you weren't intimate, then why did you both act so...so ashamed just now?"

John winced and squeezed his eyes shut. "Because she wasn't alone behind that door."

"I don't understand."

"She was, well, *working*."

Esther's furrowed eyebrows slowly rose in shock. "You mean, you interrupted..."

"Yes," he said, locking eyes with her. "So, you can understand how uncomfortable it is for the two of us to see one another again."

"Oh." Esther felt her heartbeat throbbing in her temples. "I'm so sorry. I just assumed the worst."

"Understandable, but do you believe me when I say that I have never, in all my life, visited a brothel? Well," he smiled. "At least not for that reason."

She realized that she had been the other reason he was insinuating. "I believe you," she said, smiling up at him.

He was so close, Esther wondered what he would do if she leaned in and pressed her lips against his. The desire to do so was so great, but before she had a moment to consider the ramifications of such an act, a frown clouded his face. He searched her eyes for something, but she wasn't certain what.

"I am innocent of what you have just accused me of, but I've not led a pious life. I've done many things that I regret, so many things that a woman like you would likely never forgive." He started to back away from her.

"Stop." Esther reached out and grabbed his arm.

John looked down on her. His silvery eyes scanned her face.

"Why would my opinion matter to you?" she asked

John reached up and swept a stray strand of hair off her forehead. His hand followed the curve of her cheek and he cupped her chin in his hand, lifting her lips toward his.

"Have I not been transparent enough?" he asked, dipping his head toward hers.

Esther closed her eyes, the hair on the back of her neck already standing on end, but before his lips reached hers, a loud knock on the door behind her interrupted them. Esther jumped in shock and John took a few steps backward. Taking a deep breath, she reached behind her and opened the door. Charlie Ross stood on the other side. He looked back and forth between Esther and John.

"I'm right sorry for interruptin' the two of ya."

"You didn't interrupt anything." Esther heard her own voice, sounding a pitch or two higher than usual.

Charlie eyed her suspiciously. "Mmmhmm, whatever you say, missy. I just came to say thanks to whichever one of ya got Rhonda the job. She's a good kid. I don't think she'll disappoint ya."

"I'm sure she will do very well here," Esther said, smiling at the man. "It seems we have quite the secret reunion happening at the Journal."

"Seems that way," Charlie said. "It also seems like there's lots happenin' behind closed doors here. Maybe you two should come up with a secret knock or somethin'." Charlie lifted an eyebrow at the two and turned to walk away, leaving the door open behind him.

23

A FACE FROM THE PAST

John was late. He was usually never late for anything, but his earlier interaction with Phoebe Albright had distracted him to the point of forgetting that it was Tuesday. The Reverend would be expecting him for their weekly lunch date. He only hoped the pastor didn't question him about his tardiness. He was certain the man did not want to hear that John had been closed up in an office with his daughter and had forgotten even what day it was.

When he entered the church, he didn't see anyone.

"Reverend?" he called out.

No response. John was just about to leave when a movement in the front corner of the sanctuary caught his eye. It was Mrs. Kinney, the church custodian. She peered at him from over the front row of pews.

"Good afternoon, Mrs. Kinney," John called as he made his way down the aisle. "I'm glad to have caught you..."

The woman quickly stood and, dropping the dusting rag she had been using, scooted toward the side door of the sanctuary.

"Wait," he hollered and increased his pace, his cane clicking loudly down the aisle. The woman didn't slow her steps. "Please," John called out again. "Don't go. I only want to talk to you. Please. Just give me a moment."

The woman stopped but kept her back to John. He took the pause as an opportunity to continue.

"I just wanted to thank you, for the other day. I was in a terrible way, by my own doing, mind you, and you shouldn't have had to deal with my...well, you know. That was disgusting. I want to apologize for that."

Mrs. Kinney turned her head slightly toward John, exposing the mottled scar along her left cheek and eye.

"I know a little of your story," he continued, a gentleness toward this woman overcoming him, "and I understand why you wouldn't trust me, or any man for that matter. But I want you to know that I understand better than most what you are feeling."

She didn't turn to face him, but neither did she move away from him. John stopped just behind her.

"I'm so sorry for what happened to you. I spent the first fifteen years of my life under the thumb of an abusive man and I can tell you first hand that it takes a long time to heal physically, even longer emotionally. But I did. However, not until I was willing to let go. And to let others in. I don't know if this is what you are dealing with, but if it is, I just want you to know that you don't need to run from me. I'm not going to hurt you."

The woman's shoulders slumped as she raised her hands to her face. John reached out and placed his hand on her shoulder.

"You don't need to run from me anymore."

He could feel slight vibrations coming from her small frame and knew she had begun crying. Without thinking, he turned her toward him and into an embrace. Her crying burst into sobbing once wrapped inside John's arms. He held the woman there, whispering assurances over the top of her head, until the crying that racked her body calmed to a quiet whimper.

"There, there," he assured her. He handed her his handkerchief as she stepped back from him. He smiled at her as she looked up and made eye contact. It was the first time John had been able to look fully into the woman's face. The left side was far more deformed than it had appeared to him from a distance, so much so that her eye was nearly completely shrouded by the drooping skin, but her right eye was fully intact and hadn't changed since John had last looked into it over 24 years ago, barring a few more wrinkles at the creases and underneath. His smile faded as his heart caught up with what his mind had already discovered.

"Johnny," his mother said weakly.

"You?" he said, shaking his head. "No, it can't be." He backed away from her. "How? How could it be you?"

"Johnny, I wanted to..."

"No!" he said, raising his voice. "I don't want to hear it. I don't want to hear anything you have to say!"

He stormed down the aisle and out the front door of Lansing First Church without looking back.

John pounded hard on the door. When Mrs. Albright opened it, he made no attempt at politeness. He just stormed past her and into the parlor where the Reverend sat reading.

"You knew!" he screamed. "You knew who she was, and you said nothing."

Reverend Albright laid his paper aside and laced his fingers across his barrel chest. "Yes, son. I knew," he said softly.

John clenched his teeth as tightly as his hands. "How long have you known?"

"Have a seat, John."

"How long?" John demanded.

"I said sit down." The reverend neither raised his voice nor moved at all, but something about the authority in his voice caused John, a grown man, to obey. He sat opposite him, on the edge of the chair with his hands on his knees, ready to bolt.

Reverend Albright calmly sighed. "Your mother came to me immediately after seeing you in the church that first afternoon...the day you came to lunch at my house. Do you remember?"

"Yes," he growled. "That was over a month ago. You've known for a month and you didn't tell me?"

"She asked me not to...not yet. She wasn't ready."

"Wasn't ready? For what? To face the son she abandoned? To answer for her sins? I don't suppose she would ever have been ready if I hadn't cornered her!"

"I suppose she was concerned that you would react, well, just like you are right now."

"How else would I react? That woman left me, left the five-year-old me, defenseless and alone with that beast she married. She chose to leave, but I had no choice. I had to suffer under his abuse."

"There's so much you don't know, so much you don't understand."

"Really? Then enlighten me." John crossed his arms and slammed his upper body against the back of the chair. "Well? I'm listening."

"I can't."

"You mean you won't, because you're more loyal to her than you are to me."

"I can't...because it's not my story to tell."

"And I suppose you expect me to listen to her?"

"I expect you to give her a chance."

John sat forward and rested his forehead on the heels of his hands. No matter how hard he willed the image away, he couldn't erase the picture of his mother's scarred face from his mind. Somewhere deep inside, his heart ached for her, and it angered him. Why should he care what pain she'd suffered these last twenty-four years? She hadn't cared enough about him to take him with her. She hadn't concerned herself with the suffering of her little boy. His head shook as he fought back tears. "I can't. She means nothing to me."

"Then tell her that."

John wiped his eyes with his coat sleeve and looked at the pastor. "Seriously? You want me to tell her that?"

"If that is how you feel. But only after you have given her a chance to explain herself."

"There is no excuse good enough to justify abandoning a child in the hands of that monster."

"You could be correct, but you'll never know unless you listen."

The marred face. The tortured eyes. John didn't want to spend the rest of his life haunted by them. He didn't want to be tortured by wondering anymore. He wanted relief, and there was only one real solution. He had to learn the truth. And maybe, if God were merciful, he could put this woman and all she had done behind him.

John stood up. "I'll listen, but only so I can tell her what I think of her, what I've been dreaming of saying to her for over twenty years. And then she is gone from my life forever."

It wasn't difficult to find Mrs. Kinney. She was only a few feet from where John had left her, seated on the front row of pews. Her head hung low as silent tears coursed down her cheeks. They approached her from her left side, and John was once again troubled by the emotional effect the sight of his mother had on him. He wanted to feel anger... only anger. He didn't want to feel pity for this woman.

Reverend Albright placed his hand on her shoulder. "Lucile. I've brought John back."

His mother's shocked look fell on John. Apparently, he wasn't the only one who'd thought they would never see one another again.

"It's time," the pastor said. "Time to tell him everything."

John stood, arms crossed, and waited. Pastor Albright leaned on the communion table and pointed at the pew next to his mother. "Have a seat, son."

"I'm fine right where I'm at."

"Go on, John," he said, pointing again.

The Reverend was nothing like his father, yet he commanded obedience in a way that John's father never could. Despite his reluctance, he found himself sitting down on the bench next to the woman.

They sat in silence for several minutes. Maybe she didn't want to be here any more than he did. Well, if that were the case, he could appease her easy enough.

John was just about to stand and announce his plans when he was stopped by the sound of her weak voice.

"I looked for you, you know."

"What did you just say?"

"I looked for you, after you and your father left. I looked, but –"

"You left us, not the other way around."

She raised her head, a frown settling over her one good eye. "How could you ever think that of me? How could you think I would ever leave you?"

"One day you were there, the next gone. It doesn't take much intelligence to figure it out."

She slowly shook her head. "After all the beatings I endured for you, after all I went through to protect you..."

"Protect me?" John said, his voice rising. "You never protected me!"

A tear slid down each of her cheeks. She quickly wiped away the one but left the one on her marred cheek and John wondered if she even knew it was there. Was it possible she had no feeling on that side of her once lovely face?

"Johnny–"

"My name is John."

Somehow, his words seemed to cause her even more pain. She dropped her eyes and took a deep breath.

"John," she began, "I may not have done a very good job of protecting you, but I did the best that I could. Everything you did seemed to anger him, and if I stepped between you and him, he just got angrier. But it was always worth it, if it meant I spared you any pain. Being born into that life wasn't your choosing. You were an innocent. But me...I chose your father. I might have been young and naive when he swept me off my feet, but it was my own stupidity, my own impulsiveness that caused me to marry a man I barely knew just because I was attracted to him and because he was wealthy."

Her words stirred something in him. Memories...something he hadn't allowed himself to have for decades. Memories of his father hurting his mother. Why had he forgotten that? Anger, that's why. He was so angry, he had pushed aside any thoughts of her that would have elicited sympathy. But now, listening to her voice, which, unlike her face, had not changed since he was a little boy, he could no longer block the memories.

"If you were so intent on protecting me, why leave me with him? Why leave me, alone and unprotected?"

"I've told you, I didn't leave. When they finally released me from the hospital, I came home only to find an empty house and no trace of where he had taken you."

"What do you mean 'hospital'?"

"You really don't know? After all this time?"

"Would I be asking if I did?"

"No, of course not," she said softly. "Oh, my. Where to begin."

"How about why you were in the hospital."

"Your father put me there." She took a deep breath and looked off at nothing. "You and I were playing in the backyard. Jacks, I believe. You always loved to play jacks."

John remembered that well. They always played on the veranda where the surface was hard, but the arbor above kept the sun from scorching them.

"We heard your father calling and could tell he was angry. He was yelling my name, but that didn't mean you were safe, so I took you inside and I told you to go hide under–"

"Under the stairs," John whispered, another memory crashing into him like a violent wave. "The alcove hidden behind the wood paneling."

"Yes." His mother looked up at him. "Jack didn't know about the secret cabinet. It wasn't a big space–"

"It was just large enough for the two of us. But you never hid with me."

She smiled weakly. "He would have kept looking until he found one of us, you know that."

John did know that. How many times had he huddled in the dark of that hiding place, listening to his mother's pleas for mercy as his father unleashed his wrath on her? As a child, his mother had seemed a giant, the bravest person he knew. But as an adult now, looking at her small frame, he wondered how she ever survived the beatings. Even though he knew it was ridiculous, guilt grew inside of him for hiding and letting her take the beatings meant for him.

"I hid you under the stairs and hurried in the direction of his voice. When I found him storming out of the parlor, he held a wad of silver notes gripped in his fist. He had found the money I had been stashing away."

"You planned to leave him," John said.

"Yes. It took me a very long time to save that much. Your father was just as controlling with his money as he was with his family. I was only allowed to shop at certain businesses, places where he had set up accounts. The only money your father gave me was to pay the staff. I started doing a few of the chores, like washing your clothes and some of my own. It wasn't enough for him to notice, and he never looked any of the staff in the eye, so he didn't notice when we had one less girl on staff. After about a year, I had nearly enough for you and me to start over."

"But father put a stop to that."

"He was angrier than I had ever seen him. He'd figured out what I was planning to do. He beat me, the whole while saying that the only way I was leaving was in a pine box. At some point, I began slipping in and out of consciousness. But I came fully conscious when he shoved my head into the fireplace."

The scar. John shuddered at the horror of it all.

"I still don't know how he knew about the money. I kept it hidden in an old, worn copy of *Sense and Sensibility*. He never touched a book of mine. Said I was addle minded for reading that fluff, as he called it."

"It's all my fault." John dropped his head into his hands.

"What?"

He rubbed his eyes with the heels of his hands then looked straight at his mother. "I told him about the money. I wanted a clockwork toy I saw when he took me to town earlier that morning. It was a horse and cart with a driver. I thought it was the most incredible thing I had ever seen. He told me no. I said I would just ask you for it. He laughed, that horrible, horrible mocking laugh he had, and said you didn't have any money. You were the wife. It was the men that had money. I told him that he was wrong, that you did have money. I told him you loved me and would give me money for the horse cart. I'm so sorry. I had no idea what would happen."

"You were only a child, still a baby–"

"I should have known. I should have known better than to talk back to him. He backhanded me right there in the middle of the sidewalk...sent me halfway down the street. Then he grabbed me by the collar and drug me to the carriage. I thought that was the end of it. I'm so sorry."

"You have no reason to apologize. He was a monster. You were just a small boy with no concept of what was happening around you."

"But that mistake, that is why you were in the hospital? Why you have that..." John didn't know how to say it.

"Yes," she nodded. "That is how I came to look like this. I don't remember getting to the hospital, or much of anything from the first few weeks. But, eventually I healed enough for them to send me home."

"Did no one at the hospital contact the police and report what he'd done to you?"

"Yes, they did. Mind you, it wasn't the first time your father had put me into the hospital, but I believe it was the first time that nobody thought I would come out alive. "

Realization dawned on John. "I remember seeing two police officers leave father's office. It was more than a week before we moved. Why didn't they arrest him?"

"They were waiting for me to die."

"They could have arrested him whether you died or not. The law is very clear on beating someone that badly, even if they live."

"Unless you are married to that someone. That's the funny thing about our laws. A man can beat his wife and there's nothing they will do about it. The police figure it's their own business, not the public's. If he kills her, however, that's another matter. That's why they called the police. They were certain I wouldn't survive."

"That's why he was in such a hurry to leave. I always

assumed it was his pride, not wanting to face people that knew you had left him. All along, he was running for his life...like the coward he always was."

"It took me a long time to piece everything together. I came so close to dying, and I was so frail when they discharged me from the hospital. The shock of losing you nearly finished what Jack had begun. I tried looking for you, but I had no idea where to begin. I asked the neighbors and I went to his office, but no one knew anything, or at least said they didn't. Nobody would look me in the face. I wasn't certain if it was because they were lying, or because I was so hideously scarred."

"We moved to Albany. We knew no one."

"I learned that, but not until the divorce papers arrived."

"Divorce papers?"

"Yes. But that was much later. After leaving the hospital, I tried living in our empty house for as long as I could. At least my clothing had been left behind. But the bank eventually kicked me out and sold the house. I tried finding work, but no one wanted to hire a former heiress with no experience. The church helped me for a while, but always treated me like a soiled woman, constantly insinuating that I had brought it all on myself, that my sinful nature had somehow brought God's wrath upon me. Then a letter came from my aunt in Lansing. She was ill and needed someone to care for her. I was loath to leave Buffalo. If you ever returned, how would you find me? But I had no other choice. I left my address with the church and all the neighbors, hoping you would eventually come looking for me."

Guilt twisted inside John like a dull butcher knife. He had been so angry with his mother, blaming her for his plight in life, that he'd never once thought about looking for her. He'd never considered that she was as much a victim as he.

"When I saw you that first time, here in the church, you looked so much like your father that it frightened me. I thought you were him. I was so shocked, it wasn't until you had left with Reverend Albright that I was able to tell myself that you were too young to be Jack Ward. But then, I realized, you would be just about the right age to be my Johnny."

"Why didn't you say anything?"

"I wanted to, I really did, but I felt so guilty. I've always felt there should have been more that I could have done to find you. I just never had the funds to pay for such a search. That's why the divorce papers were such a relief. I don't know how he found me, though I didn't have much family, so it probably wasn't that difficult to track me down. It had been ten years, but you were still a boy, at least in my eyes. I took what little money I had and hired a lawyer. He drew up papers that agreed to the divorce, but only if he sent you to live with me. He agreed. I was elated. I signed the papers, but then received word that you had run away. My lawyer sent the police to the house and they reported back that it was true.

"I was heartbroken. Just when I thought I had you back, that I could make up for all the lost time, you slipped through my fingers again. And you were on the streets, all by yourself. I couldn't sleep from the nightmares of what could be happening to you."

"I hopped the train until I reached Philadelphia," John said. "I got a job as a newsboy. They let me sleep in the backroom with some of the other boys, mostly immigrants. I worked hard and managed to get a job helping the typesetter. From there, I worked my way up to the news room. You needn't have worried."

"I guess God was looking out for the both of us all the while. My aunt died, and I couldn't afford the rent on her home, so I found myself in dire straits again. That's when Jasper Kinney stepped into my life. He was a neighbor of my aunt, a kind widower with no children. He offered marriage and I accepted. He passed away a few years later but left me the house and a small amount of money. That's when I started working here. It's been a simple life, my life here in Lansing, but it has been a fine one, except for the hole left in my heart from losing you."

She stood and turned to face John. "But have I lost you forever, Johnny? Can you find it in your heart to forgive me? Can you find somewhere, deep in your soul, to love me again?"

John shook his head. "I never stopped loving you, Mother. That's why it has hurt so much, all these years not knowing, wondering exactly what happened. I masked the hurt with anger, but I see now that...that—" John's words stuck in his throat.

She reached a hand toward him and everything broke loose inside of him.

"I love you, Momma." John stood and pulled his mother against his chest, burying his wet cheek against the top of her head. "Can you forgive me?"

His mother wrapped her arms tightly around his middle. "There is nothing to forgive. The past is over, Johnny. We have only the future, and we have each other. I need nothing more from this life."

24

DISCOVERED

"Why are you so happy?"

Esther stopped mid-brushstroke and looked at her sister's reflection in the mirror. "What did you say?"

"I asked you why you are so happy. You are staring off into space and have this goofy grin on your face. Something tells me that you aren't thinking about my hair."

Esther pursed her lips and returned to brushing the knots out of Sarah's curls. "Maybe I'm thinking about all the trouble you are going to get into when Mother sees your ruined dress."

Sarah looked down at the formerly white frock. "It's not ruined. Just a little dirty."

"Just a little dirty? My, yes, just like your hair was only a little disheveled. Goodness, Sarah, how did you get so many twigs and dead leaves stuck in your hair?"

Her little sister shrugged. "I don't know. I guess I got a little ruffled running from Oliver Hebert."

"Oliver Hebert? Why on earth was he chasing you?"

"Same reason all the boys do, silly," Sarah giggled. "But next time, I think I'll let him catch me!"

"Sarah Kathleen Albright! If Daddy finds out you are kissing boys, he'll tan your hide!"

Esther's warning did little to lessen the girl's obvious delight at being 'caught' by a boy. Sarah covered her mouth with her hands, but Esther's frown only caused her to giggle harder. Esther stood looking at her younger sister, hands on her hips and frowning. Suddenly, Sarah stopped laughing and looked wide-eyed at her oldest sister.

"That's it," she said. "That's why you've been smiling. It's because of a boy, isn't it?"

"What? No," Esther argued. "Don't be silly."

"That is it! Oh, Esther. Who is it? Who is it?"

"Nobody. Please stop."

But Sarah didn't stop. "Esther's got a boyfriend. Esther's got a boyfriend," she sang at the top of her lungs.

Esther laughed, despite herself. It was hard to stay angry at her little sister, especially when she had come so close to the truth.

"Alright, alright. If you'll quiet down, and if you'll promise to keep a secret, I'll tell you why I'm smiling."

Sarah whipped around and rested her arms and her chin on the back of her chair. She looked up expectantly at Esther.

"I promise!"

Esther sighed, but before she could share a single word of her secret, the sound of the front door slamming open echoed through the house.

"Esther!" her father yelled. "Esther, you come here right this minute!"

The two girls' large, saucer-like eyes stared at one another for a moment before Esther quickly opened the door of her bedroom.

"Coming Daddy," she said as she rushed to the stairs, Sarah close on her heels. When they got to the top of the landing, their father was at the bottom of the stairs, ripping his coat off.

"Sarah, you go on back to your room. This has nothing to do with you."

Their father's face was an angry shade of orange, and if there had been any defiance in Sarah, the look of anger on their father's face had surely erased it. Without another word, she sped back up the stairs and slammed the door of her room.

Her hands shaking, Esther grabbed the stair rail and descended. Her father silently motioned to the parlor. She quickly made her way into the sitting room where her mother sat, mouth agape.

"James, dear, what on earth - "

"Sit!" he yelled, interrupting his wife and pointing at a chair next to the fireplace. Esther silently obeyed.

"James. What is the problem?" Mrs. Albright asked calmly.

"The problem? The problem is that our daughter has been leading a secret life, a life that apparently includes socializing at an illegal speakeasy!"

She heard her mother's gasp and felt her eyes fixate on her, but Esther couldn't bring herself to look at her. She just stared at the floor, the shock of the situation rendering her speechless.

"Esther? Is that true?" she heard her mother ask, but Esther was too deep in thought to answer. Who had told her father? Richard was definitely vile enough to rat her out, but he was off to war. Katie certainly wouldn't say anything. She doubted John would...John. Today was Tuesday, John's day to have lunch with her father. But, why would he...

"Esther," her mother's voice raised a decibel, "answer me!"

She finally raised her head and met her mother's gaze. The hurt and disappointment she saw there cut through her soul. Tears brimmed on her lashes.

"It's not what you think," Esther whispered.

"How many times have you visited that establishment?" The veins in her father's forehead throbbed rhythmically as he spoke, and Esther knew he was angrier than she had ever seen him.

"Daddy," she began softly, "please let me explain."

"How many times?"

"I didn't drink any alcohol."

"That doesn't make me feel any better. The other possible reasons for a young woman to visit such an establishment are not any more wholesome. Answer my question!"

"It wasn't like that."

"Answer me!" he shouted.

"Four," she answered softly, biting her lower lip.

"Four! Four times? You went behind our backs and snuck out to an illegal bar to drink and do who knows what on four different occasions?"

"No. It wasn't like that! Is that what John said? He said I was drinking alcohol? What else did he accuse me of?"

"John? What does John have to do with this?"

"Isn't that who - who told you..."

If Esther had thought her father was angry before, she'd had no idea how angry the man could actually become. The muscles in his jaw flexed and sweat broke out on his brow as he stared at her, or through her would be more accurate, she thought. Without another word, he stormed from the room and grabbed his coat off the newel post where he had thrown it. Esther rushed after him.

"Daddy, wait. You have to listen to me."

When her hands gripped his arm, he jerked away and held up a finger at her.

"Girl, I am the closest I have ever been to hitting a grown woman. I suggest you sit back down with your mother until I return." He smashed his hat onto his head and left the house, slamming the door behind him. Esther ran for her coat.

"Young lady, you had better listen to your father, if you know what's best for you," warned her mother.

Esther turned back and noticed that she was crying. Returning to the parlor, Esther grabbed her mother's hands.

"Momma, you have to believe me. It isn't what you think. But I don't have time to explain. Daddy is about to, well, I'm not certain what he is about to do, but I do know that whatever it is, John doesn't deserve it."

Her mother reached out and cupped Esther's chin. "I want to believe you, but you must explain yourself to me first. Then, if I see fit, the two of us will go after your father."

Esther wanted to argue, but she knew the two of them together had a much better chance of cooling the temper of James Albright than Esther did alone. She took a deep breath and opened her mouth, and her heart, to her mother.

John was just putting on his suit coat when someone knocked on his office door. He was surprised. He thought everyone except the loading bay workers had left for the day. When he opened the door, he found his boss smiling on the other side.

"I thought I saw a light under your door," Warren said. "Don't you ever go home?"

"Not much of a home to go home to," John laughed. When seeing Warren's frown, he added. "Don't worry. I was just getting ready to leave."

"Why don't you dine at my home this evening?"

Their conversation was interrupted by a loud banging sound coming from the lobby. Warren shrugged.

"It's probably just Anna grown impatient — she's been waiting in the car for the past twenty minutes. So, what do you say about dinner?"

John stacked the papers on his desk. "Thanks for the offer, but I'm beat."

"Come on, John. Are you worried about Anna's cooking?"

"No, of course not - "

"Because you should be," Warren laughed. "My wife is amazing at so many things, but cooking is not one of them. However our cook, Mrs. Gunderson, is fantastic. Not sure what's for dinner, but I can guarantee that it will be loads better than whatever fare you'll order at the diner."

John laughed. "You'd better hope your wife can't hear you out there."

Warren shrugged again. "She's heard me say it many times. It won't matter if she hears it again."

The banging on the door grew louder and more urgent.

"You'd better get going before she leaves without you."

Warren placed his bowler hat on his head and nodded. "If you change your mind, you know where we live."

John pushed in his chair and walked toward his cane. He had gotten in the habit of leaning it near the door so that he was forced to walk short distances without it. Last night, he had gotten as far as the front door before a slight twinge in his lower back reminded him that he had left it behind. Walking was becoming so much easier that he was beginning to believe the doctors when they said he would be able to walk without it before another year passed.

He had just rounded his desk when he heard voices coming from the lobby. He recognized Warren's, though he couldn't hear what he said, but he also recognized the second voice as that of Reverend Albright, and the reverend wasn't speaking so softly.

"Where is he?" John heard him say. Again, he heard Warren speak before hearing the pastor's raised voice bellow, "Out of my way, Mallory. This has nothing to do with you."

John knew he was the only person at the Lansing State Journal this time of night that Reverend Albright could be searching for. He grabbed his cane and opened the door, intent on meeting him in the lobby, but to his surprise the older man was already there. Before John knew what was happening, the pastor had him by the collar and slammed him into the wall.

"I trusted you," the man growled in John's face. "I treated you like family, and this is how you repay me?"

John was in an utter state of shock. He understood the words the man was saying, but they didn't make any sense.

"Now, hold on, Pastor. What has gotten you so upset?"

"You are lucky that I chose to walk here, rather than drive. It gave me time to cool down a bit, but I'm still madder than a wet hen. I've come to love you like a son, and you repay me by soiling the reputation of my daughter?"

John exhaled slowly. How had he found out about the kiss? "Listen, sir, I know how it must look, and I am truly sorry. It should never have happened."

"You're right, it shouldn't have happened!" he shouted, releasing John and stepping back. John's neck was no longer held in the meaty hands of the pastor, but he felt no freer, trapped by the man's angry stare. John took a deep breath.

"Honestly, sir, I don't see how your daughter's reputation has been soiled."

"That's all I can handle," the big man said, removing his coat and rolling up his sleeves.

"Now, now, now," Warren said, stepping between the two men. "Reverend, let's not be too hasty. Whatever John has done, I'm certain the issue can be resolved amicably."

"I thought so too, at first, but this boy can't see how his actions have affected my daughter, so I'm going to have to explain it to him in a language he'll understand."

Warren looked over his shoulder at John. "Actions? What is it he has done, sir?"

"He's been dragging her off to a speakeasy, drinkin' and carousin' and who knows what else," he said, his face beet red.

"What?" John said, pushing Warren out of the way. "Is that what she told you? That I took her there?"

Reverend Albright stared confusedly at John. He was silent for a few moments. "Well, no, I don't reckon that she did say that, exactly."

It was John's turn to be confused. "Then, what makes you think I took her there?"

"Well, I - " he began, then scratched his head. "Are you trying to tell me that you didn't take my daughter to a speakeasy?"

"Yes sir, that is exactly what I am saying."

"Well, then why did she think you were the one that told me she'd been there?"

John tapped his cane against the floor. "Well, sir, I've not hidden from you my lifestyle, well, I mean my lifestyle before I became saved. I used to frequent the speakeasy you're talking about, and Miss Albright did see me there."

"How many times?"

"How many times did I visit the speakeasy?"

"No, son, how many times did you see my daughter there?"

John wasn't certain how he should respond. How much did the pastor know? Had Phoebe confessed everything? Did the man know about the day in the brothel? John didn't want to come between Phoebe and her father, but he was loathe to lie to the man. He decided that honesty was the only recourse.

"Three times."

"She said four."

John thought about that. "Well, she may have been there four times, but I only saw her there on three occasions."

The minister rubbed his chin and eyed John suspiciously. "Three times, you say? And it never occurred to you to drag the fool girl out of there? Did you even try to reason with her?"

John lifted an eyebrow at him. "With all due respect, Reverend, you know your daughter better than anyone. Do you think that there's a man alive that could make that woman listen when she already has her mind made up?"

A loud snort caused both men to look to Warren. "Sorry," he said, clearing his throat. "But we all know that's the truth."

A small smile played at the corners of the minister's mouth. "She is a bit stubborn, I suppose. Must get it from her mother," he said.

All three men laughed for a moment, but soon Reverend Albright grew serious again. He looked straight at John.

"Johnny, I'm going to ask you a question and I want you to tell me the truth."

"I've never lied to you, sir."

"What was she doing there?"

Again, John felt cornered. "I think that is a question you should ask her, but what I can tell you is what she wasn't doing. She wasn't drinking. She wasn't smoking or keeping company with men. All of the bad things that your mind has conjured up about your daughter's possible activities inside that bar, you can rest assured that she wasn't doing any of them."

Reverend Albright shook his head and rubbed his forehead. "I'm such a fool. An old, stubborn fool. Whatever possessed me to think that my little girl would ever be capable of such vile behavior. She tried telling me, but I was so angry that I didn't give her a chance to speak. What kind of father treats his daughter that way?"

"A protective one who loves her," John said. "Every young woman should be so lucky."

"I do love her, more than she will ever understand, I think." Reverend Albright grabbed his coat off the floor. He made to leave but stopped. He turned back to John, his forehead crinkled.

"Son, you apologized and said it shouldn't have happened. If you weren't talkin' about the speakeasy, what were you talkin' about?"

John held his breath. He looked over at Warren who stared back with both eyebrows lifted.

"Don't look at me," Warren chuckled. "I'm just as curious to hear your answer as the good reverend here is."

John rubbed the back of his neck, cursing his promise to remain honest. "I - I kissed your daughter, sir," he said without looking up.

The room was so still, John feared the Reverend had stopped breathing. After several awkward, silent moments, John finally lifted his eyes to meet the minister's. He wasn't certain what he would see there, but he wasn't expecting a smile. John again looked at Warren, hoping for some sort of clarification, but found him smiling as well. He looked back at the minister who broke out in a hearty laugh.

"Well, I'll be," the man said, his barrel chest bouncing up and down. "And you thought I'd be angry at that?"

"Well, yes," John said, scowling. "Of course. I'm not courting your daughter. I had no right to kiss her."

"That's true enough, but how did she react?"

John was mortified. Was he actually asking for details of their kiss?

"Sir, with all due respect, I don't think that is something a gentleman would share."

This brought on another boisterous laugh from the minister. When he calmed, he slapped John on the shoulder.

"Well, if she had slugged ya, you'd have no problem sharin' that, I'd say." Reverend Albright cleared his throat. "Son, you're right. You don't have a right to go around kissin' women you aren't committed to. However, as you pointed out earlier, my daughter isn't going to do anything she doesn't want to do. I have complete confidence that if she didn't welcome your kiss, well, she would have let you know in no uncertain terms. Since you are too much a gentleman to share, I'll assume that means she didn't smack you upside the head. So, I guess that means," he said, squeezing John's shoulder, "that I'll be seein' you around our house more often."

"Sir?" John asked. He was still having difficulty wrapping his mind around the pastor's reaction.

It was Warren that brought clarification. He stepped up to John and clasped his other shoulder.

"The man is giving you his blessing, John."

"His blessing?"

"To court his daughter," Warren laughed.

"Excuse me?" came a surprised voice from the doorway.

All three men turned to find four decidedly shocked women staring at them—three Albrights and a Mallory.

25

ADMISSIONS

John stared at Phoebe, her green eyes wide. How was it possible that she grew even more beautiful each time he saw her?

"Ladies!" Warren said, breaking the silence. He reached for his wife's hand and kissed her on the cheek. "I'm so sorry darling for making you wait so long."

"Warren, what is going on?" Anna asked.

He grinned mischievously. "So much excitement, and you'll be happy to learn that I'm not the cause of any of it."

She eyed her husband suspiciously. "I find that very difficult to believe."

"Truth be told, I caused all the excitement," Reverend Albright said. He turned to Phoebe. "Well, dear, it seems you have a lot of explaining to do."

"Yes, she does," Mrs. Albright interrupted. "And you are going to listen to her, do you hear me, James Albright."

The large man smiled sheepishly. "I know, darlin'. I will. I promise, but first, I think we need to give these two a few minutes alone."

"Alone? I don't understand," Mrs. Albright argued as her husband guided her and Sarah out the door.

Anna Mallory tugged at her husband's hand. "Come, dear."

"Must we? This is really starting to get good!" Warren laughed, crossing his arms.

Anna Mallory grabbed her husband's shoulders and turned him toward the door. "Don't worry, darling. We can eavesdrop from outside."

"Are they gonna kiss?" John heard Sarah ask excitedly.

"Sarah!" Mrs. Albright chastised.

"Sure looks like it!" Warren chuckled as he patted the girl's head.

"Warren!" Anna said.

The door closed behind the Mallorys and John was left alone with Phoebe Albright and his rapidly beating heart. She turned to him, her perfectly shaped lips agape.

"What did Warren mean - my father giving you his blessing?"

John rubbed the back of his neck nervously. "I told your father about the kiss."

"You did what!" she said, her hand flying to her mouth. "He must have been livid."

John shook his head. "Just the opposite. He seemed... pleased."

"You're teasing me."

"No, I'm not."

She looked up at him, her cheeks flushed. He wasn't certain if she was embarrassed or if she was angry. Either way, all he knew was that she took his breath away.

"Even more beautiful..."

Will Caffey's voice in his head threatened to derail what John was about to do. He wouldn't let it this time. John knew this was right.

John crossed the short distance between them. She looked

at him wide-eyed when he reached for her hands. He lifted them and gently placed a kiss on her knuckles.

"I know how I feel. I've spent weeks trying to deny my feelings. I tried avoiding you. I tried convincing myself that you were a bad person. I even tried drinking thoughts of you away, but no matter what I did, I couldn't run far enough away from my feelings for you."

"What are you saying?"

"I'm saying that I have fallen for you. I am certain of my feelings. What I am uncertain of is your feelings for me."

"I don't know what to say."

"I see," John said, releasing her hands and turning toward his desk. He stuffed his hands in his pocket to disguise their shaking. How could he have been such a fool, to actually think that a woman as good as Phoebe Albright could ever care about a man like him.

"I don't think you do see," she said. When John didn't turn around, she continued. "When we first met, I loathed you."

John chuckled. "I gave you every reason to."

"That's true. But, I don't suppose I was very kind to you either."

"I believe your first words to me were, 'You're in my way.'"

Phoebe laughed. "I forgot about that. I was thinking about that Sunday you showed up for church."

"Mmmm, yes. You were slightly more pleasant that day. I believe your exact words were 'What are you doing here?'" John looked over his shoulder at her. "Not exactly a warm welcome."

"Me? What about how you treated me on the sidewalk that day?"

John cringed. "I'm sorry. I was exceptionally rude, wasn't I?"

"I don't know if I have ever disliked a stranger so much in my life. But then, when you sat at my parents table and shared the story of your injury, when I saw the admiration you had for

Will, something in me started to warm toward you. I don't cry often, but your story really affected me."

John turned to face her fully. "You cried because of your affection for Will."

"I do care for Will, yes. He's family. But I cried for you that day. My heart ached for you and what you had been through."

"I thought you were worried for Will."

"Of course, I was...am. We all are."

John mulled over what she had just said. "I'm worried about him, too."

She moved closer to him. "When I started working here, I felt an attraction for you that I never imagined you would ever return. Then, when you risked your life to save mine, when you kissed me like that, I knew then what it has taken you so long to figure out for yourself. I realized then that I was falling in love with you. But you pushed me away. When you rejected me, I - I gave up all hope."

"I was confused. I had erected so many walls to defend against my feelings for you. When you showed up at my apartment, I wasn't prepared. And, when you kissed me back, it changed everything."

"Yes," she smiled. "Everything changed."

John took her hand in his. "We have had a very unconventional beginning, one I'm not very proud of. Do you think you'd be willing to give me another chance?"

"I'd like that very much," she smiled.

John stepped closer to her and his other hand cupped her chin and tilted her lips toward his. Suddenly, the door to his office burst open.

"Alright, you've had a few minutes," Reverend Albright said, opening the door for all those gathered in the hall to see. "That's long enough."

"Sorry, kiddo," Warren whispered to Sarah. "Not this time." Warren's eyes twinkled. "I'm starving. Let's move this party over to our house. I know Mrs. Gunderson has prepared enough for an army. You two lovebirds can ride with me and Mrs. Mallory."

"I'm a bit close to starvin' myself," the minister laughed. "Ruth, please tell me you brought the car."

"Of course," she laughed. "The women in our family aren't so foolhardy as to set out on foot all this distance."

John looked down at Phoebe as everyone exited the building. First God, then his mother, and now Phoebe. All the holes of his heart were now full. For the first time in his life, John knew what it meant to truly be happy. And nothing was going to change that.

26

BOARD MEETING

*E*arly November in Michigan meant not only colder weather but shorter days as well, but Esther refused to let the change in atmosphere keep her from her evening walk home. She relished the feel of freedom she got from the long walk after a day confined to the office. John was right. She was miserable in her job, even with the added benefit of working so closely with him.

John. She couldn't think of him without smiling. She had never met anyone like him. Never had a man evoked such emotion from her. And quite the range of emotions, Esther had to admit with a laugh. Never had another person been able to make her so angry at times, so empathetic at others, and still other moments, so passionate. She thought about how many times she had relived that first kiss in her mind and realized it was too many to count. Her heart raced at the realization that he would have repeated the kiss last night, had her father not interrupted them.

But even the thrill of seeing John every day wasn't enough to make her work enjoyable. There was nothing inherently wrong with being a secretary, it just wasn't something that

Esther felt called to do. She found no feeling of fulfillment on the keys of her typewriter. And now, with a new romance blooming between her and John, she supposed she could imagine that it might be possible that she would not be condemned to a life of secretarial spinsterhood, but even the thought of keeping a home full-time didn't completely satisfy her. Yes, she wanted to be a wife and a mother someday, but she wanted something more. She just didn't know what that 'more' was.

As she continued home, and the electric street lights clicked on around her, her thoughts drifted to Rhonda. Esther was so pleased to see how nicely she was fitting in at The Journal. Warren, despite knowing the girl's history, treated her with the utmost respect, and the other men around the office, taking the lead from their boss, followed suit. Every day, Rhonda grew a little more confident. The makeup she wore grew lighter and lighter, and she carried her head higher and higher at each passing day, appearing to take pride in her work, no matter what task they gave her. Working in the typesetting room was anything but glamorous, and the girl left the office most days with her hands covered in ink, but she didn't seem to mind. In fact, she seemed to enjoy her work. And Esther wasn't the only one who'd noticed. Just this morning she had overheard Mr. Nichols telling Warren what a fine job both Rhonda and Katie were doing in the typesetting department.

Katie. Another name that brought a smile to Esther's face. Who would have thought a few short months ago that the woman who broke up Esther's engagement would one day become one of her dearest friends? Esther was so happy she had been able to help Katie find work, even if it is only temporary. She didn't know what would happen once Katie had her baby, but for now, she had a job and a place to live, and Esther praised God for his hand in Katie's life. He had brought her this far, and Esther trusted that He would take care of her in the future, despite how the circumstances looked to Esther. Society didn't welcome women like Katie with open arms. As far as the men who put women like her into the situation were considered, well, maybe their involvement would be frowned upon, but they could move on and live a normal life - work, marry, have a family. But women like Katie weren't so lucky. She would forever be labeled, ostracised, condemned, as would her child. It broke Esther's heart.

As she rounded the corner onto her street, she was surprised to see a number of cars and a few buggies in front of the church. It was Tuesday evening. Nothing ever happened at church on Tuesday evenings. As she walked closer, she recognized most of the vehicles. Warren's father, the senior Mr. Mallory's Oldsmobile was there, as well as Mr. Hugh's. There was an RE Olds that she believed belonged to Ralph Boyd and one of the buggies she recognized as Lottie Arthur's. Another Oldsmobile, older than the Mallory vehicle, Esther recognized as the vehicle of Elmer Baxter. All board members of Lansing First Church, Esther realized, but this was not a normally scheduled board meeting night.

Esther knew that she should walk past the church and just go home, but she had a feeling in the pit of her stomach that would not let her do so. She crept around the back of the building, unlocked the basement door and slowly opened it. The downstairs classroom area was dark, but she knew the hallways well and navigated them quickly and quietly. She made her way to another staircase leading to the first floor. At the top of the stairs, she could see light coming from a crack in the door leading to the stage and indiscernible voices trailed out to the small passageway. She crept closer to try to hear what was being said.

"It's deplorable, just deplorable," Mrs. Arthur was saying. "To think, the daughter of our own pastor, acting in such a matter."

Esther cringed. Her instinct had been correct — this impromptu meeting was all about her. And seeing Mr. Baxter sitting there smugly removed any doubt Esther may have had as to who had informed her father of her speakeasy association.

"Now, Lottie, let's not jump to conclusions," Reverend Albright said calmly. "Unless we talk with Esther herself, we don't know the whole story."

"Story?" the old woman cackled. "What 'story' could that girl offer that could ever justify her actions? She is an embarrassment, I say, to you, your wife and this entire congregation! Something has to be done about her."

"I have to agree with Mrs. Arthur. For some time now, I've noticed your daughter has been putting on airs. And the way she dresses, all those fancy clothes, not at all the way a preacher's daughter should dress. I've noticed how her skirts keep getting shorter and shorter."

Short skirts! Is he insane? Esther thought. Her skirts were a good two inches longer than most women her age.

"Now hold on there, Roy," Winston Mallory spoke up. "My daughter-in-law makes most of Miss Albright's clothing. Are you saying her skirts are too short as well?"

"Your daughter-in-law is different. She's not a pastor's daughter."

"Does that make a difference?"

"Of course, it makes a difference," Lottie Arthur broke in. "Her actions and her attire reflect on this entire church. She is held to an entirely different standard."

"That seems a bit unfair. She's a young woman just like any other young woman in this church. You've got a daughter, Les. What do you think?"

"This isn't about my daughter. I agree with Mrs. Arthur. Miss Albright is held to a different standard."

"Standard or no standard, Esther's actions are inappropriate for any Christian woman."

"What actions exactly are we speaking of?" Winston Mallory asked.

"Mr. Baxter?" Lottie Arthur said, nodding her head in his direction.

Elmer Baxter crossed his arms and leaned back. "I have it on good authority that not only was Miss Albright in an illegal speakeasy, she was also found in a room for prostitutes."

Esther watched all of the color drain from her father's face. It had been late last night when they had returned from dinner at the Mallory's home, and her father had already been out of the house when Esther came downstairs this morning. He hadn't returned before she'd left for work, so she'd assumed they would have their talk tonight over dinner. She hadn't had a chance to tell her father her entire story.

"Is that true, Reverend?"

Her father sat quietly for a moment, then took a deep breath. "She has admitted to being in the speakeasy. This is the first I have heard of the other."

"She admitted it! How did you punish her?"

"There's been no punishment. Yes, she admitted to being there, but we haven't had time to discuss it fully."

"What on earth is there to discuss?"

"I want to hear her side of the story. I have a hard time believing Esther would have anything to do with prostitutes."

"Oh yeah?" Elmer Baxter said, leaning forward in his seat. "Then why did I see her having lunch with a prostitute just the other day?"

"How do you know she's a prostitute?" Reverend Albright asked, leaning forward in his seat as well.

"She is a woman commonly known around town as a harlot!"

Esther clenched her jaw. *Around town, my foot,* she thought. Esther knew exactly how Elmer Baxter knew Rhonda's occupation.

"Oh dear," Mrs. Arthur said. She leaned back in her seat and fanned herself with her handkerchief. "Our own pastor's daughter, associating with a fallen woman."

"No wonder those two boys broke off their engagements to her. What good, upstanding man would put up with this kind of behavior? Who would want to be married to such a hussy?" another board member said.

The small gathering of board members erupted in murmurs and chatter. Esther wanted desperately to walk straight up to the group and tell them exactly what she thought of this entire tribunal, but she knew better. Interrupting a closed meeting that she was not supposed to be at would only worsen the case against her.

Reverend Albright cleared his throat. The board members quieted and looked at him. "I trust my daughter. If she says she's done nothin' wrong, then I believe her, and until she has told me her side of the story, I won't be passin' judgment on her."

"Well, Reverend, I'm not so certain I trust you to be the proper person to handle your daughter."

"What's that supposed to mean?"

"I mean, with the way you have been associating with unsavory people, I don't think you have the right perspective."

"Elmer, if you are accusing me of somethin', you'd best get to it, because I won't sit here and listen to you make idle accusations about me."

"Fine. I, as well as many other members of this congregation, have noticed how much time you spend with people of an unsavory nature. Sinners and heathens of all sorts. People that don't even attend church here. People that don't tithe to this church, either, I might add."

"Are you telling me that you're upset I'm reaching out to the lost?"

"Reaching out to the lost is one thing. Spending all your energy on those who would pull you into their world of sin is quite another. Many of us have noticed how little time you spend calling on the members you already have, tithe-paying members. The people of this church pay your salary, or have you forgotten that?"

"No, Elmer. I haven't forgotten that," Reverend Albright said coolly.

"I'm beginning to think that the issue we have with your daughter is more of a symptom to a much larger problem."

"And what problem is that?"

"That it might be time we started looking for a new shepherd for our little flock here at First Church, one who understands the needs of our people, rather than ignoring them altogether."

Esther stopped breathing. The look of absolute defeat on her father's face as the board once again began muttering tore her heart. This was all her fault, yet she had no idea how to fix it.

Winston Mallory rose from his seat. "Now, hear, hear. This is getting us nowhere. This meeting was called to discuss rumors we had heard about the Reverend's daughter, not the Reverend himself." He held up a hand to stop someone from interrupting him. "I'll not hear another argument until we settle this business about Miss Albright. Reverend Albright has said that he needs to speak with his daughter. The least we can do is give him time to do that. I say we adjourn and meet again in one week."

With half-hearted agreement, the gathering dispersed. When the room had mostly cleared, Winston Mallory laid his hand on her father's shoulders and spoke, but Esther could not hear what he said. She saw her father nod his head, then the senior Mr. Mallory followed the rest of the board members out of the back of the sanctuary.

Esther watched as her father rested his head in his hands. She had never seen him look so defeated.

Dear God, please help me to fix this, she prayed silently. She quietly stepped backward toward the back stairwell.

"You can come in now, Esther," her father called from the sanctuary.

~

SHE RETRACED her steps and slowly opened the door off the side of the choir loft. "How did you know I was here?"

"I heard the downstairs door creak open. Since only you and Phoebe know where the key is hidden, and Phoebe is hundreds of miles away, it wasn't hard to figure out."

"I'm sorry. I know I shouldn't have eavesdropped."

"Come. Sit," her father said, ignoring her apology.

Esther did as her father said, descending the few stairs of the platform and sitting in a pew opposite his chair. She expected to find him angry, but his blank expression was worse than any angry stare.

"Is it true?"

Esther folded her hands in her lap and sat ramrod straight. Her heart was breaking for her father right now, but she refused to have a repeat of last night's argument. "Are you willing to listen to my entire story, or are you going to fly off the handle and refuse to listen to me?"

Her father crossed his arms across his barreled chest. "Alright, girl. I'll listen, if you promise to tell me everything. I don't want to be blindsided like I was tonight ever again, you hear me?"

"I understand, Daddy, and I would have told you everything before. And, if you had told me about this meeting, I would have left work early so you wouldn't have been blindsided."

"Are you tellin' me there's truth to what Baxter is sayin'?" he asked, shock evident by his gaping mouth.

"You are getting angry, but you promised to listen to me."

"Well, then, child, I suggest you get to it, because I've had a long night of holdin' my temper. I'm doin' the best I can."

Esther dove straight into her story, beginning with Richard and ending with her visit to save Katie.

"Daddy, the man I barged in on was Mr. Baxter. He was in the brothel as a customer. He's the 'source' that saw me there."

Reverend Albright rested his elbows on his knees and rubbed his eyes with the heels of his hands. He said nothing, just continued to rub whatever image Esther had given him away from his mind.

"Daddy, say something," she said softly. "Are you angry?"

"Yes, but I'm not sure who I should be angry with." He stopped rubbing his eyes and sat up, looking at his eldest daughter. "Honestly, girl, I don't know whether to throttle you or pat you on the back. I'm so angry that you did all that without tellin' me. Why didn't you trust me enough to tell me what was goin' on?"

"You were out of town, but even if you had been here, you would have been angry."

"Of course, I would have been, but at least you wouldn't have gone on your own. What if John hadn't shown up?"

"I'm afraid to think about it."

"As well you should be! Good grief, girl! What were you thinkin'?"

"I was thinking that Katie was in trouble. Don't tell me you wouldn't have done the same thing if you were in my place."

Reverend Albright sighed. "Of course, I would have. You know that better than anyone, because you are my girl, one hundred percent." He smiled sheepishly at her. "You may look like your momma, but inside, you're all me."

Esther laughed. "I'm so glad it's not the other way around."

Reverend Albright threw his head back and laughed heartily. "You'd do fine with your momma's temperament, but lookin' like me wouldn't make you too pretty, now would it?"

The two laughed for a moment. Esther knew that statement wasn't completely true, since her sister Phoebe, with her dark hair and brown eyes, favored their father, yet Phoebe was a beauty. But it was still funny to imagine her father in feminine form.

"Well, Daddy," she said, rising. "We best get home for supper before Mother begins to worry."

"One more thing," he said as he stood. "What about that last bit Elmer was talkin' about - you havin' lunch with a prostitute. Was he talkin' about Katie? I thought you said she never prostituted herself?"

"No. He wasn't talking about Katie. He saw me at Steuben's Diner with Rhonda, a *former* prostitute. She is a friend of Katie's who wanted to leave that life but had no one to turn to. She sought me out for help. We had breakfast and I helped her get a job at The Journal. She is doing splendidly, Daddy. I'm still trying to convince her to come to church, but she's afraid she'll be judged. After tonight's meeting, I'm not so certain she won't."

Reverend Albright grabbed his daughter by the shoulders. "Well, praise God, darlin'! Look at how God is using you to further His kingdom!"

"I only helped a woman in need."

"Exactly. Think about it, sweetheart, if you hadn't made all the choices you've made over the past few months, that girl wouldn't have known anything about you. She wouldn't have had anyone to turn to when she needed someone. But God put you within reach of her, just because you were willing to go somewhere that most Christian women wouldn't have dared go. God's given you a ministry, child."

"A ministry?"

Tears brimmed in the big man's eyes. "Yep, a ministry. You've done somethin' I could never have done. Do you think if I would have gone there and dragged Katie out of that mess that this Rhonda would have came lookin' for me? Never in a million years. I'm a man, a minister at that, and that poor girl's experience with men is not what it should be. I'll bet she hasn't had a man in her life she could trust in years, if she ever did. But a woman, one about her age, now there's someone she could feel comfortable with. Esther, God has opened a great door of opportunity for you. Do you think there are other girls like Rhonda looking for help?"

The sight of his tears brought some tears to Esther's eyes as well. Her hair stood on end as she thought about his question. "I never thought about it, Daddy, but I'm sure there are. You're right. This is a mission field. But, how on earth can I find these women? The speakeasy has been raided and closed down."

"You don't," he smiled knowingly. "But I bet Rhonda knows where to find 'em."

A feeling unlike anything she had ever felt coursed through Esther's veins. Yes, of course there were other girls like Rhonda. Girls who were lost and had no one to care about them or reach out to help them. They needed someone, and although she had no idea what she was going to do or how she would go about it, she wanted nothing more than to be that someone.

27

GOING HOME

"So, you told your father everything?" John asked incredulously.

"Everything," Phoebe said.

John frowned for a moment. "What exactly did you tell him about the kiss?"

Phoebe laughed. "I thought you told him about the kiss."

"No, well, not entirely. I did admit to it, but I didn't offer any details."

"Well, I'm glad to hear that," she laughed again. "I didn't mention the kiss. He knows it happened. I don't think it's necessary to tell him that I brazenly took a cab to your apartment unchaperoned for a passionate exchange."

It was John's turn to chuckle. "No. I don't think that's necessary."

She squinted at him. "Are you blushing?"

"I think one of us should be! Good grief, doesn't anything embarrass you?"

"I'm not sure. I'll let you know if I come across anything," she said with a wink. She flounced toward the door. "Now, boss, if there isn't anything further you want from me, then I will return to my desk."

John came up behind her and placed his hand on the door. "There is something I want from you," he said huskily in her ear.

She kept her back to him but turned her head slightly in the direction of his face. "Why, sir, whatever could you mean."

"Turn around, and I'll show you."

His heart beat wildly in his chest when, much to his surprise, she did just that. Slowly. The torture was almost unbearable to him as she took her time facing him, but when her mischievous green eyes finally rose to meet his, he knew he would wait however long it took to be this near to her. His free hand reached up to cup her face and, with just as much leisureliness and deliberateness, he traced the contour of her cheek with his thumb. If she wanted to play this torturous game, he was more than willing to give her as much grief as she was giving him.

When he thought he couldn't take the torment another minute longer, he dipped his head toward hers. A loud knock on the door behind her caused Phoebe to jump, and rather than lips meeting lips, Phoebe's forehead connected with John's nose.

"Ouch!" John exclaimed.

"Oh, no!" Phoebe said, delicately reaching her fingers toward the hand clutching his nose. "I'm so sorry, I didn't mean -"

Her words were interrupted by another knock, this one louder and more urgent.

"Mr. Ward! Mr. Ward, are you in there?" Katie called from the other side.

John looked at Phoebe with knit eyebrows, but she only shrugged. Why would Katie be looking for him?

Phoebe stepped aside and John opened the door.

"Yes, Miss Feegle. What can I do for you?"

Katie spotted Phoebe immediately.

"I'm so glad you are both here. She asked for Mr. Ward, but I'm sure she'd want both of you to come. Hurry. We must hurry," the woman said frantically.

"Katie, stop!" Phoebe called, following the woman out of John's office. "What are you talking about? Who are you talking about?"

Katie whipped around to face them again. "Mrs. Caffey. She's not well. I tried to get her to go to the hospital, but she refused. She just told me to come get Mr. Ward, and said he would know what to do."

"What's the matter with her?" Phoebe asked.

"I don't know. She was well last night, said she was just a little worn out, but this morning, she's in an awful state. She has a fever and is having trouble breathing."

Phoebe whipped around to face John. The look on her face was a perfect representation of the dread he was feeling.

"I'm sure everything is fine," he reassured her, despite his own fears. "I'll speak with Warren about taking his car to check on her." John gave the women his most confident smile, even while he battled his own doubts. "Remember, Mrs. Caffey is a strong, healthy woman. I'm sure she's just eaten something that didn't agree with her. She'll probably be all better by the time we get there."

But, when the three arrived at the little yellow house, Mrs. Caffey wasn't better. She had grown worse.

The two women entered the bedroom first. John almost knocked Phoebe over in his rush to enter. She had stopped and stood frozen. John caught himself in time, then followed Phoebe's path of vision. He stopped breathing all together when he saw what had caused Phoebe's paralysis. Mrs. Caffey lay on her bed, barely breathing. Her skin was an odd bluish shade and her cheeks had unmistakable telltale spots on them.

Although he had never seen it in person, he had seen enough news reports to know what he was looking at — the Spanish Flu.

John and Phoebe's eyes locked and he knew that she recognized the signs of the disease as well. He didn't know what to say. He didn't know what to do.

"Mr. Ward, do something," Katie cried, tears coursing down her cheeks. "She said you would know what to do, so do something." Her body trembled as she choked out the last words.

John looked at Katie's tear stained face, then down at the buttons pulled tight across her belly, a reminder of the new life growing within her. He turned back to Phoebe.

"Get her out of here," he commanded, pointing at the woman's newly distended belly.

Phoebe turned to her friend and a small cry escaped from her. "Katie, you shouldn't be here. The baby!"

"I'm not leaving! She needs me!"

"There's nothing you can do," Phoebe argued, grabbing Katie by the arms.

"What do you mean? What's wrong? What are those spots? She didn't have them when I left. I should never have left her. I should have - "

"You must go," John said sternly. He grabbed Katie by the arm and pulled her back to the front entry.

"I don't understand," Katie cried hysterically.

John turned her to face him and shook her a little. "Listen to me. You and your baby are in danger. Mrs. Caffey isn't just a little sick. She has the Spanish Flu, and it doesn't look good."

All color drained from the woman's face as she stared open mouthed at John.

"No, oh no. My baby!"

"You must leave," he said, then turned back to Phoebe. "Take her to your parents, then come back with a doctor. And hurry."

Phoebe nodded, tears brimming on the lashes of her eyes. "She has to get better. She can't die."

"You must pray. That's all I know to do."

Phoebe took the keys to Warren's car and rushed Katie out the door.

John stood staring at the closed door, but his mind was no longer in the little house. It was thousands of miles away in the battlefields of France.

"God, I know I don't have any right to ask you for anything. You've already given me so much more than I deserve, but I beg you. Don't take her. Not before Will gets home. Make her well, Lord."

'Those who walk uprightly enter into peace; they find rest as they lie in death.'

"No, please. I don't want to hear that." Of all the times for the scriptures of his youth to resurface, now was not a welcomed one. "Will has been through too much, suffered too much in that disgusting war. Please don't take his mother away."

'My grace is sufficient. My power is made perfect in weakness.'

Before John could argue with God again, he heard a weak voice call to him. He rushed down the hallway and found Mrs. Caffey awake in her bed. He knelt beside her.

"I'm here," he said gently.

"John, I'm going home," she said with a weak smile. Her eyes were glazed over and she stared at the ceiling.

"Try not to talk. You need your energy if you're going to fight this."

"I'm done fighting, son. I'm going home."

"You're just confused, ma'am. You're already home."

Mrs. Caffey turned weakly toward John's voice, but he wasn't certain she saw him or even understood who she was talking to.

"No, John. I'm going home. I'm going to be with Jesus."

She had such a peace about her, such a calmness, that although John wanted to argue with her, to demand that she fight for her life, he knew it was pointless. She was going home, and she was happy to be going.

"Yes, ma'am," he choked. He felt a tear fall on the hand that held hers and realized he was crying. Mrs. Caffey reached a weak hand up and touched his cheek.

"You know, Will loves Phoebe."

John's breath caught in his throat. "Yes. He's told me."

"They'll make a lovely couple. They both love God so much. I'm so happy for them."

John didn't answer her. Why argue with a dying woman?

"Is Will here?" she asked, frowning at John.

"No, Mrs. Caffey. Will's still in France."

"Oh, that's right," she said. She turned her head back toward the ceiling. Her breath became more labored. "John, will you tell my boy that I tried waiting, but it was too hard..." She coughed then wheezed. When she could breathe again, she asked, "Will you tell him that?"

"Of course."

"Tell him I'm with his father, and I'm alright. Will you tell him that, too?"

"Yes, ma'am. I'll tell him everything."

The woman nodded and smiled.

"Tell Phoebe I love her as well. My, how I miss that girl."

John rested his head on their joined hands, willing what strength he had within him to flow to her. Mrs. Caffey had grown delirious. He knew it wouldn't be long now.

"And Esther," Mrs. Caffey continued. "Esther deserves happiness, too. Is Esther here?"

"No, ma'am," he said.

"Tell Esther that I love her, and that God has a special plan for her."

"I will." John had no idea who she was talking about, but he would say anything to ease the woman's pain.

His words seemed to calm her and her breathing, though labored, settled into a peaceful rhythm. Once or twice he thought she had stopped breathing, but she would cough, a horrible, gurgling sound, then settle back into the peaceful, heavy breathing.

It felt like hours before Phoebe returned with the doctor. Reverend Albright was also by her side. John had never met this doctor, but prayed he could work some sort of miracle. But, within moments of seeing her, John saw the same sad, defeated look on his face that he was certain graced his own.

After listening to her heart and taking her pulse, he looked up at the three of them and just shook his head. A small cry escaped Phoebe and John jumped to his feet to catch her before her knees gave out. John held her close as she sobbed uncontrollably.

With a quiet grace that seemed so strange for such a large man, yet so appropriate at the same time, Reverend Albright walked around to the other side of the bed and sat on its edge.

"Bessie, you're pretty sick," he said softly.

Mrs. Caffey reached up and patted the minister on the shoulder. "I know, James. But for just a little longer. Jesus is taking me home, then I'll be all better."

"I know, I know," he said. John watched a single tear fall down the man's cheek and onto the bedspread. "Do me a favor, will ya?"

She nodded silently.

"Tell that husband of yours when you see him that he still owes me a fishin' trip. I gotta believe there's some pretty good streams up there."

"You tell him yourself," she said, smiling. "We'll be waiting for you."

The minister chuckled and nodded his head.

"I'm going to see Jesus," she said softly.

"You go to him, Bessy. Don't mind us. We'll all see you real soon."

"James?"

"Yes."

"Tell Will I love him."

"I will, but he already knows it, darlin'."

And that's how it ended, the life of Elisabeth Caffey, smiles and jokes, and expressions of love.

ESTHER WRENCHED herself from John's arms and ran out of the room. This couldn't be happening. She had to get away.

She threw open the door but made it no farther than the front porch before her strength gave out. She threw herself against a column and wrapped her arms around it. She sobbed uncontrollably, and she didn't care how she looked or who saw her. Her eyes stung, and she squeezed them tight, hoping to block out the world around her.

The events of the morning seemed surreal. Mrs. Caffey couldn't be dead, she just couldn't. She must be dreaming. But even as Esther cried out to God to wake her from this horrible nightmare, the pain in her chest told her that this was no nightmare. This was real. Painfully real.

A touch on her shoulder brought her back to reality. Without opening her eyes, she turned and fell into the waiting arms. Recognizing his cologne, Esther knew before her tear-stained face hit his strong chest that it was John.

"She can't be gone. This isn't real," she sobbed against him.

She felt his hands gently rub her back as his husky voice offered words of encouragement.

"I know," he said. "I know it hurts."

"How could God do this? How could he take her? She is

such a good person, so loving, so kind. How could he let her die? She didn't deserve this."

"Deserve this? She didn't see this as a bad thing. Why should we?"

Esther pushed back from John and opened her eyes. His own blue-gray ones stared back at her, red and puffy. John was crying as well.

"I can't see this as a good thing. Her dying...that's not a good thing. I don't want to lose her."

"I don't either," he said. "But I wouldn't keep her from heaven for selfish reasons."

Esther hadn't thought about that. Yes, she wanted Mrs. Caffey back, but she knew Mrs. Caffey was in heaven now. No matter how much she hurt, she would never wish her to be pulled away from paradise.

"Didn't you hear her in there?" John continued. "She's with Jesus now. Did you notice the peace that settled over her when she talked about Him?"

Esther had noticed. Mrs. Caffey always had a certain joy about her when she spoke of Jesus, but today, on her deathbed, that joy was mixed with such an unexplainable peace. A peace Esther had never seen before, and remembering it warmed her aching heart.

"And she couldn't wait to be with her husband," John said.

Esther smiled a little. "She's lived so many years without him. I know she has missed him."

John nodded. "I wasn't with my father when he passed, but I know he didn't have the peace, nor the enthusiasm for going, that Mrs. Caffey did. We can be grateful for that."

Esther reached up and wiped a slow-moving tear off his cheek. She didn't know what to say. John had been through so much, so much more than she'd ever had to endure. Anything she thought to say sounded so trivial.

"I never thought I could feel love for another person, especially a woman," he said. His gaze was no longer fixed on her but stared intently at nothing in particular on the deck of the front porch. "When I first met Will's mother, I wanted nothing more than to fulfill an obligation to Will. But, within the first few minutes, I was drawn to her. I tried to fight it, tried to keep her in the same category as my own mother, but no matter how hard I tried, I couldn't distance my feelings for her. I came to love her. Does that sound silly?" He looked at her, tears once again forming on the brims of his lashes.

"Not at all," Esther whispered.

John shook his head. "But, every woman I have ever loved, God has taken away."

"But you have your mother once again."

"For how long? God could take her from me tomorrow."

"Nothing in this life is for certain. All we can do is appreciate the time we have with those we care about."

John didn't seem to be listening. "Maybe it would be easier if I didn't allow myself to love."

Esther gasped. "Don't say that."

"First, Mrs. Caffey wormed her way into my heart, then you. Now, God has taken her from me. What if he takes you as well?"

Esther clutched the lapel of his jacket. "I'm not going anywhere! John Ward, you listen to me. I love you. Do you hear me? And I'm not going anywhere!"

John's arm snaked around her waist and he brought his lips to meet hers. Tears fell down both their cheeks, but Esther didn't mind the saltiness of the kiss. In her heart, she knew the words she had just spoken were the truth. She was in love with John Ward. She loved him like she had never loved another man before, and she knew that no matter what life threw their way, nothing would change that love. She was now and forever his.

28

WILL

John rocked back and forth on his heels while he waited for the train. He had decided he didn't like Michigan in November. Its gray skies and cold winds chilled not only a man's fingers, but his soul as well. But, he rationalized, the weather alone may not be the reason for his melancholy mood.

Will's train was late, but John wasn't disappointed. As eager as he was to see his friend home, safe and sound, the arrival of the man brought no small amount of anxiety to John.

It had been a surprisingly simple task locating Will. The War Department had known exactly where he was, probably due to the heroics he was carrying out for them in France. In less than a day, John had received a telegram from Will saying he was on his way home.

It killed John knowing that his friend had received the news of his mother's death while on the frontline. That's the kind of thing a man should hear from a friend, especially someone like Will, a good man who deserved better than what life had given him lately. The silver lining to the cloud, if one could be found, was that Will was able to come home and leave the horrors of war behind him, even if only for a little while.

John's guilt over Will's circumstances was only worsened by the knowledge that he would have to reveal to his best friend that he had stolen his girl. He hadn't spoken to Phoebe about it, although he had tried, but the days since Will's mother's death had been so busy, with preparations for the funeral and his responsibilities at the paper that he and Phoebe had not had a single moment alone. And John had tried. Hard. And not just to discuss Will, but since their encounter on the front porch of Mrs. Caffey's house, when Phoebe had confessed her feelings for him, John had wanted nothing more than to be near her, to drink in her beauty, and, if he were to be honest, kiss her perfectly shaped lips. Never had he felt this way before. But Phoebe was different. Phoebe's heart belonged to him. And, he was almost certain, she owned his heart just as fully.

In the distance, a long, black train chugged toward the station. John decided that he wouldn't say anything to Will about Phoebe until after the funeral. Let the man deal with one heartbreak at a time. He couldn't imagine that Phoebe would say anything to Will about it, either. The next couple of days would be about supporting Will in his mourning, not gushing about a new relationship. And if she did, John thought, maybe that was for the best. Maybe it would be better for him to hear it from her, knowing how he had built up such a fantasy about his future with her. Maybe hearing it from her personally was the only way to bring Will back to reality.

The train screeched to a stop. John hung back while throngs of people crowded the platform, eagerly seeking loved ones departing the train. He scanned the cars, looking for any sign of Will. He finally caught sight of a soldier dressed in doughboy khaki exiting one of the last cars. The soldier stepped onto the platform then reached up to assist a woman. John watched as he reached up and again gave his hand to another woman, and then another.

"Typical," John said under his breath. He chuckled and made his way through the crowd toward his friend.

By the time he'd made it to the end of the platform, the crowds had thinned. Will smiled when he caught John's eye, and John felt a swelling in his heart he wasn't accustomed to.

"Johnny," Will said, before clasping John in an embrace.

They stood there, two grown men, embracing one another in public, but neither of them cared. John could feel slight vibrations coming from the other man. John tightened his grip.

"Were you with her?" Will asked brokenly.

"Yes," John said, his voice raspy as well.

"Did - did she suffer?"

"No. It was very peaceful. She wanted me to tell you that she loved you and that she is with your father now."

John felt Will's body relax as he let go of emotions he had most likely been holding inside for days. John clasped him tighter as he sobbed, wishing he could take away his pain.

After several moments, Will's crying subsided, and he pulled away. He wiped his face with the back of his sleeve and smiled weakly.

"You'd think I'd be a little more hardened by now," Will chuckled.

"I'd be disappointed if you were. Don't be embarrassed. I've done my share of crying since she passed. A good woman like her is worth crying over."

Will's eyebrows shot up. "That doesn't sound like the John Ward I know."

John smiled and clapped him on the shoulder. "I'm not the same John Ward."

"Please tell me that means what I pray it means."

John nodded as a lump formed in his throat. Where had all

these emotions come from? "I'm a new creation, Will. You were right. Lansing was just what I needed. I found God here."

Before John could protest, Will grabbed him again and wrapped him in another embrace. Both men cried once more, but this time, the tears were founded in joy.

When the men eventually separated, Will reached for his haversack and threw it easily over his shoulder.

"They're much lighter on this side of the pond," John remarked, indicating the army-issued bag.

Will nodded. "Yeah, without my shelter half and other gear attached, I hardly know I'm wearing it."

The two men made their way off the platform toward a cab waiting on the street. John gave the driver the address, but Will interrupted him.

"I want to go to the Albright's. I'm not ready to go home."

John gave the driver the address and looked away, hoping his face didn't betray the momentary dread he felt. Of course, John realized, Phoebe would be the first person Will would want to see. However, John wasn't certain he could handle the guilt of watching his best friend get rejected by the woman he loved. Maybe it wasn't right for John to keep the truth about his relationship with her from Will. John owed him his life. The least he could give Will in return was the truth.

"Will —" John began.

"How did you find me so quickly?"

John turned to find Will staring blankly out the window, his face pallid. He looked completely spent.

"It helps that you're on the list to receive the Medal of Honor. Seems your escapades have had you in the War Department's sights for some time. They knew exactly where to find you. Tell me, did you really capture 110 Germans at one time?"

Will shrugged. "Not single-handed. There were other men."

"Other men aren't being awarded the Medal of Honor."

"They should be," Will said, staring off at the passing buildings. "Every single man over there should receive some sort of medal or something for enduring the anguish."

John nodded in agreement. "No one here truly understands, except former soldiers. The government has the news from the front so tightly controlled, nobody stateside has a clue what our boys are really going through."

"I'm glad," Will said. He turned back to look at John. "I'm glad my ma didn't know what I was going through. I couldn't have handled her knowing the truth."

The trip from the Michigan Central Railroad Depot to the Albright's home was not a long one, and the two men finished the ride in silence until the car pulled up in front of the two-story parsonage.

Will had barely stepped out of the vehicle when the front door opened, and Phoebe came rushing down the front porch stairs. John watched as Will dropped his pack and rushed forward to scoop her in his arms and lift her off the ground. Phoebe's arms were wrapped tightly around him, and her face was buried in his shoulder, but John could still make out her words.

"Oh, Will. I've been so worried. I'm so glad you're home safe. I've missed you."

Something in John's gut twisted. He couldn't hear Will's words. His words didn't matter. The sight of Phoebe in Will's arms, the tears coursing down her cheeks, her words "I've missed you," spoken so lovingly, it all caused more pain than any bayonet could ever inflict. John turned to the cab driver.

"Hold on a minute."

Within moments, Sarah, Mrs. Albright and the Reverend joined Phoebe.

"Good grief, girl, let the boy breathe," Reverend Albright laughed.

"Yes, it's my turn," Mrs. Albright said, pulling Phoebe aside. "Oh, look at you! How handsome in your uniform!"

While Mrs. Albright fawned over Will, Phoebe moved to John's side. His head had begun to pound. He was afraid to look at her, worried to see the look of regret - regret for declaring any affection toward him, yet desperately needing to see if it was true. But, he knew it must be. How could she not realize what a mistake she'd made, John thought, now that Will was home.

"I haven't told him anything about us," he whispered without looking at her.

"I was just about to ask you not to," she whispered back. "It's probably best if we - "

"Don't say it," he interrupted. "You don't need to say it."

"John, I - "

He ignored her and stepped closer to Will.

"Sarah?" Will was saying. "You can't be Sarah. Sarah is a little twig of a girl. You, why you're almost a young woman."

The girl blushed, then hugged Will quickly before retreating to her father's side. John took the opportunity to speak.

"I'm going to go home now so you all can have some time catching up."

Everyone frowned.

"Why, John, you're one of the family," Mrs. Albright argued. "Stay. I've made a huge dinner."

"Thank you, but I really should be going."

"Nonsense," Reverend Albright said. "You'll want to catch up with Will as well."

"I will later. Thank you for the offer," he said. He tipped his hat and turned back to the waiting cab. He had just touched the handle when Will placed a hand on his shoulder.

"Everything alright, Johnny?"

When John turned to look at Will, he could see Phoebe standing behind him, a frown on her face. John nodded.

"It will be," he said. He offered Will a weak smile before climbing into the cab.

"Where to?" the cab driver asked as he pulled away from the curb.

"How long would it take to drive to France?" he asked, dropping his head to the seat behind him.

DINNER WITH WILL was a joyous occasion. Esther's mother's cooking was delicious, as usual, but it was the company that made the evening so enjoyable. Will had always been like a brother to Esther and having him home was nice, even if the circumstances for his return were anything but pleasant. However, when the conversation did turn to Mrs. Caffey, which it did most of the night, there was just as much laughter as there were tears.

"Do you remember that time that our mothers took us with them to the hat shop?" Will asked over dessert.

"I remember it!" Mrs. Albright said, looking not too happy. "I've never in my life been thrown out of a shop before that day."

"We weren't that bad," Esther laughed. "That salesgirl was just too uptight."

"I'd be uptight as well if three unruly children knocked over half of my hat stands in a blink of an eye."

Both Esther and Will burst out laughing at Mrs. Albright's angry face.

"I thought you were going to kill us," Esther said, trying unsuccessfully to stifle her laughter.

"I would have if Bessie hadn't intervened. I swear, that woman could sweet talk a lion out of eating her for supper. She couldn't seem to sweet talk the salesgirl, though."

"I remember her trying to set the stands back into place, but the salesgirl just shooed her out with the rest of us. Said she didn't want to see us ever again," Esther chuckled.

"And she didn't! We had to start shopping at the hat store across town."

"Well, we had to polish all the pews for that. It took us a whole week. Do you remember that, Will?"

Will nodded. "Yeah, but it was totally worth it. I'll never forget the look on Phoebe's face when that purple hat full of feathers landed on her head. I'd polish a hundred pews to see that again."

The stories continued well into the evening, but even through the laughter and the tears, Esther couldn't keep her thoughts from John. Something had obviously been wrong this afternoon, but she didn't know what. He had seemed distracted, distant even, when she'd drawn near to him. Then, when they spoke, he'd become upset. She had played her words over and over again in her mind, trying to figure out what she had said that would have bothered him, but she couldn't think of anything. All she had said was it was best to wait to tell Will, when the three of them were alone and could really talk. Surely, he couldn't be annoyed by her desire to wait until after the funeral to share their good news.

"Well, I'd best be going," Will said as Mrs. Albright cleared the dessert plates. He pushed away from the table and stood.

"I'll drive you home," Reverend Albright said, standing as well.

"Thank you, sir, but the walk will do me good. Besides, I think I need the extra time to prepare myself, you know, to be there without her."

"Will, dear, why don't you stay with us tonight. You could stay in Phoebe's room."

"It's fine, really. I have to face that empty house eventually. I'd rather do it tonight than after the funeral tomorrow."

"Are you sure you wouldn't like us to go with you?" Esther asked.

Will smiled. "Thanks, but no. But I would like to speak with you for a moment in private, if you wouldn't mind."

"Of course not," she said, rising and taking her coat from the coat tree near the front door. "I'll walk you out."

Esther stepped onto the front porch. The days were growing short, and although it was only early evening, the street lamps had already flickered on to illuminate the darkening night. Will, campaign hat once again atop his head, shrugged into his olive drab overcoat and shut the door behind them. He had changed somewhat, Esther mused, yet still the same Will.

"You look older in your uniform," Esther said. "I might not have recognized you had John not brought you directly to our front door."

Will nodded. "In some ways, I feel like I've aged twenty years. War will do that to you, I suppose."

"I'm glad that it hasn't changed you entirely. You're still the same old Will," she said with a smile.

"I'm glad to hear you say that. I would hate to think the war had changed me so much that I wasn't me anymore. I kind of like who I am," he said with a wink.

Esther chuckled. Yes. Same old Will.

The conversation quieted, and Esther watched as Will leaned on the porch post and fidgeted with the buttons of his overcoat. Will was seldom at a loss for words, yet he seemed unable to move the conversation forward.

"Will," she began, "there was something you wished to speak with me in private about?"

Will gave her a crooked smile and looked at her sheepishly. "I guess we didn't need privacy, I - well, I guess I didn't feel comfortable talking in front of everyone."

Now Esther's curiosity was piqued. What on earth would

Will have to say that he wouldn't want to say in front of her parents and Sarah?

He straightened to his full height and stared off into the distance.

"Is Phoebe coming home for my ma's funeral?"

"Oh, Will," Esther said, laying her hand on his arm. "Daddy tried desperately to get word to her. He reached out to the college, but the school is on fall break and Phoebe is traveling with a group of student evangelists. They said they would try to get word to her, but we haven't heard anything."

Will dropped his head and nodded.

"I know she would want to be here. Your mother was very special to her, just as she was to me. I'm so sorry."

"It's okay. I was just curious, that's all." He continued to stare at the boards of the porch.

Esther was confused. "Will, why didn't you want to ask my parents about Phoebe? Surely, they would have told you..."

As she spoke, Will lifted his eyes to meet hers. His brows arched sheepishly over his blue eyes. He said nothing, but his eyes spoke volumes.

"Oh," Esther said. A smile slowly spread across her face as she began to fully understand his meaning. She raised her own eyebrows in response. "Oh, I see."

"Right there is the reason I didn't want your entire family privy to this conversation."

"What? I don't know what you are talking about," she said, covering her mouth with her hand in a sad attempt to disguise her mirth.

"I would have received the same reaction from all four of you. One of you is bad enough. I don't need four Albrights busting my chops over it."

"That's not fair," Esther said, placing her hands on her hips. "Four Albrights, my foot. We both know mother wouldn't tease you for the world."

"That's true," Will agreed.

"But she would start making wedding plans immediately."

Will smacked himself on the forehead. "That would be worse!"

After they laughed for a few moments, Will once again grew serious.

"You have to promise me you won't tell your family I asked about Phoebe."

"I'll promise, but I think it's silly. They'll learn soon enough, since I assume you plan to eventually make your intentions known."

"Eventually, but eventually isn't right now. Right now has its own worries."

Esther sobered remembering what they all faced tomorrow. "Agreed. I promise. Your secret is safe with me."

"Thank you. Now, on to the second issue."

"There's more? I can't wait to hear what will follow your last revelation," she laughed.

"Not a revelation. A question. What's wrong?"

"Excuse me," she asked, confused.

"It's obvious something has been bothering you all evening."

"It's nothing," she said. How could she tell him she was bothered by John's attitude and departure that afternoon without revealing her feelings for him?

"Come on, you know it will make you feel better if you talk about it. It always does."

Esther smiled. Will had always been a good sounding board when life was a struggle. She wasn't ready to tell him about John, but there was another matter she wished to discuss with him.

"The church board met recently to discuss me."

"What does that mean, 'to discuss' you?"

"They met to discuss what they deem as immoral behavior."

Will crossed his arms and threw his head back in laughter. When he realized Esther wasn't laughing, he sobered.

"You're serious?"

Esther nodded her head. "It was terrible. I snuck in through the basement and eavesdropped from behind the choir loft door. I realize that would probably qualify as immoral behavior in and of itself, but I couldn't help myself."

Will held up his hands. "Whoa, now. Hold up. I don't understand. You're going to have to start at the beginning. What immoral behavior?"

"It's kind of a long story, and it's cold out here, but the short version is that I have made a couple of visits to a speakeasy." Esther waited for Will's response.

"Go on," he said calmly, staring at her intently.

"You aren't shocked? Disappointed? Appalled?"

"Should I be? You're the girl who knocked over the hats and let us all take the blame for it, after all," he laughed. "But, seriously, I'm not going to jump to conclusions. You haven't told me the whole story. Did you have good reason to be there?"

"Yes, well, I believe so."

"Would God condemn you for your actions?"

"Certainly not! I did nothing to destroy my testimony."

"Well, then why would I, or anyone else, condemn you if God wouldn't?" he said matter-of-factly. "What did they say when you told them your side of the story?"

"They never asked for my side. They just made assumptions... completely false assumptions."

"They didn't ask you, but you were there. Didn't you interrupt them and tell them the truth?"

"No, of course I didn't. I'm not a board member. I wasn't supposed to be there."

Will placed his fists on his hips. "Let me get this straight. You were there. They were talking about you, but they had the story wrong. Yet, you did nothing about it? That doesn't sound like the Esther I know."

Listening to Will's plain but keen words, Esther had to agree. It didn't sound like the Esther she knew, either.

"It's getting cold, and it's late. You should get back inside. Tomorrow is going to be a long day. How about we talk after the funeral. I want to hear the whole story, but something tells me that we don't have time now."

Esther agreed, especially since John played such a large role in the story she wished to share with Will.

"Thank your mother for dinner again for me, will ya?" he said before nodding and bounding down the porch steps. He stopped and looked up at her. "You know, I thought you were upset about something entirely different."

"Oh, yeah? What's that?"

"I thought you were upset that ol' Johnny boy didn't join us this evening."

Esther gasped. Will smiled a huge grin, winked at her, and turned down the sidewalk, whistling a tune as he disappeared into the distance.

29

FUNERAL

*S*leep had eluded John for most of the night, so when the little slumber he was able to find was interrupted by a knock at his apartment door, he wasn't all that inclined to be kind to the young boy he found on the other side.

"Ernie? What the - " John caught himself. Old habits were hard to break. He took a deep breath to still his frustration. Ernie, a newsboy who occasionally ran errands for the paper, twisted his cap in his hands.

"I'm sorry, Mr. Ward, but Mr. Mallory sent for ya."

"In the middle of the night?"

"It's not the middle, sir. But it is pretty early. Come on, he said it was urgent. Sent me in his car with his driver and everything."

Warren had never summoned John from his home, so, whatever the reason, it must be important. He quickly dressed and followed the boy down to the waiting car.

When they arrived at the office, it was apparent that John wasn't the only employee called in early. Newsboys, sleepy eyed and sluggish, milled around, waiting for some sort of task. John

251

headed straight for Warren's office and was almost run over by Mr. Nichols, the typesetter, as he rushed from the room.

"Sorry, Mr. Ward," the man said as he pushed by John. He called over his shoulder. "Mr. Mallory sure will be glad to see you."

Warren Mallory rose from his desk chair and crossed the room when John entered.

"What's happening?" John asked.

Warren didn't respond verbally, just handed John a piece of paper. John read the words on the page. Then he read them again. After a third reading, he looked at his boss.

"Is this real?"

"Now do you see why I sent for you? I figured you'd want to be the one to write it."

John stared at the piece of paper as a smile broke across his face. God had answered everyone's prayers.

"Well, don't just stand there gawking. Nichols is already reworking the front page. I want to get the morning edition out as soon as possible. We need to be *the* paper everyone is reading today."

John lifted his eyes again and chuckled. "I've been waiting to write this article since I moved to Lansing. Give me half an hour."

"You've got twenty minutes."

John wrote it in fifteen. Never in his life had he been so keen to finish a story and see it in print. In his excitement, he hovered over Mr. Nichols as he prepared John's story for print on the front page and stood at the end of the press to collect the first copy. Without waiting for the ink to dry, he grabbed the paper and his coat and ran out.

The sun was just beginning to rise when he knocked on the Caffey's front door.

After several moments, the front door opened a crack. "Good morning, Mr. Ward," a startled Katie said.

"Katie!" The shock of seeing the pregnant woman in Will's home made John forget propriety. "I - I was expecting to see Will."

"He slept in the garage last night. I offered to go to a hotel, but he insisted I stay. Said he'd be just fine sleepin' in the garage."

"I'm sure it's a much better arrangement than what he's been accustomed to."

"But it's been so cold."

"I'm sure he's fine," John said, turning and heading down the front stairs.

"Tell him I'm leaving for the morning," she called out to John's retreating body. "I'm going to help Mrs. Albright with the funeral dinner preparations. There's coffee on the stove."

It took John's eyes a moment to adjust to the dim interior of the garage, but when they did, he saw no sign of Will. The garage was mostly empty, save the Model R parked in the middle of it. John peered in the car and found his friend curled up on the seat, his coarse wool overcoat serving as a blanket.

"You plan on sleeping the day away, soldier?"

Will jerked to an upright position, then slouched back in the seat when he saw John. "Good morning," he said sleepily. "I know you've missed me, but couldn't you have waited another hour or two to visit?"

"This couldn't wait," John said, happily shoving the early morning edition of the Lansing State Journal in front of Will's face.

Will read the headline then looked at John.

"It's over?" he said, smiling. "It's really over?"

"Yes sir. Wilhelm abdicated, and the new German government signed the armistice on the 11th. We did it, Will. We won."

Will whooped and threw the paper into the air. "It's over. The war is finally over!"

"And there's coffee on the stove. Let's get you inside where it's warm."

Once inside, the two men sipped coffee and discussed the end of the war that had brought them together.

"You know what this means?" John asked excitedly. "You don't have to go back. You're home for good!"

A shadow crossed Will's face. "Home for good," he said, rising from the kitchen table. He turned and walked into the sitting room. John followed him.

"This is what you've wanted. It's what you've prayed for, what we've both prayed for."

Will nodded. "Of course. It's an answer to prayer, but, it's just that, well..." he said, sweeping his arm across the room. "This doesn't *feel* like home, not without her."

John understood. "It will eventually. Maybe not today or tomorrow, but someday the mourning will end, and you will move on."

"But, it's not just that. Of course, I miss my ma, but being here, it just doesn't feel right. What is there for me here?"

"I could speak with Warren Mallory. I'm sure he could use a smart kid like you at The Journal."

Will smiled weakly at John. "That's your life, not mine."

"Well, then you have to find your life. Trust me, Will. There is life after war. If anyone knows the truth of that, it's me. You'll find work, you'll fall in love, start a family. This is just the beginning."

"But that's just it. I'm already in love. I'm not worried about finding someone and starting a life with them, because I've given that to God and I know he is working it all out according to His plan."

John said nothing, just stared at the ground. Images of yesterday — of Phoebe in Will's arms — played in his mind's eye.

"I guess it's my purpose that I'm struggling with," Will said.

"In France, I knew what I was doing. I was fighting for our country, protecting those I love. But I also found purpose in my dealings with the other soldiers. The war department may have sent me to a battlefield, but God sent me to a mission field."

Will walked to the small table that sat between his mother's and father's chairs and picked up a small framed photo of his parents and him when he was a small child.

"I remember when this was taken. I hated that suit. It was so scratchy," he laughed. "My dad always said that a man wore his identity in Christ the same way he wore a fine suit - proudly." He turned to John. "Who am I if I no longer wear the olive drabs of the U.S. Army?"

"Will, are you saying you're considering being a career soldier?"

"No, I don't think so. I wouldn't subject that life on any woman." Will replaced the picture on the table. "I wish Phoebe were here right now. She always has the right words."

Yes, she does, John thought.

"Well, that's enough worrying for now. How about some breakfast?"

"I really should head home and change before the funeral."

Will followed John to the door.

"Thanks for coming by, John. It really is good news. The war is over!"

John nodded and laughed. "The war is over. Praise God."

THE MORNING of Mrs. Caffey's funeral was cold and gray. *Even the weather is mourning the woman's death*, John thought.

He had taken his time readying for the funeral. He wanted to be one of the last ones to arrive in hopes of avoiding any conversation with Phoebe. He was still trying to process how he felt about having seen her and Will together, and he didn't want any of those same feelings resurfacing this morning.

For a man who had spent the majority of his life refusing to feel anything other than contempt, the past twenty-four hours had proven to be a whirlwind of emotional experiences for him - joy and anxiety at Will's return, devastation at the sight of Will and Phoebe's reunion, joy at the news of the armistice signing, and now sorrow as they prepared to put to rest Will's mother. John never thought it was possible for him to love anyone, but Mrs. Caffey had been the first person to break through his cracked barrier. And now, she was gone, leaving a sizable hole in his heart.

John slowly climbed the stairs of the brick-sided building, his mood growing as gray as the skies. He wasn't a happy man before he accepted Jesus into his life, that was for certain, but this side of salvation wasn't exactly a walk in the park, either.

Help me through this, Lord, he prayed.

'The Lord is nigh unto them that are of a broken heart.'

The inside of the church was more packed than the Sunday service John had attended. Every pew was filled. Will stood at the front of the sanctuary greeting those who had come to pay their last respects. He was dressed in his military uniform, not his Sunday best. John couldn't help but smile knowing that was exactly how Mrs. Caffey would have wanted it. She always said her boy was going to return home a hero. He only wished she had lived long enough to see it herself.

Will lifted a hand in greeting, then motioned for John to join him in the front pew. John politely shook his head and found a place to stand in the back of the room. Will motioned again, and John almost relented. But when he saw a slender hand reach up and grab Will's tunic sleeve, he stopped himself. He watched as Will took his place for the service, seated next to Phoebe.

Music filled the church signaling the start of the funeral,

but John didn't notice. He was too engrossed with the sight of Will and Phoebe sitting close to one another. It looked so perfect, his dark head lowered as he listened to the soloist, her fair head leaning close to him, whispering something. They really were perfect for one another, Will and Phoebe. John only wished he had realized that before falling in love with her.

In love. It was the first time he had truly admitted it to himself. Yes. He was in love with Phoebe Albright, and it hurt.

Reverend Albright took to the pulpit and began the eulogy. John tried to concentrate on his words, but his mind kept traveling back to the front row of the church. As the minister spoke, John watched Will lean forward and rest his head in his hands. His body began to shake, a son sobbing for the loss of his mother. A sharp pain shot through John's chest as Phoebe wrapped her arm across Will's back and laid her head on his shoulder.

John's gaze drifted over the others in attendance. Some he recognized, most he didn't, but each one of them had something in common - a love for Mrs. Caffey. They also had something that John did not have - a shared sense of belonging. These people belonged here, in this church, worshiping together, mourning together. John did not belong here. And he most certainly did not belong with Phoebe.

Yes, he loved her. He loved her enough to want her to have the best possible life. Will could give her that life. And Will deserved Phoebe. John did not. It had taken Will's return to make him see that. They would make a wonderful couple, and John was determined to no longer be a barrier between them.

He slipped out the back door as Reverend Albright prayed the closing prayer. He flipped the collar of his coat up to guard his neck from the cold. A wet iciness touched his nose. He looked up into the gray clouds that covered Lansing and was reminded of the scripture he had read that very morning:

'For as the rain cometh down, and the snow from heaven, and

returneth not thither, but watereth the earth, and maketh it bring forth and bud, so shall my word. It shall accomplish that which I please, and it shall prosper whereto I sent it.'

John nodded silently at the sky. He trusted God to see him through this. As painful as it would be, John no longer wanted to walk outside of God's will. If Will was God's plan for Phoebe, as both Will and Will's mother believed, then he must believe it as well.

John turned down the sidewalk and headed away from the church, and, he hoped, away from any feelings he had for Phoebe Albright.

30

WILL AND ESTHER

*E*sther gathered some empty dishes and bowls and carried them into the kitchen. A few mourners remained, milling about and offering Will words of condolence. She knew they all meant well, but Esther wished they would just leave already. It had been a long day and Will had been pleasant and attentive to each person all afternoon. After traveling a week to get home, surely, he could use some rest.

But as the last person left, Esther was surprised to see Will, tunic removed, walk into the kitchen, rolling up his sleeves.

"No you don't," she said, shaking her head. "You get on out of here, Will Caffey. I'll take care of these dishes."

"There's no reason for you to do all this on your own."

"Sarah will help me," Esther said, craning her neck to look out of the kitchen. "I just need to find her."

"She left with your mother. They are driving Mr. Peck home."

"Why didn't Daddy do that?"

Will pointed his thumb toward the parlor. Esther leaned out and saw her father in his chair, fast asleep.

"Hmph. I thought I heard snoring."

"Come on," Will said, shouldering her out of the way. "I'll wash. You dry."

"Really, Will. I don't mind. You should head home and get some rest."

"I'm not ready to go home," Will said.

Esther understood exactly what he meant. She remembered the emptiness she'd felt being in the house after Mrs. Caffey had passed. She slid over and picked up a towel.

"It's just not the same," he said and handed her a teacup to dry. "Besides, doing dishes sounds more relaxing that curling up in the seat of Dad's Oldsmobile for the night. Better than the cold, hard ground of Chateau-Thierry, but still not luxury."

Esther laughed. "Will, why on earth would you sleep in a..." Her hand flew to her mouth. "Katie! Oh, no! I didn't even consider...oh, Will. She can stay here so you can go sleep in your own home."

"She's already back at the house."

"Then you should stay here. Mother wouldn't hear of you sleeping in a car."

"It wasn't so bad. Besides, it would only be for one more night."

"Oh? Where is Katie going?"

Will scowled as he handed her a wet plate. "Nowhere. Do you really think I would put a pregnant woman out on the street?"

"Well, no, but you said..."

"I'm going somewhere."

"Where?"

"Your dad mentioned that a lot of the boys would stay at the State Constabulary barracks when they were home on leave. So, I stopped by there this morning before the funeral."

"But it's your house," she argued.

Will shrugged. "She and her baby need it more right now."

Esther nodded. "It's becoming obvious now, isn't it?"

"What? That she's with child? I'd say so. I'd also say it's time for some different clothes. She looked mighty uncomfortable today. What about Etta Curran? Didn't she and Harvey just have a baby? Maybe she could loan Katie some things?"

"That's a great idea. I don't know why I didn't think of it."

"So, tell me about Katie. How did my mother come to board a woman in her condition?"

How much should she tell him? She longed to tell Will everything, but how could she and still keep her relationship with John a secret? She decided to tell him as little as possible

"I introduced them. Katie was Richard's mistress."

Will dropped the cast iron skillet he had been scrubbing in the sink and scowled at her. "Richard? But you are friends with this Katie, aren't you?"

"I am now. He lied to her just as he lied to me. She was as much a victim as I was."

Will went back to scrubbing. "I never thought he was right for you. You deserve a much better man than that."

Esther nodded, but said nothing. They worked in silence for several moments. With the last of the guests gone, the mask Will had worn so bravely all day began to slowly slip away, exposing a face worn out by exhaustion and sadness. Esther wished she had words to soothe Will's pain, but Will had accepted countless words of sympathy and encouragement today from well-wishers to no avail. No. Will had heard enough words today. Silence was the best she could offer her friend in this moment.

"Phoebe would have liked the funeral, don't you think?" Will said, breaking the silence.

"Yes," Esther said sadly. Poor Will. In his deepest moment of mourning, the one person he wanted to comfort him was nowhere to be found. This loss was most likely made worse by the absence of his best friend. His brusque departure yesterday was rude, but not showing up for Mrs. Caffey's funeral was downright inexcusable.

"Yes. Phoebe would have liked it very much," Esther said, turning her thoughts away from John. "I fear she'll never forgive herself for missing your mother's funeral. She loved her very much."

"She's doing God's work. My mother would have expected nothing less. Neither do I."

Esther nodded. Mrs. Caffey would never have wanted Phoebe to leave the mission work to come home for her funeral. But that knowledge would be little consolation to her sister.

"You won't say anything, will you?" he asked without looking up from the tea cup he was washing.

"Say anything?"

"To Phoebe. It's really no secret how I feel, but knowing your sister the way that I do, I don't think she'll take too kindly to the entire family knowing my intentions before I've made them clear to her."

Esther laughed. "No, I don't suppose so. And you wouldn't want her to be upset with you. Once she is upset, it's really difficult to change her mind. She's kind of stubborn like that."

Will smiled and winked at Esther. "You leave that up to me. I can be pretty convincing when I want to be."

She laughed again. Yes, she was certain that if there were anyone in the world capable of breaking through her sister's hard exterior, it was Will Caffey. The thought warmed Esther's heart.

"I think I quite like the idea of having you as a brother-in-law. I mean, you're already family to us. It would just make it official."

"Then we'll just need to get ol' Johnny boy to propose, and the family will be complete."

When she whipped her head in Will's direction, she saw the

corners of his mouth twitch and she realized she had fallen into his trap. Any words of denial that had begun to form in her mouth faded away.

"So, I'm right. There has been some romance brewing between the two of you."

"I have no idea what you are talking about."

Will chuckled. "Oh, yeah? Look me in the eye and tell me nothing is going on."

Esther looked him straight in the eye. "I find John Ward to be one of the most stubborn, insulting, and patronizing men I have ever met in my entire life." Esther grabbed the wet bowl from Will and turned away.

Will laughed harder. "Now, that doesn't exactly answer the question I asked, does it?"

Esther continued to dry but said nothing.

Will eyed her for a few minutes more, then turned back to the dishwater.

"Alright, if you're going to be like that." He chuckled and shook his head. "But I couldn't be happier about the idea of two of my closest friends falling in love."

"Closest friend? Aren't you angry with him?"

"Should I be?"

"I would be. If my best friend didn't attend my mother's funeral, I'd be furious."

"He was there."

Esther stopped drying. "Where?"

"In the back. I saw him before the service began."

"I never saw him," she said angrily. "And what happened to him afterward? Least he could have done was make an appearance at the dinner."

Will shrugged. "I expect he had to get back to the paper on a day like today."

"Hmph. What's so special about today that couldn't be put off until tomorrow?"

Will finished rinsing the last plate and handed it to Esther. She was nearly finished drying it before she realized he was staring at her.

"What?" she asked.

"You don't know?"

"Know what?"

"I know today was a busy day and all, but surely you heard people talking?"

Esther placed the clean plate and hung the towel on the hook. "Talking about what, Will?"

Will rested his hands on his waist as a slow smile spread across his face.

"Out with it, Will Caffey! You look like the cat that ate the canary."

"It's over."

"What's over?"

"The war, silly. The war is over."

Esther just stared at him. "What did you say?"

"I said the war is over. News broke today that an armistice was signed on the 11th."

Esther clasped her hands in front of her. "Honestly? Will, this isn't anything to tease me about."

He grabbed her by the shoulders. "I would never tease about this. We won."

"Does that mean...you aren't going back?"

"Looks like it."

Esther threw her arms around his neck. "Oh, Will! I'm so happy. You're home for good! You must be thrilled!"

"You're choking me," he laughed.

She pulled back. "This calls for a celebration!" She opened the door of the refrigerator.

"I don't think I could eat anything..." Will said but stopped when he saw Esther pull out two plates, each with a slice of pie. "Except your mother's famous coconut cream pie!"

Esther giggled. "Mother put these aside before the dinner began...one for you and one for Daddy. She figured you would both be too busy to stop for pie before they were all gone." Esther peeked around the corner at her sleeping father. "And since he doesn't seem in the mood for pie..."

Will laughed as they both sat at the little kitchen table. He took a huge forkful. "Man, you don't get pie like this in the trenches."

"Well, you have many years ahead of you to enjoy my mother's cooking."

Will shrugged his shoulders. "If I stay in Lansing."

Esther stopped, fork halfway to her mouth. "Why wouldn't you stay in Lansing?"

"No reason, I'm just not sure what God's plan is yet."

"Don't be ridiculous. Of course, God's plan is for you to stay here."

"You're probably right," he said, shoveling in another forkful. "Sorry for my manners," he said between bites, "but this is so good, I can't slow down."

Esther chuckled. "How about some milk to wash it down?"

"Yes!" he said with a full mouth. "Another seldom seen luxury for a soldier."

Will polished off the last bite of his pie as Esther poured them both a glass of milk. He leaned back in his chair and rubbed his midsection.

"So, tell me about this other girl you met. What did you say her name was? Rhonda?"

"Yeah, Rhonda."

"What's her story?"

Esther took a sip of her milk. "What do you want to know? I don't know much about her past. Well, other than her previous, er, occupation."

"I'm not talking about her past. How is she doing now? Is she working out at the Journal?"

"Well, mostly. She is a hard worker...when she shows up."

"Does she miss a lot of work?"

"Some, but I don't know if she is completely to blame. She is trying to get on her feet and stays with friends until she wears out her welcome. It's hard to show up for work when you are constantly looking for another place to live."

"Why didn't my ma take her in?"

Esther looked at him, shocked. "I never introduced her to your mother. I figured I had already asked a lot of her by asking her to take Katie in."

Will eyed her as he took another sip of milk. "She should move in. I'm sure Katie could use the company."

Esther laughed. "Katie can't stay, Will. Especially now that you're home for good."

"I stopped by the State Constabulary this morning, remember?"

"But that's just temporary."

"More than temporary. They offered me a job."

"A job?"

"Yep. General Vandercook himself spoke with me."

"But, with the war over, there's no need to secure our state. What will you do?"

"Vandercook wants the state to make the constabulary a permanent fixture, a police force for the entire state."

"And who better to recruit than a young war hero?"

Will smiled and shrugged. "Something like that." He took his dessert plate to the sink. "I'll be in training for weeks, then after that, I could be sent anywhere in the state. It doesn't make sense for the house to sit empty."

"Anywhere in the state? But...what about Phoebe? What if you are stationed somewhere other than Lansing? What does that mean for you and Phoebe?"

Will sighed. "I don't know exactly. But I know that Phoebe is God's plan for me. I also know that taking Vandercook's offer, and giving my house up for the sake of those women, it all just feels...right."

"I don't understand."

Will rinsed his plate and turned to face her. "This Rhonda, and all the others like her...they need a place to stay. I want you to use my mother's house."

"And what if this constable job doesn't work out for you?"

"But that's the thing...I know that it will. Phoebe, the state constabulary...it all seems to be God's plan for me. A calling, in fact. I've never felt more certain of anything." Will returned to the table and picked up her empty plate. "And something tells me that you might have found your calling as well. My mother would've loved nothing more than for the home she loved to become a refuge for women that need a second chance."

Esther said nothing as Will washed and put her plate away, but his words rang over and over again in her ears. *Calling.* Could helping these women actually be a calling for her? They certainly needed someone to champion them in this world, and although she did not share their life experiences, she did understand what it felt like to be rejected. But who was she to take on such a responsibility? She was just a two-bit secretary with a temper who had a tendency to act before thinking.

For such a time as this. Queen Esther, the brave woman she was named for, must have felt inadequate for the task when faced with the responsibility of saving the lives of God's people. Yet, with prayer, she did just that.

Despite all Esther's questions and doubts, something deep inside assured her that it would somehow work out.

The idea felt...right.

31

GOODBYE

"**I**f I hadn't been there to witness it, I wouldn't believe you were ever injured," Will said. He pointed at John's leg. "Your limp is barely noticeable."

"Yeah, the doctor wants me to continue using the cane, but it's more of a hindrance than a help at this point."

The two men stepped out of Maudie's restaurant into the crisp, windy afternoon. John flipped the collar of his coat, his new habit to guard himself against the cold. Will seemed undeterred by the weather and John wondered if he would ever adjust to the harsh winters of Michigan. He shook his head, remembering that he wouldn't need to adjust.

"Hey, do we have time for a short detour?" Will asked. "I need to run into this shop for a second."

John unbuttoned his coat and pulled his watch out of his vest pocket. He still had plenty of time left before the afternoon edition went to press. He shrugged his shoulders and followed Will into the tiny store.

He hadn't paid attention to what shop Will was dragging him into, but the glaring reflection of the numerous glass cases filled with sparkling gems quickly brought John to his senses.

Will had brought him into a jewelry store. The acids in John's stomach began to roil. There was only one person Will would purchase jewelry for. It was hard enough living with the mental image of Will courting the woman John loved, quite another thing to watch the process begin.

"I really need to get back to work," John said, buttoning his jacket.

"This will only take a moment," Will insisted.

An older gentleman emerged from the back room. "Ah, Mr. Caffey. I have your necklace all ready for ya."

"Glad to hear it, Mr. Anderson. Was it difficult to repair?"

"Not at all. Just a broken clasp. The new one is much stronger, so you won't have to worry about it breaking too easily," the little fellow said cheerfully.

John watched as the jewelry store owner produced a rather plain, sturdy looking gold chain for Will's approval. Will paid the man, and John saw his friend pull something from his pocket and slide it onto the chain. He put the necklace on and unbuttoned his top collar to drop the chain inside his shirt but stopped when he saw the confused look on John's face. He pulled the necklace back out and held the trinket attached to it out for John to see.

"It's my mother's wedding ring."

"And you're going to wear it around your neck?"

"Yes, to keep her close to me, but only until I give it away," he said with a wink.

John winced. "Are you going to propose to Phoebe?" He felt the muscles of his chest constrict as he spoke the words and hoped they sounded more casual than they felt.

Will laughed. "Well, I think that's a little premature, but, yes, that's my hope, someday. Phoebe's the kind of girl that would appreciate receiving my mother's ring, rather than a new, trendy one. Sentimentality is far more important to her than modern fashion."

John's eyebrows furrowed, and he had to keep from shaking his head in response to Will's statement. Though he didn't doubt that the sentimental gesture would mean a great deal to Phoebe, he was shocked that Will was so oblivious to Phoebe's obvious bent toward stylish things, especially clothing and jewelry.

"I'm sure you two will be very happy." He could feel the muscle in his jaw flinch and he tried to force his mouth to relax. "Make sure you write to me all about it."

Will stopped dead in his tracks. "What do you mean 'write to you'? Are you going somewhere?"

John turned on the sidewalk to face his friend. "It's time. I'm ready to move on."

"Move on? What are you talking about?"

"With the war ending, Warren has a whole slew of men returning from Europe."

"Did he fire you?"

"No," John admitted. "He wants me to stay, but I said no."

"I don't understand. Where will you go?"

"I've got a connection in San Francisco. I figure I'll give the west coast a try."

Will crossed his arms and stared at the ground, scowling. "It doesn't make sense, Johnny. There's nothing for you there." Will lifted his eyes. "What about your mother? You've only just found her, and now you're going to leave her?"

"She's not happy, of course, but I've convinced her to visit once I'm settled. I'm hoping I'll be able to persuade her to stay in California once she's there."

"But her life is here. Her church is here, her friends." Will rubbed the back of his neck and shook his head. "John, your life is here. Your church. Your friends."

"I've never been one to put down roots, you know that Will. Surely, you must have known that this day would come."

"I had hoped Lansing would be different. I honestly thought

that once you were here, once you met the Albrights, once you met – ." Will stopped mid-sentence and looked apprehensive.

"Once I met who?" John asked.

"I guess it doesn't matter now. I just thought you would find, well, that you would find your home."

Home. John breathed in slowly. Never had a word sounded so appealing yet so unattainable at the same time. "Lansing is your home, Will. There's no place for me here."

Will just kept shaking his head. "And there's nothing I can say that will change your mind?"

"Just say that you will be the husband that Phoebe deserves and that you will be happy. That's all I want you to tell me right now."

Will raised an eyebrow at his best friend. "That's a strange request," he chuckled, "but, God willing, that is exactly what I plan to do."

"That's all I ask."

PHOEBE LAUGHED as she swept into the office. "I was just in the press room and I heard the most ridiculous rumor. The men down there seem to think you are going somewhere."

John paused merely a second at the sound of her voice, but quickly returned to packing the box on his desk.

"Wh-what are you doing?" he heard her say. The mirth was gone from her voice.

John refused to look up. He was afraid to. "I'm packing."

"What do you mean you're packing? Where are you going?"

"San Francisco. I got a job at The Chronicle."

"You can't be serious!" she huffed, a sound that sounded like the beginning of a laugh but fell short. John knew that sound. Reality was setting in. His chest constricted.

"Very serious. Never been one to pass up a good opportunity," John said, trying desperately to sound far calmer than he was.

John's packing was halted by the sound of his office door slamming behind him.

"You turn around and face me, John Ward!"

This was it. He knew this was the moment that counted most, and it was the moment he'd dreaded most. If he didn't pull this off, all would be ruined. He had to leave Lansing with no ties and leave Phoebe with no hope of a future with him.

He turned. "Is there something you need, Miss Albright?"

"Yes, there is, Mr. Ward...an explanation!"

Her eyes burned a hole into his soul and he nearly lost his nerve. But he loved her too much not to follow through with his plan.

Will's girl.

"What exactly would you like explained? I'm packing my belongings. I'm moving to California. What is so confusing?"

She stared at him, mouth agape, saying nothing for several moments.

"Were you planning to leave without speaking with me?" she finally said.

"It wasn't a plan, exactly. I just figured I'd see you on my way out the door. If not, I would have left you a note. I'm not a complete jerk."

She gasped. "Is that all I mean to you? A note left behind? I - I love you, John. I thought you loved me, too."

He couldn't take this. From the first moment he'd seen her in the speakeasy, he'd been captivated by her beauty, cheeks flushed, eyes blazing in anger. Then, the first time he'd seen her smile he'd thought his heart would never slow to a normal pace. But this...this was more than his heart could take. Her beautiful face...those green eyes furrowed, those delicate lips quivering...to see her beauty marred by such a look of anguish, an anguish he caused, broke him somewhere deep inside. Yet, even in her agony, she was still something to behold.

She was radiant.

He wanted nothing more than to protect her from the pain of this world, but here he was...the cause of her pain. How could he have done this to her? Why hadn't he kept his distance from her like he planned? Why had he fallen in love with her? Worse yet, why had he let her fall in love with him?

"I never said I loved you." It wasn't a lie, though John had never felt more deceitful in his life. He placed the last item in the crate. When he looked back at her, tears brimmed at the corner of her eyes. *Don't cry. Oh, please! Don't cry.* John swallowed hard and delivered the final blow. "Come, now, I'm not the first man to fool you into thinking you were loved."

John wanted to vomit as the words left his mouth, but the statement produced the desired effect. The tears dried as flames of anger jumped in her green eyes. *That's my girl*, he thought with pride. This was the Phoebe he loved, the spitfire that wouldn't take any guff from anyone. This is the Phoebe he'd wanted to face today... had needed to face today, because this is the Phoebe that would survive the hurt he was causing and would come out the better for it.

He saw her fists clench and unclench but was still caught off guard as her delicate palm sliced through the icy air of the office and connected with his left cheek.

"How dare you! You are the most repugnant, arrogant, loathsome beast of a man I have ever met."

With every fiber in his being, John longed to reach out and pull her against him and assure her he meant nothing he'd just said. Instead, he reached for the box, turned away from Phoebe Albright and everything she meant to him, and walked out of The Lansing State Journal.

32

CONFRONTING THE ENEMY

"*I*f it's going to snow, I wish it would just get on with it," Esther said with a shiver. She tightened her grip on her shoulders as she stared out of the bedroom window.

The unusually pleasant weather they had been experiencing of late seemed to have slipped away overnight, leaving behind clouds as gray as her mood.

"Don't take your anger out on the sky. It hasn't done anything to you."

Esther sighed. As happy as she had been to discover Phoebe in the parlor when she arrived home yesterday, she wished the timing had been better. All Esther wanted was a day or two to wallow in her sorrows. But that was near impossible with her sensible sister nearby.

"I can't help it. Winter is so...depressing."

Phoebe shrugged. "I don't have issue with it. It reminds me of Mrs. Caffey. She was always writing to me about the beautiful snow in her letters."

Esther's shoulders, and attitude, softened as she turned toward her sister. "Yes, she did love the snow. Funny how I forgot that."

Phoebe smiled weakly. "I feel terrible that I missed her funeral."

"We tried contacting you. The college said they would get the message to you post haste."

"Which was yesterday, apparently. I wish they would have told me the message was a week old. I read the note saying to come home immediately, and I did just that."

Esther sat on the bed next to her sister. "Like I told Will, his mother wouldn't have heard of you leaving your mission work for her funeral."

"I know, but had I known the funeral was over, I wouldn't have wasted the money on such a short trip."

"Do you really need to leave today?"

"I really do. I have to finish the semester early if I'm to join the evangelism meetings in Kansas City."

"You know you broke Mother's heart when you told her you wouldn't be home for the holiday break."

Phoebe sighed. "I know, but I prayed long and hard over this. I don't know why, but God told me I am supposed to do this."

"And you aren't scared to speak in front of all those people?"

"I'm more frightened than I have ever been! That's how I know it's God's will, because it certainly isn't my own desires chasing after this opportunity. I've prayed for God to shut the door on this, but he just keeps opening it wider and wider."

"Maybe he's training you for your future."

"I don't think so. I have no desire to be an evangelist."

"Maybe he's preparing you to be a pastor...like Daddy."

Phoebe laughed. "Hardly! I have a hard enough time stomaching the idea of speaking in front of a crowd, let alone all of the other things that come along with being a pastor. Honestly, all these boys I go to college with think they are ready to enter the pastorate, but they have no idea what that really means."

Phoebe's words were a chilly reminder of what was

happening next door, and Esther went to the window once again to watch yet another car pull up in front of the church. Five vehicles. Two more people to arrive, then the board meeting would begin. The meeting that would decide her father's fate at Lansing First Church.

"No," Esther said. "Unless you've been raised in a parsonage, you have no idea what being a pastor really entails...until you become one yourself, I suppose." She considered momentarily that she should share what was happening with her sister, but they had so little time together, and she didn't want to waste it with such an unpleasant discussion. She turned a smile toward Phoebe. "I don't suppose one of those ignorant, young pastors-to-be have caught your eye?"

"Goodness, no! I've said it before and I'll say it again, I didn't go to college to get married."

"Right. Why go to college for a husband when there's a perfectly good one waiting at home?" Esther said with a wink.

Phoebe chuckled. "What's that supposed to mean?"

"Oh, nothing," Esther said. "I just think your prospects are brighter here than at that stuffy college you've been sequestered at for the past three and a half years."

"Here? Doubtful! If that were true, how come you haven't snagged one of these 'bright prospects'?"

Esther knew her sister's words were only meant as a good-humored quip, but the newness of her broken heart was too raw for her to keep her emotions in check. Her chest constricted as the pain sliced through her heart once more. Esther leaned her head against the frame of the window as tears coursed down her cheeks.

Within seconds, Phoebe was by her side.

"I was only teasing. I didn't mean to upset you. Please don't cry. Richard isn't worth your tears."

Esther shook her head. "Richard is a dolt. I'm glad to be rid of him."

"Then why are you crying?"

"John."

"John? Who is John?"

"The man I'm in love with."

Phoebe's brows knitted over her dark eyes. "If you are in love, why are you so sad?"

"Because he doesn't love me."

"Then he is the dolt."

"What?"

"Any man who wouldn't thank the Lord for a woman as great as you is a fool."

"He's no fool."

"Did he actually say that he didn't love you?"

"Yes. Well, no, not in so many words."

"Then maybe you haven't given him enough time. I swear, some men–"

"He's gone."

"What do you mean, 'he's gone'?"

"He left. I told him I loved him, we kissed, and the next thing I knew, he'd accepted a job in California and left."

Phoebe led Esther back to the bed and sat, wrapping her arms around her as she cried.

"Romans 8:28," Phoebe whispered into the top of Esther's head.

Esther pulled back slightly and looked at her sister. "What did you say?"

"Romans 8:28. All things work together for good to them that love God, to them who are called according to His purpose."

"How is any of this good?" she asked in anguish, breaking into new sobs.

Phoebe pulled her sister back into her arms and rested her cheek on top of her head. "I don't know. And it breaks my heart to see you so hurt. But what I do know is that none of what is happening right now is a surprise to the Lord. And none of it is outside of His ability to use it for good."

Esther couldn't imagine how God could take her shattered heart and make anything good from it, but she had little time to consider her sister's words before the knocking on the front door interrupted the women.

"Your cab!" Esther said. "Your train! You're going to miss it!"

Phoebe sighed. "I suppose I could take the morning train."

"Nonsense," Esther said, rising and wiping her eyes with her handkerchief. "You have too much to do, isn't that what you just told me?"

"But that was before I knew...before you told me about what has happened. I can't leave you now."

"You can...and you must! Come now." Esther grabbed Phoebe's hand and pulled her off the bed. "You don't want to miss your train!"

"But Esther–"

"No! I'm fine. Or, at least I will be. But I won't be fine if I know I ruined your chance at being a part of the evangelism meetings in Kansas City. Now, get!"

Within minutes, Phoebe was waving frantically from the cab and Esther stood in the doorway, waving back, using all of her willpower to hold back the tears that once again threatened to fall. The car pulled away just in time and Esther quickly closed the door and let the tears come.

She wasn't certain how long she leaned there, tears falling freely down her cheeks, but after several moments, she straightened herself and wiped at her eyes again. She had just finished drying them when someone else was at the door knocking.

When she opened the door, she found Will on the other side.

"It's dinnertime. Thought I might stop by and see if your mother would like to invite me to stay."

Will's effervescent smile was contagious, and Esther found herself smiling back at her friend.

"I'm sure she would...if she were here. But she and Sarah are visiting shut-ins. They should be back soon if you'd like to come in. I'm sure whatever we have, there will be plenty for you as well."

"Great," he said, stepping inside. "I'll just visit with your dad. I haven't had much time to catch up with him."

Esther shut the door behind him. "He's not here either."

Will motioned toward the church. "He next door?"

Esther nodded.

"I saw all the cars. What's going on?"

Will had asked at the wrong time. With her emotions so raw, Esther was unable to keep her feelings at bay and she found herself once again in tears.

Will looked at her wide-eyed. "Woah! I've seen my fair share of weeping girls, but I've never seen *you* cry." He led her to the parlor. "I think you better sit down and tell me everything."

And that is exactly what Esther did, from her first visit to the speakeasy confronting Richard, to her mission to save Katie, and John's subsequent saving of her.

Will stood up and paced the small room. When he stopped, he turned a wrinkled brow toward Esther. "What were you thinking? Of all the foolhardy, knuckleheaded things...do you know what could have happened to you?"

"Yes, Will–"

"I don't think you do," he said, raising his voice slightly. "Esther, you don't know men the way I do. Those kind of men aren't like the men you are used to. You have no idea what he would have done to you."

Esther stood to her feet as well. "I may not be a woman of the world, Will, nor a soldier of war, for that matter, but I do know that man's intentions. I know what could have happened, had God not protected me."

Will nodded. "Thank God for John."

Esther winced. Yes, John had saved her that day, but the pain he had caused her afterward would leave a deep wound for certain.

"To think, if John had never moved here...well, I don't want to think of what could have happened."

Esther bit her bottom lip as tears once again fell down her cheeks. She had lost all control of her emotions, a state of being she was not accustomed to.

Will looked at her, confusion etched across his face. "You're not telling me everything."

Esther shook her head. "No, I'm not. There's so much more."

Will led her back to the settee. "Tell me."

Esther covered her face with her hands. How could she tell Will everything? She couldn't even look at him without melting into a sobbing mess.

"Esther, I've never seen you like this. You have to tell me."

It was useless, fighting against the tears, resisting Will's kind words. She lifted her face and the words began pouring out. She left nothing out. She told Will everything, about her feelings for John and her declaration of love, the words he had said to her. Then she told him about the confrontation in John's office yesterday and about John leaving. When she finished, she felt a huge weight lifted from her shoulders. But when she looked at her friend, she felt as if she had placed that weight directly onto his.

Will rose and stood in front of the fireplace, his back to Esther. He said nothing, but his body was rigid, and he clenched his fists at his side.

"Will? Say something."

He just shook his head.

"Say something. You have me worried."

"I did this," Will said, barely above a whisper.

"What did you say?"

"I did this. This is my fault. If I hadn't brought him into your life, he never would have hurt you like this."

"Oh, Will. This isn't your fault. You aren't to blame for John's actions. How could you have known this would happen?"

"I prayed for it," he said. "Not for him to reject you, but I did pray that you would fall in love with him. I thought that there was no way he wouldn't fall in love with you, you were so perfect for him. But, I never considered that things could end like this. I spent so much time telling John how amazing your family was. I convinced him to move to Lansing. This is all my fault. And he isn't around for me to make it right."

Esther smiled and shook her head at him. "You needn't worry about defending my honor. My honor is intact, Will."

"But it isn't right that he played with your emotions like that. And I'm the one that needs to teach him that lesson." Will's eyes traveled to the window that faced the church. "What does that meeting next door have to do with all of this?"

"The board is meeting about what disciplinary action to take against my father. They feel that my visits to the speakeasy reflect poorly on him."

"Even after hearing your side of the story?"

"They've never asked for my side of the story."

Will crossed his arms. "Let me get this straight...the same woman who marched into an illegal speakeasy to confront a cheating fiancé is the same woman sitting in her parents living room waiting for an invitation to tell her side of the story to a bunch of stiff-necked board members?"

Esther blinked several times. "But, it's a closed board meeting — no one but board members and the pastor are allowed."

"So? The Esther I know would never let that stop her. Nor would she let some pathetic excuse for a man cause her such grief."

Esther chuckled. "He is pathetic, isn't he?"

"He's a dolt."

Esther threw her head back and laughed. "That's exactly what Phoebe said."

"You've spoken with Phoebe?"

Esther's hand flew to her mouth. "Oh, Will! Phoebe was here!"

"Here? Where is she now?"

"On her way to the train station. Hurry! If you leave now, you can catch her."

Will's head snapped toward the door. He stared at it for a few moments, then took a deep breath.

"I'll see her the next time she is home."

Esther frowned at him. "But that will be months. She isn't coming home for Christmas. She's doing more evangelistic work."

Will winked at her. "She's worth the wait."

Esther smiled and reached her hand to Will's cheek, then quickly frowned as she smacked him upside the head.

"Hey! Why'd you do that?"

"I did it to get your brain functioning properly, because you have obviously lost your senses. Go!"

"But, Esther–"

"I'll be fine. Hurry, Will. At least one of us should have a happy ending."

Will frowned at her, turned and looked at the door, then back at her. "Are you certain?"

"Yes! But you'll have to hurry if you are to catch her before her train leaves."

Will jumped from his chair and kissed Esther on the forehead. "I'll check back in on you later tonight."

"You'd better!" she called after him as he reached the door. "I want to hear all about your little reunion!"

Esther laughed as she watched Will rush out the door and down the front steps just in time to hail a cab that, as luck would have it, was just passing by. *No,* Esther thought. *Not luck. God.*

God does work all things out for good, Esther thought. Will had no idea that he would need a cab when he'd come by the Albright's home that day, but God had known, long before Will had run down those steps. And God had known that Esther would need a savior that day in the brothel, so He'd sent John to Lansing months before she found herself in that harrowing situation. And that same God knows what lies in the future, she realized. Even though she couldn't see how, she knew in her heart that God would take her brokenness and work it for good...for she loved God and she was called according to His purpose.

Esther's gaze floated once more to the cars parked in front of Lansing First Church. Will was right. It wasn't like her to sit back and let injustice happen, especially when it affected her family. God had given her a bold spirit and she had never faltered in using it. Esther was called according to His purpose, and she wasn't about to ignore that calling anymore.

ESTHER THREW OPEN THE LARGE, wooden doors of the church with a resounding thud. She hadn't intended to make such a grand entrance, but her raging emotions had a greater impact on the trajectory of the doors than she had anticipated. Intended or not, she had made her presence known in a very loud manner and she wasn't about to shy away now. She proudly strode down the aisle, straight to the pews full of gaping board members.

"Miss Albright, you have no right to barge in to this meeting," Elmer Baxter said.

"Right or not, I'm here, and I have something to say."

"Well, we don't want to hear what any woman who

frequents speakeasies and keeps company with prostitutes has to say! Shame on you." Lottie Arthur said.

"No, shame on *you*, Mrs. Arthur. Shame on all of you for *not* frequenting speakeasies! And, yes, I have been keeping company with former prostitutes, because if I don't, who will? Certainly not any of you pompous, sanctimonious hypocrites, content to keep yourself cocooned inside your safe little Christian world, unwilling to share any of God's blessings with those you see as 'unfit'. In God's eyes, *you* are the unfit."

When the gasps quieted, she continued. "Who do those poor girls have to turn to in order to escape their life of sin? Rhonda is just one of dozens, maybe hundreds, of girls that have no one telling them about the transforming love of Jesus. So, if my keeping company with the likes of Rhonda and other girls like her is seen as inappropriate by the members of this church board, then so be it. Condemn me. Fire my father. Do whatever you feel necessary, but understand this, it will not stop me from spreading the Good News to those who need to hear it most."

"Calm down, darlin'," Reverend Albright said, lifting his hand. "They aren't going to fire me, because I just resigned."

"You what?"

"I can't continue in a church with such a closed mindset. You're right dear. Reaching the lost is much more important than pleasing this church board. So, I submitted my resignation."

"A resignation that we have yet to accept," Winston Mallory interrupted.

"I'm ready to put it to a vote," Elmer Baxter said, crossing his arms.

"I second," Mrs. Arthur said. "It must go to vote now."

Winston Mallory rubbed his forehead and sighed. "Pastor, would you excuse us while we vote on the matter?"

"Gladly," the reverend answered, pushing away from the

table. He strode down the aisle toward the still slack-jawed Esther. He placed his hand on her back and led her toward the exit.

"Wait!" Esther stopped in the middle of the aisle and turned to face the board one last time. "I have one more thing to say."

"You've had your say," Mr. Baxter barked. "It's time you left."

Esther placed her hands on her hips and glared at the balding man, but she spoke to the board as a whole. "The one thing I find so baffling in this whole situation is that not a single one of you has asked yourself who exactly was this informant? Who exactly saw me in the upstairs brothel of that speakeasy, and what exactly was he doing there himself? Don't you find that odd that none of you have wondered that?"

"I've wondered," the small voice of Mrs. Henrietta Stuart said. It was the first time she had spoken in either meeting and all members of the board looked at her. She folded her hands in her lap and looked directly at Elmer Baxter. "I've also wondered how you knew the young woman that Miss Albright lunched with was a woman of ill repute. I personally wouldn't know a woman like that from any other profession and I doubt anyone else around this table could confidently say that they could recognize a prostitute out in the light of day. Yet, somehow, you knew the woman. How is that, Mr. Baxter?"

"Come along," Reverend Albright whispered to Esther as he guided her down the aisle.

"That's a very good question," Esther could hear Winston Mallory say before the door of Lansing First Church shut behind her and her father.

33

───────

LEAVING LANSING

The inside of the Michigan Central Railroad Depot was nearly empty as John made his way to the ticket window. He looked at the board. His train wasn't scheduled for another hour, but he had nothing better to do than to hang out at the station and wait for it to arrive.

John turned away from the window, intent on finding a bench to spend the remainder of his tenure in Lansing on, but instead found himself directly in the path of a young woman hurrying toward the ticket agent. She seemed oblivious to John's presence and had he been more nimble on his feet, as he had been before the war, he could have avoided the collision, but as it were, he found himself helpless to avoid her from slamming into him. She stumbled back, eyes wide in shock, and John had to grab her by the shoulders to keep her from landing on her backside.

"Whoa there, miss," he said. "Are you alright?"

The girl's valise, which had flung from her hands in the collision, lay at John's feet. He bent to pick it up.

"That isn't necessary," the brunette said, reaching for the case.

"Let me help you," John said smiling. "My train isn't for some time, and you seem to be in quite a hurry."

The woman straightened to her full height, which, next to John's lanky stature looked rather ridiculous, and spoke haughtily. "Sir, do I look too weak to carry my own case?"

"That's not at all what I said."

"No, not with words," she said. She lifted an eyebrow, waiting for John to comply with some unspoken demand. She reminded him so much of Phoebe, except this woman was brunette with brown eyes. Nothing at all like Phoebe. John shook his head. Would he spend the rest of his life haunted, seeing glimpses of her in the face of every woman he met?

"Well?" she asked impatiently.

"Well, what?"

She threw out her hand and raised her eyebrow another notch in silent answer. John handed her the valise.

"I apologize if I in any way offended you," he said.

The woman, who had already reached the ticket window, turned and sighed.

"I'm sorry. I've had a stressful day. Thank you for your offer, but I can assure you, I am in no need of a man's assistance."

John made his way to the nearest bench and leaned against a post while he watched the stubborn young woman purchase her ticket then hurry out the door to the waiting train. As the train pulled away, he smiled. Spunkiness. That must be what reminded him of Phoebe. No matter how hard he tried to forget, he kept finding himself drifting off to another place, another person, one with flaxen curls and green eyes.

John rubbed his face and turned to look at the clock over the ticket window. Five o'clock. Still an hour until his train. Then he would be on his way to a new life. A life without her. A life he didn't want.

John's attention was drawn to the entrance when a man came rushing through the doors and the sight of him made

John's gut clench. Will's eyes searched the depot frantically, but when they landed on John, his face darkened. John knew at that moment that Will had discovered his betrayal.

Will moved toward John, his steps growing longer and faster the closer he drew. The force of Will's fist, coupled with the speed at which he ran, was enough to send John flying to the floor behind him.

"How could you? I trusted you! I thought you were my best friend." Will yelled. "Get up!"

John rubbed his jaw. He deserved everything that Will could dish out. He slowly rose to his feet, but before he could straighten out, he received a blow to the midsection. He bent over from the force and Will took advantage of his position to punch him once more in the face. Unlike the first blow, which was fueled more by speed than accuracy, this blow was well calculated and found its intended mark directly below John's left eye. John's vision went black for a moment but was quickly replaced with streaks of red as fierce as the pain raging in his head.

"I deserve that," John said.

"You're darn right you do." Will grabbed John by the shirt and punched him squarely in the nose.

John fell back against the wall behind him, the metallic taste of blood coating his lips.

"Take that outside!" the ticket collector yelled from his booth.

"Gladly," Will growled. He grabbed John by the coat and shoved him through the door.

Once outside, the cold air seemed to do nothing to chill Will's anger. On any given day, John could hold his own against the younger man. But John refused to fight back, feeling the need to pay the penalty due for hurting this good man.

After a few more blows, however, self-preservation kicked

in and John pushed him off, slamming Will's shoulder into the brick wall.

"Stop, Will," John panted. "I don't want to fight you."

"I trusted you," Will said, rubbing his shoulder.

"I'm sorry," John said. "I tried resisting. I didn't mean to fall in love with her."

Will stopped. "Love? You're in love with her?"

John pulled out his handkerchief and wiped his face. "I'm sorry, Will. I really am. But, yes. I'm in love with her."

Will's eyebrows knitted over his blue eyes as he rubbed the back of his neck. "Then why are you leaving? Why break her heart?"

He can't be serious, John thought. *Would Will really give up the woman he loves just because I fell in love with her too?* Then another thought occurred to him. *Well, that's what I'm doing, isn't it?*

"Listen, Will. I might be scoundrel enough to have feelings for my best friend's girl, but I'm not monster enough to steal her out from under him. So, I'm leaving. I love you like a brother, and I hope the two of you have many years of happiness, but I'm sorry. I can't stick around and watch it."

John stared at the ground, waiting for Will's next move. He wasn't certain whether he was ready for another punch or not, but he was certainly not ready for Will's apparent confusion.

"Phoebe. You think you've fallen in love with Phoebe," Will said.

John couldn't believe that Will was making him repeat it. "Yes, Will. That's what I said. I've fallen in love with her and I'm sorry. You'll never know how sorry I am. I wish I had never come to Lansing."

A slow smile spread across Will's face. "You poor, tortured wretch. How did you continue for this long under such a delusion?"

He could endure whatever physical abuse Will wanted to

dish out, but he wasn't in the mood for verbal abuse. "Delusion? *I'm* under a delusion? That's rich coming from a man who is in love with a fantasy. You think you know her, but you know nothing about who Phoebe really is. If she was the woman you think, the woman God has intended for your wife, would she have kissed me while you were off fighting for her freedom?"

Will's eyebrows shot up. "You kissed her? Really! How was it?"

"How can you make light of this?" John took a step toward Will. "I'm sorry if you think that my feelings for Phoebe are delusional, but I assure you they are not. They are very real. So real they are killing me."

The smile faded from Will's face. "You misunderstand me, John. You aren't deluded as to the intensity of your feelings. The delusion that you have been under all these months is who you think you are in love with. You aren't in love with Phoebe. You are in love with Esther, her sister."

"What?" John said, confused. "Phoebe's sister's name is Sarah, and she is a child."

"Yes, Sarah is the name of her sister...Phoebe's younger sister. Esther is her older sister."

John stared blankly at the ground. "Esther? Phoebe has an older sister?" He spoke more to himself than to Will. The events of the past weeks flooded his consciousness. "If she's Esther, then where is Phoebe?"

"Well, she came through here just a moment ago. That's why I'm here. I was trying to catch her before she left for Bible College again."

John stared at him. "What does Phoebe look like?"

Will smiled. "Think of Esther, but even more beautiful, with silky dark hair and eyes to match. You couldn't miss her."

John turned and stared at the now empty track in the direction the train had just gone. "Esther? All this time...she was Miss Albright, only Miss Albright, at work and at church...I thought she was Phoebe, and all this time, she was..." John shook his head.

"Miss *Esther* Albright. Blonde-haired, green-eyed, slap-you-as-soon-as-look-at-you Esther Albright."

"Not Phoebe?"

"Not Phoebe. Phoebe has been away at Bible College, and is on her way back there now, by the look of things."

Hadn't he thought the woman with the valise reminded him of Phoebe...*no, Esther. Her name is Esther*, he reminded himself.

Will laughed. "How did you manage all these months without figuring that out?"

John swore under his breath. "The things I said to her, the way I treated her. She's never going to forgive me. Will, what am I going to do?" John swore again.

"Well, my first suggestion...don't use language like that in front of her."

John scowled at the ground and continued shaking his head. "She'll never forgive me. Even if she wanted to, I don't deserve her. I'm not like you Will. I'm not a good man. She deserves someone like you. Someone so much better than me."

"I'm a clay vessel the same as you," Will said. He reached out and clasped John on the shoulder. "Just because you have a different pattern of cracks and flaws running through your vessel doesn't make you any worse than me. We all have scars left by our sins. But inside that hard, cracked exterior of yours is a new creation. God has redeemed you, John. And because of that redemption, you have the same treasure within that I do, and that Esther does, and Reverend Albright. Jesus has made you a new man. It's time you started realizing that."

"But I've made so many mistakes. I don't deserve Phoebe," he stopped and shook his head. "Esther. I mean Esther. I don't deserve Esther."

"That's the truth," Will laughed. "She's a very special person.

I doubt there's a man in the world that deserves her. But, for some unknown reason, your ugly mug is the one she chose to fall in love with."

John laughed despite the misery he felt inside. "No accounting for taste, I guess."

"I guess," Will agreed. "John, there is a woman just across the river that is completely shattered by your departure. I'm no expert, but if my hunch is correct, she'll not only forgive you, she'll welcome you back with open arms."

"Do you really think so?"

"Scars and all. She really loves you, John. You've stopped running from God. It's time to stop running from love as well." Will laughed at him. "Go on. If my story doesn't have a happy ending tonight, yours at least should. Go to her."

34

THE SWEETEST NAME

The blast of cold air caught Esther by surprise as she and her father stepped out of the church. The surge of anger and confidence that had fueled her tirade only moments ago swept away with the icy, November wind. With the adrenaline gone, the reality of what had just happened, of what she had just said and done, gripped her heart. She turned to her father who stood buttoning his coat, looking more tired and defeated than she had ever seen him in her entire life.

"Oh, Daddy!" Esther cupped one hand over her mouth as she reached for her father's arm with the other. "I'm - I'm sorry."

"You've nothing to apologize for," he said, patting her hand.

Esther shook her head. "It isn't right. You did nothing wrong. How could God do this to you?"

"God didn't do this to me, darlin'. We live in a fallen world full of fallen people."

"But God allowed this to happen."

"Esther, do you think any of this came as a surprise to Him?"

"Of course not."

"Then, don't you think he will take care of us?"

Esther pondered that. Of course He would. He always had.

"We are so blessed in our lives, dear. We have more happiness than most. Let's focus on the good in our lives, not on what Satan would use to tear us down."

Happiness. Would she ever know what happiness felt like again? Esther sighed. "Daddy, I have something I need to tell–"

But she didn't have a chance to say anything before their conversation was interrupted by the heavy wooden door crashing open as Elmer Baxter came flying out of the church. He neither looked at Esther nor her father, nor did he say anything to them, but his bright red face and the speed of his departure spoke volumes. Not far behind him was Winston Mallory who stopped short when he saw the two of them on the front stairs.

"Oh, I thought I was going to have to hunt you down. The board would like to speak with you, Reverend. If you would join us again..." Mr. Mallory opened the door and held it for Reverend Albright.

"I've said my piece, Winston," her father said.

"And now it's our turn," Winston said. "Jim, please come back in. We've voted to not accept your resignation."

Reverend Albright smiled and shook his head. "Nothin' you got to say can stop me."

"How about 'I'm sorry'?"

Reverend Albright rubbed the back of his neck and continued to smile and shake his head, but he said nothing.

"Come hear what we have to say, at least. You can give us just a few more minutes, can't you?"

Esther watched his shoulders slump slightly and she could see that Mr. Mallory had won the argument. She was not surprised. Her father was famous for giving people second chances.

Mr. Mallory looked at Esther as the Reverend crossed in front of him. "We'd like you to join us as well."

"With all due respect, this is my father's business, not mine.

I believe I've meddled enough with the affairs of the church board."

"I disagree, but I'll respect your wishes. If I dally out here much longer, he might change his mind."

The door sounded heavier and more solid than ever as it closed behind the man. A shiver ran down Esther's spine, but she felt no dread for the impending meeting her father was now a part of. God was taking care of her father, just as he predicted.

Something wet touched her cheek and Esther jumped from the cold shock. She touched her face but found nothing. She raised her eyes to the sky and the mystery was solved. The cloudy, overcast sky that covered the entire city like a gray canopy had just begun to release tiny, white speckles of snow.

The first snow. Esther sighed. Even these sparkling fragments, one of her most favorite signs of the fast approaching holiday season, could do nothing to lighten her heart.

The snow thickened, and the fluffy flakes began to accumulate on the grass and branches of trees that had long ago shed their summer leaves. Esther extended her hand in an attempt to catch a flake or two, but the particles melted the instant they came in contact with her warm skin, leaving tiny dots of cool water in their place. She chuckled. Nothing she reached for seemed willing to stay once in her grasp. Three men, three heartbreaks, nothing but melted snow.

Mother had been right. She had never been in love with Richard, and certainly not with Leonard. She'd had no idea what love was before John Ward came into her life, and she wished she could go back in time so that she wouldn't know love now, either. No, that wasn't true. If she could change things, she wouldn't. As painful as it was, loving John had shown her that she was capable of real love. She was a different woman now, a better woman, and she wouldn't change that for the world.

Beneath her sleeves, she could feel the hair of her arms stand on end, reminding her that in her rush to reach the church board in time she had neglected to grab her coat. The lights from a vehicle that had just turned onto her street also reminded her that the day was fading quickly, for which she was grateful. She looked forward to crawling into her bed and hiding away from the troubles of this day.

She rubbed her hands up and down her arms, then started down the stairs. She stopped suddenly when the car, a cab, came to a halt in front of the church. A familiar face emerged from the vehicle.

"Hello, Will," she said. "Did you find Phoebe at the train station?"

"No." He shut the car door. "But I found the next best thing."

Esther's smile quickly faded as the door behind the driver opened and out stepped John. Her heart beat wildly in her throat and she stopped breathing all together.

"I believe you know my friend, John," Will said, sweeping his hand dramatically toward the other man. "But, apparently, he has yet to meet you...well, properly that is. John, this is my good friend, Miss Albright...Miss *Esther* Albright."

"Esther," John said, barely above a whisper.

He stared at her intensely, almost painfully. She didn't know what to do or what to say. She didn't understand what was going on or why Will had dragged him back to her.

It was Will that finally broke the silence. "Well, I think I will go on over next door and see what kind of sweets your mother has hiding in the cookie jar."

If Esther had something to throw, she would have hurled it at the head of that traitor as he quickly departed, leaving her awkwardly staring down at the man who had broken her heart. John said nothing, only stared at her with that pained look on his face. And his face did look painful, fresh bruises decorating his left cheekbone and eye, convincing Esther that Will had followed through on his promise to teach John a lesson. The silence finally got to her and she blurted out the first thing that came to her mind.

"I thought you left already."

"Esther?" he asked, placing a foot on the first stair tread.

"Yes?" she said impatiently. She took a step backward.

He smiled, seeming pleased with her simple response.

"Esther. Your name is Esther," he said matter-of-factly, taking another step.

"I'm well aware of that!" She backed up again and found herself at the top of the stairs.

John continued climbing the stairs and Esther's heart raced even faster. "Is...is that all you have to say? My name?"

"But it's such a beautiful name to say," he said, his smile spreading wider across his handsome face. "It's the most beautiful name I've ever heard." He stopped at the last step, bringing him eye level with her.

Esther shook her head. "What are you doing here, John?"

"I'm here to ask for forgiveness from you, Esther."

"Why would you desire my forgiveness? You made your feelings very clear yesterday in your office."

"I've been such a fool. A stupid, confused fool." John reached out and ran his knuckles down the side of her face. "But confusion is no excuse for how I've treated you." His hand trailed down her arm and took her hand in his.

Her skin tingled along the trail his hand left and her hand felt warm in his. "No, it isn't," she said, pulling her hand back from his grasp.

"Esther, my love, please don't–"

"What did you just say?"

"Esther, my love." He took her hand in his again. "I love you, Esther Albright."

"You have an odd way of showing love, John Ward."

"I've been a fool."

"That's putting it kindly. So now, all of a sudden, you decide you're in love with me?"

"No, Esther, I've been in love with you ever since the first moment I saw you knock a man off a barstool."

She laughed in spite of herself. "Every man's dream...a woman who can throw a punch."

John laughed as well. "Dreams...nightmares, they're hard to separate sometimes."

She had to bite her bottom lip to keep from smiling back at the rake. But she wouldn't be fooled by his charm again. "Then why did you leave?"

"I thought you deserved someone better than me, someone like Will."

"Will! You thought I was interested in Will?"

"I thought it was a possibility."

"But, Will loves Phoebe."

John threw his head back. "Oh, I'm well aware of that!"

"Then, what would ever make you think...how would leaving Lansing make...You aren't making any sense."

"I know. I've acted horribly and nothing I say could excuse what I've said and done to you. I was blind, but I see the truth now."

"Oh, really? And what do you see?"

"I see you, Esther Albright, and I see love...the love you have for others, especially those whom society rejects, the love you have for God, and the love I have for you. And I hope I still see a glimmer of love for me left in your eyes."

Esther continued to scowl at him. She lifted one brow at him. "Say it again."

"Say what again?"

"Say that you love me."

John climbed the last step and stood looking down at her. "I love you," he said huskily. "I love you, Esther Albright. I will love you until my final day on earth, and I will tell you that I love you, multiple times, every day, until the moment God takes me home." He cupped her face in his hands and bent his lips toward hers.

"John?"

He pulled back slightly. "Yes, Esther?"

"Why do you keep saying my name over and over again?"

John laughed heartily. "Because the sound of your name is the sweetest sound I have ever heard."

And with that, he took her lips with his and kissed away any thoughts of hurt that had engulfed her. A strong pressure grew in her chest as he kissed her, not from the knife-like pain of betrayal, but from the growing emotion that was exploding within her...love. A love for John Ward, the most infuriating, insulting man she had ever met, and the only man she wanted to spend the rest of her life with.

35

EPILOGUE

"What is the matter, my love?"

Esther looked up at her handsome husband and smiled. "Married only a few hours and already you read me like an open book."

"If only that were true, then I would already know what was upsetting you. You haven't found marriage to be disappointing already, have you?"

Esther laughed. "Not yet! And you? Have you grown tired of your bride?"

"How could a man married to the most beautiful woman on earth ever tire of her?"

"Keep flattering me so, and I will be a very happy wife indeed."

"That is my plan...to make you happy every day of our life together. But apparently, I am already failing at that goal. Tell me, why such a sad face on our wedding day?"

Esther touched his cheek. "It isn't you. I'm just missing my sister."

"I was afraid you'd regret not putting off the wedding until Phoebe came home."

"Oh, no, I don't regret it at all. Goodness knows when she'll come home again. I just miss her. We may not see her until after graduation, and there was no way I was waiting that long to...John? Why are we stopping here?"

He said nothing as he stepped out of the car. Although she knew the neighborhood well, she was certain she knew no one on this street. She had walked past these homes each time she'd visited Will's mother. Who on earth did John know here and why was he visiting them when they were supposed to be beginning their honeymoon?

John held open her door and offered her his hand. He led her down the sidewalk of a beautiful Victorian home, more than twice the size of her parents' parsonage.

"John," she whispered as they neared the front door. "Who lives here?"

He leaned close to her ear and whispered back, "You do."

Dumbfounded, she stared at him, mouth agape, as he pulled out a key and opened the door. He turned back to her and held out his hand.

"Welcome home, Mrs. Ward."

She allowed herself to be led into the beautiful, two story home. Shiny oak floors greeted them as they passed through the foyer and into a large living room. The room was bare, save for the fire glowing in the fireplace.

"Oh, John! It's beautiful."

"I looked at a few brand-new homes, but they were much smaller and the location of this home was too perfect to pass up."

"Location?"

"If you are going to be working at the Caffey home every day, I thought it would be best if we lived nearby, to lessen your travel time."

Esther did indeed find herself often occupied at the new

mission for troubled women the church had established. It had been one of the conditions her father had demanded in exchange for withdrawing his resignation. He'd insisted that the church not only accept Esther's work with wayward women, but that they also support her efforts financially. Will offered his house to the church, since he himself would be kept busy at the Michigan State Constabulary. As one of their first hires for the position of State Police officer, he would have to live in the state barracks anyway. In the few weeks since that fated board meeting, not only had Rhonda joined Katie in the house, now lovingly referred to as Bessie's Beacon of Hope, but two other former employees of the speakeasy had joined them as well. Esther spent her days sharing not only God's Word with the women, but also the skills she learned in secretarial school. Working alongside her mother and other women from the church, the women of Bessie's were taught skills like cooking and sewing, skills they could use to find honest work. Even John's mother volunteered her services, teaching the women gardening.

"I - I can't believe you bought this place," she said, still in shock.

"Did you seriously think I was going to take you home to that hole of an apartment I've been living in?"

"But, this house is so grand! I know you do well at the paper, but even at that, how can we afford a place so...large!"

"Well, Warren did give me that raise to keep me from leaving."

"A raise generous enough for a home like this?" she asked incredulously.

"That, and, of course, there is also the matter of my inheritance."

"Inheritance?"

"My father was a wealthy man, Esther, and when he died, it

all came to me. I gave most of it to my mother. Goodness knows, she deserved it. But I kept enough for us to start our life together, including this house."

Esther left his side and slowly walked up the oak staircase. At the top, she called down to him, "Look at all these doors! How many bedrooms?"

"Five, I believe."

She laughed. "Goodness! What are we going to do with that many bedrooms?"

"Fill them with children, I suppose."

Esther turned and smiled down at him. "First, we'll need to fill this place with furniture, unless you enjoy sitting on the floor."

"Well, I did have one of the rooms furnished already."

"Really? I don't see any –" She stopped when she caught sight of the room at the end of the hall. It had a large double bed, bedspread folded down. Their bedroom.

"Oh, I see." She could feel heat gathering in her cheeks, a warmth she was not accustomed to. She clasped her hands in front of her and turned back to her husband. To her great surprise, he looked as nervous as she felt, with his eyes averted and his hands stuffed into his pants' pockets. Her giggle made him look up. He bolted up the stairs, taking the treads two at a time.

"What, my dear Mrs. Ward, do you find so funny now?"

"You." She wrapped her arms around his neck. "I never know what to expect with you. Just when I think I have you figured out, you surprise me."

His arms encircled her waist and pulled her body against his. "Well, one thing you can be assured of...this is your new home."

Esther smiled. "It is a beautiful house, John. Thank you."

"I wasn't talking about the house," he said as he brushed a stray golden curl off her forehead. "I meant here, in my arms."

And as he captured her lips in a kiss, one of passion meant only for husband and wife, she knew without a doubt that they had both found their home.

Love in Lansing, Book 3

Chapter One

COMING HOME

"Next stop – Lansing!"

The landscape flew by, just like it had so many times before, but Phoebe didn't notice. How many times had she taken this trip? Too many to count, but this time was different. This time was the last. This time, she was coming home for good.

So here she was, a Bible College graduate, bound for home to begin the rest of her life. She only wished she knew what the rest of her life looked like.

"Lansing!" shouted the conductor, startling Phoebe. She

was so lost in her own musings that she hadn't realized how close she was to home. She finally looked out her window at the scenery that she had been ignoring. Farmland stretched out, like an ocean of tilled dirt, touching the sky where the Earth seemingly dropped off and the sky took over. There was little to differentiate this land from the countless miles that she had already passed, except for the occasional oak standing in the middle of a field, left untouched by the farmer. The crops just circled around these massive trees, as if giving respect to their impressive elder.

Phoebe then looked at the ground closer to the train. At the speed in which the train traveled, the vegetation close to the tracks looked like nothing more than a blur, and Phoebe couldn't help but think that it was exactly the opposite in life. God only allows us to see right in front of us, but beyond today and tomorrow, it is all a blur.

The train began to chug and slow its pace, indicating that they had reached their destination. A woman across the aisle began to rise to gather her things, but Phoebe knew better. She had taken this train far too many times to fall for the deceivingly slow pace the train was now making. She kept her seat and watched as the woman, valise in hand, stood, then lost her balance as the train jerked to its final stop. Had it not been for the gentleman who sat behind her jumping to her aid, she would have surely fallen flat on her backside.

The woman thanked the gentleman. He said something in return, which caused her to blush, and then the flirting began. It took everything in Phoebe's whole being to not roll her eyes at the display. She had never been one to participate in such ridiculous fawning. But, maybe, she should have tried. Maybe then…oh, it didn't matter anyway. God could have provided, but he chose not to. There was no use dwelling on what wasn't meant to be.

Phoebe gathered her things and headed for the exit. The

sun shone bright as she departed the train, and she had to squint to see around. She couldn't help but be reminded of her earlier observation.

'*Well,*' she thought, '*my future may be blurry, but with God's help, I can handle whatever lays directly in front of me.*'

With a new-found resolve, Phoebe squared her shoulders, lifted her chin and took her first step into her future. Unfortunately, that first step got caught somewhere in her skirts and she fell out of the train. She flew, unable to slow her decent, and would have landed in a very unladylike manner had God not intervened and landed her into the arms of a Michigan State Constable.

"Oh, my!" was all she was able to sputter. He had saved her from a nasty fall, for which she was very grateful, but the fact that he still held her in his arms was beginning to make Phoebe very uncomfortable. "I'm so sorry…"

"No apologies necessary. Are you alright, Phoebe?"

In shock, she looked into the face of her savior. Beneath the khaki Montana campaign hat were two of the brightest blue eyes Phoebe had ever seen. She searched his face, wondering who this man was. He certainly knew who she was.

Phoebe's confusion seemed to delight the officer.

"What's the matter, Pheebs? Don't you recognize me?"

Her eyes grew wide as suddenly Phoebe did recognize the man whose arms held her.

"Will Caffey?" she gasped.

"Oh, good. I was beginning to think that you had forgotten all about me," he said, smiling down at her.

Forgotten? Will Caffey? How could she forget the boy who had teased her relentlessly her entire childhood? The adolescent that chased her around the playground every day at school. The teenager that had captured her behind the church and…

She longed to slap the mischievous grin off his face. If she had had any difficulty connecting the little boy of her memories with the handsome, and now very grown up, man of today, that smirk erased all doubt. This was the same, obnoxious Will Caffey she had always known.

"Put me down, sir." She struggled to free herself from his arms. "People are beginning to stare!"

"Sir?" Will chuckled, and gently righted Phoebe to an upright, balanced position.

She straightened her skirt, gathered her things, then looked up at him.

"Thank you for saving me from a vicious fall. For that, I am very grateful." She looked frantically for her father, wishing to escape the embarrassment of the situation as quickly as possible. "But your prolonged embrace, that was unnecessary and has only delayed me further. So, Mr. Caffey, thank you, but good day."

"Sir? Mr. Caffey?" Will chuckled again. "Well, I guess if we are being formal, then the name is Constable Caffey now, *ma'am*," he replied with exaggerated gallantry, tipping his hat and bowing to her.

"I stand corrected," she said, picking up her valise. "Let me try again. Goodbye…*Constable* Caffey." She turned to leave.

"C'mon, Pheebs. You aren't still mad about that kiss, are you?"

Phoebe stood frozen. "Kiss? I have no idea what you are talking about," she lied.

"So, you are still sore."

She twirled around. "Sore? Mad? Why would I be upset about having a kiss roguishly stolen from me when I was still a child? I couldn't care less!"

"Oh, that's apparent."

"What's apparent is that you haven't changed…not one bit. You are still the most annoying boy I have ever known. I've wasted enough of my time with the likes of you. Good day, *Constable!*"

She turned and strode toward the depot, anxious to find her father. All she wished was to be home and the last thing she wanted was any more banter with the likes of Will Caffey.

"I wouldn't dismiss me so quickly if I were you," she heard him yell after her.

"Oh," Phoebe called over her shoulder. "And why is that?"

"Because it's a long walk home from here."

A CALLING FOR PHOEBE COMING SOON!

A MESSAGE FROM JEN

~

When I first decided to stop dreaming of being an author and started to sit down and actually make it a reality, I thought I had one novel in me that I had to get onto paper. But as I wrote Phoebe and Will's story (which is now Book 3 in the series), I couldn't stop wondering about these two minor characters I had written. Esther intrigued me. She was diametrically opposite of Phoebe, not only in looks but also in mannerism, and I wanted to know why. I also wanted to know more about John, who he was, how he came to live in Lansing, and why he had a limp. I knew the events of Esther's story might impact Phoebe's story, so I determined to put Phoebe on the back burner while I delved into her older sister's life.

I realize this novel does not begin the way a normal romance might, but I believe it was very important to begin where both main characters felt life was ending because it is often at these points in our lives that we finally surrender and allow God to take us in a new direction. Thus, the opening scene featuring John and Will was born. I wanted to accurately portray the battle scenes in the novel, but, being a romance novelist, I wanted to be very mindful of how graphic those war scenes were while still keeping them historically accurate. I was blessed to happen across letters, poetry, and accounts from actual World War I soldiers that were instrumental in the descriptions I used. Every detail John shares is taken from these accounts, including his retelling of Will's heroism. Will's war story is based on the real-life WWI hero, Alvin C. York, a highly decorated Army sergeant. As you read the chapter *Remembering*, you may have thought his heroics seemed unrealistic, but I encourage you to Google "Sergeant York" and see that a hero like Will Caffey actually existed in real life.

Speaking of real life, there is another character in *Avoiding Esther* that is modeled after a real-life hero of mine. The bigger than life personality of Reverend Albright was largely patterned after my own grandfather, a Church of the Nazarene minister and southern transplant in Michigan who loved and influenced everyone blessed to have known him. Although not an exact replica of my grandfather, James Albright was such a fun character to write. All I had to do was close my eyes, remember my grandfather, and Reverend Albright came to life on the page.

As in all my novels, I strive for historical accuracy. Esther's story, set in 1918, takes place two years before National Prohibition took effect in 1920. However, the state of Michigan passed its own prohibition amendment in 1916, with Ingham County being one of the thirty-six counties to pass a local prohibition law six years prior to that. So, if you raised your eyebrows at the prohibition issues in the novel, no fear. Speakeasies and rum runners were commonplace in Michigan by the fall of 1918 when Esther first confronts Richard in one.

I hope you have enjoyed Esther and John's story as much as

I have enjoyed writing it. If you have, you'll be happy to know we get a further glimpse of their life together in the next book of the Love in Lansing series, *A Calling for Phoebe.*

All my love and gratitude,

Jen

ACKNOWLEDGMENTS

~

Always first and foremost, to the author and creator of my life and of each story I write. Thank you, Lord, for never giving up on me. You continue to bless this very flawed woman in ways I don't deserve. May this book be a blessing to others in Your name.

To my husband and my children. Your love and support mean more to me than I could ever express in words. It is because of you that I am able to be an author, and I pray that God will bless each of you for your sacrifices, which made writing this novel possible. I love you with my whole heart.

To Mom and Dad, the unsung heroes of my family. You have supported everything I have ever done in my life, including when I made the decision to become a full-time mother and author. You've been there every time I've needed you and I can never thank you enough

To the ladies of the Christian Indie Writers' podcast, J.R. Nichols, Christina Cattane, and Rhonda Hagerman. You are my writing partners, my accountability keepers, and my friends. I love and appreciate you all!

To J.R. Nichols, for saving the day and picking up the revision of this book when others left me hanging. Without you and your editing skills, as well as your constant encouragement when I needed it most, Esther's story may never have made it to publication. I don't say it enough, Jamie, but your friendship means the world to me!

To Jennifer McNab, whose attention to detail fine tuned the final draft and made Avoiding Esther print ready. Thank you so much!

And last, but never least, to Kayla Korpi, for allowing your beauty to grace the cover of this book. You are lovely inside and out, and you are the only person I would want to portray Esther. Thank you!

ABOUT THE AUTHOR

Jenifer Carll-Tong is the author of historical Christian romances. She is a graduate of Boston University's College of Communication. Searching for Anna is her debut novel.

Jenifer lives in Michigan with her handsome husband, three beautiful daughters and two lazy dogs. She also has three adult stepchildren who have left the nest, but not her heart. When she isn't writing kissing scenes between devilishly handsome heroes and strong, independent heroines, you might find her napping or wearing sandals in the snow. You probably won't find her cleaning her house. Unless company is coming over.

Learn more about Jenifer and her books HERE or you can join the fun over at Jenifer's Facebook group, Jenifer Carll-Tong's C.I.R.C.L.E. of Readers. (Heads up...that's where the giveaways happen.)

And don't forget to sign up for her newsletter to stay up to date on the latest news and releases. Visit https://goo.gl/Qur2sU and you will also receive the Searching for Anna ebook absolutely free for signing up!

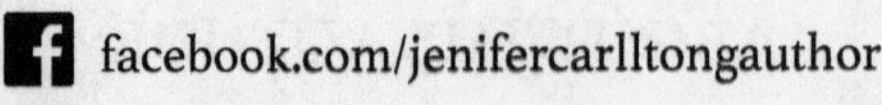

facebook.com/jenifercarlltongauthor

twitter.com/jencarlltong

instagram.com/jencarlltong

ALSO BY JENIFER CARLL-TONG

Love in Lansing Series

Book One

Searching for Anna